MURDER IN THE SOHO GRAVEYARD

EMILY ORGAN

Storm
PUBLISHING

Ebook ISBN: 978-1-80508-884-4
Paperback ISBN: 978-1-80508-886-8

Cover design: Ghost
Cover images: Adobe Stock

Published by Storm Publishing.
For further information, visit:
www.stormpublishing.co

ALSO BY EMILY ORGAN

The Baker Street Murders

Death in Kensington

Churchill & Pemberley Series

Tragedy at Piddleton Hotel

Murder in Cold Mud

Puzzle in Poppleford Wood

Trouble in the Churchyard

Wheels of Peril

The Poisoned Peer

Fiasco at the Jam Factory

Disaster at the Christmas Dinner

Christmas Calamity at the Vicarage (novella)

Writing as Martha Bond

Lottie Sprigg Travels Mystery Series

Murder in Venice

Murder in Paris

Murder in Cairo

Murder in Monaco

Murder in Vienna

Lottie Sprigg Country House Mystery Series

Murder in the Library

Murder in the Grotto

Murder in the Maze

Murder in the Bay

ONE

February 1889

The tall gates of St Anne's churchyard stood ajar. Clara Clifton peered through the bars. A set of grimy steps led up to the neglected burial ground with its sunken tombstones and knotted weeds.

A strange sense of trepidation crept over her, but she did her best to ignore it. She was used to places like this. There was no reason to be uneasy. And yet something felt wrong.

The early morning rain had cleared and water trickled steadily from broken guttering and uneven roofs. Here in Soho, the buildings were packed tightly together. The churchyard was hemmed in by cramped, decaying housing and overlooked by the lofty bell tower of St Anne's church.

Clara pulled her notebook out of her bag and read the notes she'd made to remind herself of the burial ground's history. The churchyard had been consecrated two centuries ago. Since then, more than 100,000 people had been buried here. Clara caught her breath as she read this. It was difficult to comprehend. She looked up from her notes to peer through the bars of the gate again.

A clue lay in the height of the churchyard. Over the years, it had been raised several feet above the level of the street to accommodate the burials. The steps had been constructed over time as the ground had risen. Coffins had been piled on top of coffins. The dead layered like bricks. The ground had become foul and unsanitary until burials finally ceased thirty-five years ago.

Clara pushed against the heavy gate. It groaned on its hinges.

'You're not going in there, are you?' came a voice from behind her.

Clara turned. An old man stood watching her, wrapped in a filthy, threadbare coat. He had a jaundiced face and a set of grubby toes poked through a tear in his boot.

'Yes, I am,' she replied.

'I wouldn't if I were you. It's no place for a lady.'

'I know what I'm doing.'

The man gave a cackling laugh and shuffled off down the street, muttering and shaking his head.

Clara stepped through the gate and climbed the steps. She'd visited overcrowded burial grounds before but there was something unsettling about this place. The air was still, muffled. There was no trace of the noise of London beyond the iron gate. Just the steady drip of water somewhere nearby. A silence that felt too complete.

Some graveyards were peaceful and serene and Clara found them pleasant places to visit.

But not this one.

It gave her a chill on the back of her neck. The air smelled dank and fetid.

The headstones leaned at awkward angles, their lettering worn and their surfaces coated in slick green moss. Thick tendrils of ivy crawled across the ground and clambered over the stones. Clara stepped carefully, watching her footing on the uneven, saturated ground.

Discarded rubbish was strewn here and there – sodden papers, a broken lamp, fragments of rusted metal. She spotted a small heap of bones, long and narrow. A bird, perhaps. Or something larger.

She winced as her feet sank into the damp ground. Stopping

beneath a skeletal tree, she opened her notebook and made a few quick observations. She didn't want to be here any longer than was necessary.

Ivy is growing profusely, she wrote. *Poorly maintained. A great deal of rubbish.*

The air was so damp that the corners of her page began to curl. Clara folded her notebook closed and pushed it into her bag.

Then something caught her eye among the tombs and weeds. A flash of something red.

A piece of fabric, perhaps, blown in from the street.

She turned to go. But something – curiosity, unease – drew her back. She stepped carefully across the spongy ground. Brambles tugged at her skirt. Damp soaked through her shoes.

The red fabric had a sheen to it, like satin. Her stomach gave a lurch when she realised it had a form.

She took another step forward and saw it was a dress. Then she caught sight of something pale. White skin.

A lady lay on the ground. Her skin was waxen, almost blue. Her mouth hung open in a silent cry. Her eyes stared blindly up at the slate-grey sky.

Clara felt a cold bolt of horror shoot through her. She staggered backwards, clasping her hands to her mouth. She fell against a tombstone, the hard stone bruising her hip.

'Help!' Her voice sounded weak in the damp, oppressive gloom. 'Someone! Come quickly! Help!'

TWO

Emma Langley smiled as her pupil, Beth, finished a graceful rendition of Bach's 'Minuet in G Major'.

'Well done,' she said warmly. 'That was beautifully played.'

Beth swung her legs beneath the piano stool and gave a shy smile.

'I played it better,' declared her twin sister, Harriet, from her seat in the armchair across the music room.

'You both played it very well,' Emma replied diplomatically.

'But mine was better,' Harriet insisted.

'No, it wasn't!' Beth turned in her seat, frowning.

'It's not a competition,' Emma said gently, although she quietly thought Beth had played it with more expression and control. 'What matters is that you're both making excellent progress. I can tell you've been practising diligently, and that's far more important than who plays something better on any given day. You should both be very proud of yourselves.'

Neither girl looked entirely convinced. Emma sensed that praise shared equally wasn't what either had hoped for.

She glanced at the gold carriage clock on the mantelpiece. 'Well, that brings us to the end of today's lesson,' she said. 'Keep practising, both of you, and I have no doubt you'll impress me even more next week.'

Rising from her chair, she could still feel the undercurrent of rivalry between the girls. She wondered if all twins were this competitive.

She retrieved her music bag and turned to them with a parting smile. 'I'll see you both next week.'

After updating the twins' governess on their lesson, Emma stepped out of the tall townhouse on St James's Place and began her walk towards Piccadilly Circus to catch an omnibus home. The February afternoon was bleak and damp, the sky a heavy blanket of grey. A steady drizzle had left the streets slick and shining, and a chill crept beneath her coat as she turned up her collar.

Her route took her through St James's Square, where bare trees stood like skeletal sentinels and the statue of King William III proudly sat on horseback, his bronze form streaked with grime. The flowerbeds beneath him lay empty, the soil dark and sodden.

As Emma passed along the path, her eyes fell on a bench occupied by a solitary woman. She sat with her head bowed, her shoulders hunched and a large bag resting beside her. She looked to be around thirty, dressed in a black overcoat and a velvet bonnet. Something in her posture – a quiet collapse of spirit – made Emma pause. She might have had an argument, Emma thought, or perhaps received bad news. Whatever it was, she looked desperately sad.

Emma kept walking, not wishing to intrude. But then she heard it – a soft, unmistakable sob.

It seemed cruel to walk past. Taking a breath, she turned back. 'Is everything all right?' she asked quietly.

The woman looked up and quickly dabbed her eyes with a handkerchief. 'Yes. Fine... Actually... not really.'

'Do you mind if I sit?' Emma gestured to the bench.

The woman moved her bag without hesitation. 'Please,' she said. 'But don't worry about me. I'll be all right.'

Emma sat beside her. 'You don't look all right,' she said.

The woman gave a small, tired laugh. Her fair complexion was pale with a reddened nose and cheeks. Her wide-set blue eyes shimmered with the remnants of tears.

'I've just had a bit of a shock,' she said. 'Something rather upsetting.'

'I'm sorry to hear that. Would you like me to walk you somewhere? I hate to think of you sitting here alone.'

'Thank you, but truly, there's no need. I don't want to trouble you.'

'It's no trouble. I've just finished my last lesson for the day.'

'You're a teacher?'

'A piano teacher,' Emma replied with a smile. 'My name is Mrs Langley.'

'I'm Mrs Clifton,' said the woman. Her eyes flicked to Emma's black coat and gloves. 'You're in mourning.'

Emma nodded. 'My husband passed away four months ago.'

'I'm terribly sorry,' said Mrs Clifton. 'You must think I'm being very silly, sitting here crying. I've just spent quite a bit of time at Vine Street police station.'

Emma blinked. 'The police station?'

'Yes. I needed some air after that place. It's so... bleak. I walked here to sit down for a moment and gather my thoughts.'

'You don't have to tell me what happened if you'd rather not, but I'd be very willing to listen if it might help,' Emma asked curiously.

Mrs Clifton looked down at her gloved hands as she twisted her handkerchief. 'I found a woman this morning.' Her voice was tremulous. 'In a disused churchyard. She was lying there... dead.'

Emma gasped. 'Oh my goodness. How awful!'

'I called for help and the police arrived quickly. They think she was murdered.'

A cold shiver ran down Emma's neck. 'How dreadful.'

'I just wasn't prepared for it,' Mrs Clifton whispered. 'I spend a lot of time in old graveyards, you see. That probably sounds strange.'

Emma gave a small shake of her head. 'Not strange... Just unusual.'

'It's my work,' Mrs Clifton explained. 'I'm documenting London's disused burial grounds for the Metropolitan Public Gardens Committee. They're trying to restore public open spaces.'

'Well, that's admirable,' replied Emma. 'And it must be fascinating... if a little morbid.'

Mrs Clifton managed a faint smile. 'I started a few years ago, and I've seen some rather grim places... But nothing like today.'

Emma was silent for a moment, absorbing the weight of what she'd heard. 'Do you know who the woman was?'

'The police told me her name was Mrs Melbourne, but I don't know anything more about her. Why was she there? And who could do such a thing?'

Emma shook her head slowly. 'Some people are capable of cruelty I'll never understand.'

'Apparently there's going to be a memorial service for Mrs Melbourne at six o'clock this evening at St Peter's, Eaton Square in Belgravia,' said Mrs Clifton. 'I think I might go.'

'That's a good idea,' said Emma. She wondered about going herself; she was intrigued to find out more about the victim. Would it be odd for her to attend when she hadn't known Mrs Melbourne? She reasoned it was a church service which everyone would be welcomed to.

A gust of wind swept through the square, and both women shivered.

'It's really too cold to be sitting here,' Emma said. 'Would you let me treat you to a cup of tea?'

Mrs Clifton hesitated only a moment before nodding. 'I'd like that very much. Thank you.'

THREE

Miss Lydia Jackson approached St Peter's Church in Eaton Square, its columned portico illuminated by the soft glow of street-lamps. A steady stream of mourners stepped inside, their hushed voices mingling with the crisp evening air. She straightened the collar of her overcoat and followed the crowd. She had nearly reached the door when a voice, deep and unmistakable, called her name.

'Lydia?'

She froze. The voice sent a shiver down her spine. A voice so familiar and yet one she'd never expected to hear again.

Her breath caught, her heart thudding in her chest. For a brief moment, she closed her eyes, bracing herself before turning to face the man she'd not seen in twenty years.

He stood a few paces away, his face illuminated by the gaslight. Time had changed him only slightly – his frame was a little broader, and there were threads of grey in his neatly trimmed whiskers. But it was unmistakably him.

'Mr Ashford.'

Their eyes met, and in an instant, the years fell away. For a fleeting moment, she was no longer standing in the cold outside a church, but walking along a riverbank on a golden summer evening, her hand locked in his and their laughter carrying on the breeze. She realised she was smiling.

'Do call me Christopher,' he said gently. 'How are you? How have you been?'

She hesitated. 'I've been all right.' Instinctively, she covered her left hand with her right – hiding the disfigurement she'd carried since birth.

He studied her for a moment. 'Are you still Miss Jackson?'

'Yes. I never married. If that's what you mean.'

'I see.' He nodded, his expression unreadable. 'Well, you look very well.'

She gave a small, hollow laugh. 'Do I? I'm not sure I feel it.' She glanced towards the church entrance. 'It's terribly sad news about Mrs Melbourne, isn't it?'

'Yes, dreadfully sad. She was my godmother, of course. And the manner of her death...' He ran a gloved hand over his whiskers. 'It doesn't bear thinking about.'

A pause followed. The sound of footsteps and murmured conversations filled the space between them as more people filed into the church.

'Your wife,' Lydia said at last. 'Is she with you this evening?'

Christopher hesitated. 'I'm afraid not. She died last year.'

A silence hung between them.

'I'm so sorry,' Lydia said softly.

'Both she and the baby,' he added. 'It was... a very difficult time. But I managed. You know how it is.'

A sharp pang twisted inside her. She clasped her hands together to still them. 'Oh, absolutely,' she murmured.

'So you returned to London?'

'Yes,' she said, unsure why he'd asked the question. 'I never left.'

'Didn't you? Oh...' The line between his brows deepened. 'Perhaps I misheard... Are you living locally?'

'I was, but I'm currently searching for a new position so I'm staying at a guesthouse on Buckingham Palace Road.' She smiled.

'The name sounds glamorous but it's not. The house backs onto the railway lines from Victoria station.'

He smiled. 'Not far from here then.' He cleared his throat. 'Did you see much of Mrs Melbourne in recent years?'

She gave a slight nod, reluctant to recall her last encounter with her. 'I saw her recently... briefly. I didn't see her for a long time, but then a new job brought me back to this part of London, and I met her again.'

'Are you still a governess?'

'I am.'

'Well, that's good,' he said.

She gave a small, measured nod. 'Yes. Things have worked out as well as they possibly could.'

They stood in silence, watching the last of the mourners enter the church. A cool breeze whispered through the square, and Lydia felt its chill seep into her bones. The weight of unspoken words pressed upon her. This was a man she had once known so well – better than anyone. And yet, here they were, speaking in pleasantries, formal and distant.

She wanted to reach for his hand, to take a walk as they once had. She wanted to tell him that his absence had left a wound that never fully healed. But what would be the point? His life had moved on, even through grief. Any feelings he'd once had for her were long buried. This meeting was nothing more than a polite exchange between two people who'd once meant something to each other.

The church bells struck six.

Christopher exhaled and straightened. 'Well, I suppose we'd better go in.'

Lydia nodded. 'Absolutely.'

'And judging by the number of people here this evening, Mrs Melbourne was a popular lady.'

'Yes,' Lydia said, forcing a smile. 'It seems she was.'

FOUR

After finishing her lessons the following day, Emma travelled by omnibus to St John's Wood and then walked to Penny Blakely's house.

Back in her Fleet Street days, Penny had covered her fair share of murder cases. Although her life was now very different – married, with two small children and no shortage of domestic demands – her curiosity and sharp instinct for mysteries hadn't faded. Emma felt sure her friend would have thoughts about Clara Clifton's disturbing discovery.

By the time Emma stepped off the omnibus in St John's Wood, the light was fading and the afternoon had turned colder. A newsagent already had the evening editions on display. One bold headline caught her eye: *Murder Mystery in Soho Graveyard*. She bought a copy, folded it under her arm and quickened her pace, eager to discuss the story with Penny.

Penny greeted her with a warm, if slightly exasperated, smile. Her hair was coming loose from its pins and there were shadows under her eyes.

'Florence started crawling a few days ago,' she said as she ushered Emma into the sitting room. 'And now I can't stop her.'

'Go away!' came a shrill voice from the hearthrug, where two-year-old Thomas was trying to defend a neat row of tin soldiers from his younger sister's advances. Florence, determined and undeterred, crawled straight for the toys, her eyes shining with mischief.

'If you put them on the table, Thomas, she can't reach them,' said Penny, with the patient tone of someone who'd repeated this advice a hundred times already.

'I don't want to put them on the table!'

Penny sighed, scooped up Florence and placed her on her hip. The baby responded with a loud protest, kicking her legs furiously.

'All she wants are the soldiers,' Penny said, giving Emma a weary glance. 'I try to tempt her with her own toys, but she has no interest whatsoever.'

'Hello there!' Emma said brightly to the baby, pulling a funny face in the hopes of distracting her. Florence paused and studied Emma's face with great seriousness for a moment, then burst into a wail and began flailing again.

'She's tired,' Penny said. 'But won't sleep, of course. I'll fetch her a rusk. Sometimes that gives me a few minutes of peace.'

'I want a rusk!' Thomas cried.

'And what do we say when we want something?' Penny prompted, already halfway to the kitchen.

'Please!'

A short while later, the children were happily chewing their rusks. Florence perched on Penny's lap, content for the moment, dribbling biscuit down her mother's sleeve. Emma, watching the scene, felt a quiet warmth. She imagined herself as a mother one day – but not yet. The sight of Penny's tired eyes was reminder enough of the demands of motherhood.

Once the children were settled, Emma mentioned her encounter with Clara Clifton and the discovery in the graveyard. Penny listened attentively, her brow furrowed.

'The poor woman,' she said when Emma finished. 'How dreadful. A disused graveyard is unsettling enough on its own, but to stumble upon a murder victim there... It must have been harrowing. And the police will have questioned her extensively; she must be quite drained.'

'I thought so too,' said Emma. 'I picked up a copy of the evening paper on my way here.'

She unfolded the newspaper and pointed to the front page. Penny leaned closer.

'Well?' she asked. 'What does it say?'

Emma skimmed the article and read aloud the key details. 'The victim was Mrs Eleanor Melbourne, sixty-four years of age, widow of the industrialist Patrick Melbourne. She lived in Belgravia. The police believe she was killed sometime during the night. They're trying to determine who last saw her and when.'

'Hmm,' said Penny, sitting back. 'At least they've identified her – that's something. The widow of an industrialist, you say? She sounds like a woman of some standing. What on earth was she doing in a disused graveyard in Soho in the middle of the night?'

Emma shook her head. 'It doesn't make sense.'

'No, it doesn't. And a woman of her position would almost certainly have household staff. They'll know when she left the house and whether she mentioned where she was going. With luck, it won't be too difficult to piece together her last movements. I expect Scotland Yard will be involved soon. James will probably hear something before long.' Penny shifted Florence gently on her lap. 'Would you like some tea?'

Emma looked at Florence who was contently sucking her biscuit. 'Yes, please. But let me make it. You shouldn't move while she's happy.'

Penny gave a soft laugh. 'Thank you, Emma.'

Over a cup of tea, Emma told Penny what she'd learned after attending the memorial service for Mrs Melbourne the previous evening.

'They lived in Belgravia – Upper Belgrave Street, I believe. After her husband's death, it appears Mrs Melbourne kept a fairly quiet, respectable life. She was charitable, too. She gave away a good deal of her fortune to various causes. Churches, schools, hospitals… you name it. She was a regular worshipper at St Peter's in Eaton Square which explains why the service was held there. There were a lot of people there so she was clearly popular. She was a good friend of the reverend too. Reverend Underhill. He conducted the service. From all accounts, she was a devout and generous woman.'

'Which makes the crime all the more baffling,' Penny said. 'Why would anyone want to harm her?'

Penny's husband, James, arrived home while she and Emma were halfway through their second cup of tea. He stepped into the sitting room, unbuttoning his coat and loosening his scarf.

'How was your day?' Penny asked. 'And tell me – have you been drawn into the Melbourne case yet?'

'Not yet.' James greeted the children then sank into an armchair. 'Inspector Paget from C Division is handling the case for now. Unless it proves more complex, Scotland Yard won't be stepping in just yet. They're still trying to piece together Mrs Melbourne's final movements. What we do know is that she left home two evenings ago, supposedly to dine with a friend. She was attacked with a long-bladed knife.'

Emma winced at the thought.

'The doctor estimates she died around midnight,' James continued. 'But she wasn't found until early the following morning. It's a rather overgrown burial ground and her body wasn't visible from the street. The woman who found her happened to be surveying the graveyard.'

'That was Clara Clifton,' Emma said. 'I met her yesterday. She was sitting on a bench in St James's Square. She'd just come from Vine Street police station and looked terribly shaken.'

James raised his eyebrows. 'Did she tell you what happened?'

'She didn't go into much detail, but she said she'd found the body while working. Apparently, she's cataloguing abandoned burial grounds for some kind of conservation society.'

'Poor woman,' said James, shaking his head. 'I hope she's being properly looked after.'

'She seemed very even-tempered and sensible,' Emma said. 'But I imagine the shock will catch up with her.'

'Does Paget know why Mrs Melbourne was attacked?' Penny asked her husband. 'Was it a robbery gone wrong?'

James shook his head. 'Unlikely. Her jewellery and money were still on her. Nothing had been taken. It doesn't look like theft was the motive.'

'So it was personal?' Penny asked, frowning.

'Possibly.'

Emma thought of the people she'd seen at the memorial service the previous evening, could Mrs Melbourne's murderer have been among them? 'I spoke to Mrs Melbourne's housekeeper after the church service,' she said. 'Obviously it wasn't the right time to ask her questions about her employer's death, but it's possible she knows something.'

'What's she like?' asked Penny.

'Quite stern and sombre. Her name's Agnes Black and she's in her mid-forties. I realise she was sombre because of the occasion, but she looks like the sort of lady who's serious even at the best of times.'

'Inspector Paget will be speaking to all the staff in the household,' said James. 'If the housekeeper knows anything about Mrs Melbourne's death then Paget will pick up on it.'

'Are you sure?' asked Penny.

'Of course I'm sure. He's in charge of the investigation.'

Penny's expression was sceptical. 'I wouldn't be so sure about him, he wasn't much good at investigating Augustus Forster's death, was he?' She recalled the investigation she and James had been involved with five years previously. Mr Forster had been murdered in St James's Square and Inspector Paget and his men had failed to catch the culprit.

James sighed. 'That was five years ago, Penny. I'm sure the chap has been managing perfectly well since then.'

Penny gave Emma a sidelong glance which suggested she doubted this was true.

FIVE

Agnes Black retired to her attic room that evening. The day had been long and filled with unspoken tensions. She felt grateful now to be alone. She removed her keys from her belt and placed them on her bedside table. Then she opened the little window from where she had a clear view over the Belgravia rooftops. It was a sight which had always brought her a measure of comfort. The mist from earlier in the day had lifted, revealing a crisp, cold night. The air was tinged with coal smoke and a bright crescent moon hung in the sky, casting silvery light over the city. She stood still in the darkness, making no move to light the lamp. There was something reassuring about the night, about watching the world outside while remaining unseen.

For thirty years, this house had been her home; its familiar walls and winding staircases were as well-known to her as the lines on her hands. But now, everything was uncertain. Change loomed ahead.

A carriage rumbled by in the street below, its wheels clattering over the cobblestones. A man called out to a friend, his voice carrying through the still air. Somewhere in the distance, a woman laughed, the sound high and brittle.

A single tear traced a slow path down Agnes's cheek. She

focused on the sensation, on the way it tickled before turning cold against her skin.

The tear was not for Mrs Melbourne – of that, she was certain. She would never weep for her former employer. The years of service, the sacrifices, had all amounted to nothing.

Her fingers instinctively sought the cross that hung from the silver chain around her neck. She traced its familiar edges, finding solace in the cool metal as her mind recalled the conversation with Mrs Harwell. Every word struck her anew, as sharp as a blade. The weight in her chest was heavy and unrelenting. It felt almost suffocating.

She drew in a deep breath, but the air wouldn't come. No matter how hard she tried to fill her lungs, it wasn't enough. A wave of dizziness took over, and she stumbled back, collapsing onto her bed.

As more tears fell, she clutched the cross to her heart. The night stretched on around her, vast and indifferent. The city continued to hum with life beyond her window.

But here, in the quiet solitude of her attic room, Agnes Black was utterly alone.

SIX

After teaching a piano lesson in Marylebone the following day, Emma joined Penny for an afternoon walk in Regent's Park. Penny was pushing the perambulator with Florence inside and Thomas walking alongside. It was a clear, sunny day but cold.

'Thomas, where's your hat?' asked Penny.

'I took it off.'

'Where did you put it?'

'Over there.' He stopped, turned, and pointed to a bench about ten yards behind them.

Penny sighed. 'Please go and fetch it and put it on your head, Thomas. You have to wear a hat out here to keep your head warm.'

Wearily, Thomas trudged over to the bench, fetched his hat and marched back with it in his hand.

'Would you like Emma to put it on your head for you?' asked Penny.

Emma smiled, feeling sympathy for him. He looked up at her sullenly and said nothing.

He held the hat out for Emma, and she took it from him. 'This is a lovely hat,' she said. 'I wish I had a hat this colourful and warm.'

He continued to say nothing and kept his sulky expression as she carefully placed it on his head and pulled it down over his ears.

'I wonder how the police are getting on with the investigation into Eleanor Melbourne's murder,' said Emma. 'I didn't notice any police officers attending the service two nights ago. If I were a detective, I would have gone to see who turned up. It's possible the murderer was there.'

'Yes, I think it is possible,' said Penny. 'You hear of strange tales like that, don't you? Sometimes a murderer returns to the scene of the crime and sometimes they attend their victim's funeral. A murderer can present himself as a concerned family member or friend. I've come across it before.' She paused to check on Thomas who was stomping up ahead, still sulking that he'd had to put his hat back on. 'From what you've told me, there were a lot of people at the service. Even if a police officer had attended, I'm not quite sure where he would have begun. At this stage of the investigation, I can imagine the police are making a list of the people who were closest to Mrs Melbourne – family, friends and staff.'

'Who benefits from her death?' asked Emma.

'A good question. According to James, Christopher Ashford inherits Mrs Melbourne's estate. He was her godson and she was very fond of him. I'm not suggesting he murdered his godmother, of course, but he's now inheriting a fortune and a large house in Belgravia.'

A squirrel scampered across their path and Thomas squealed with delight as it scampered up a tree.

'And does James know what Mrs Melbourne was doing in the churchyard?' asked Emma.

'No, that remains a mystery. Apparently, she dined at a restaurant in Haymarket that evening with her friend Margaret Harwell. Both ladies went their separate ways and, for some reason, Mrs Melbourne ended up in St Anne's churchyard.'

'Did they actually go their separate ways?' asked Emma. 'Or is that just what Mrs Harwell says?'

Penny laughed. 'I can tell you're suspicious of everyone!'

'But you have to be, don't you?'

'I'm afraid you do. Investigating murders can make you extremely sceptical about people's words and actions. Although we're not investigating Mrs Melbourne's death, are we? It's up to the police to solve it.'

Emma couldn't help feeling disappointed about this. She and Penny had solved her husband's murder, and they'd also been able to solve the murder of Lord Harpole. Although both cases had been difficult, Emma had enjoyed the challenge of solving them. Like putting together the pieces of a puzzle. 'Are you finding it difficult not to get involved?' she asked Penny.

'Yes!' Penny's eyes sparkled with enthusiasm behind her spectacles. 'Very difficult! When I was a news reporter, discovering the truth was part of my job. And now, I don't have an excuse for investigating what happened to Mrs Melbourne.' She sighed, her fingers tapping impatiently on the handle of the perambulator. 'I'd like to investigate, but we can't involve ourselves in every case, can we? I'm a mother and you're a piano teacher. We don't have any right to look into this in more detail.'

'It would be good to come up with a reason, though, wouldn't it?' replied Emma.

'Yes, it would. We need to have a think about it. Oh, Thomas!' She stopped. 'Where's your hat gone now?'

The little boy gave her a sheepish look. 'Over there,' he said, pointing to a bare-branched shrub. The colourful woollen hat dangled from one of its branches.

'Go and fetch it,' said Penny with an exasperated sigh.

He did what he was told and Emma helped him put it on again before they continued on their way.

'My next article for the *Morning Express* newspaper is going to suggest hobbies for mothers,' said Penny. 'All the things I don't particularly enjoy myself... Sketching, needlework and charity work. But perhaps I could suggest other pastimes for mothers?'

'Such as what?' asked Emma.

'Solving murders.'

Emma laughed. 'I may be wrong, Penny, but I think there's only one mother capable of doing that.'

SEVEN

'I've forgotten how difficult it is to play the piano,' moaned Mrs Solomon that evening. 'I learned a lot of songs as a young woman, and I thought I'd remember them still. I can recall a few notes here and there, but it's a shame because I appear to have forgotten just about everything.'

They sat at the piano, which Mr and Mrs Solomon had recently bought for Emma.

'I'm sure you'll find the songs come back to you after a few lessons,' said Emma. 'Let's start with something easy.'

Emma placed 'Für Elise' by Beethoven on the music stand.

Mrs Solomon leaned forward and squinted at it. 'I can't play that,' she said.

'Haven't you played it before? It's a popular piece for piano students.'

Her landlady shook her head. 'I don't recognise it. And I certainly don't remember music looking that complicated.'

Emma gave an inward sigh. She'd been led to believe Mrs Solomon's musical knowledge was greater than it now appeared to be. 'Can you remember any musical notation?' she asked patiently.

'Let me see now.' Mrs Solomon peered even closer at the music. 'That's a C, isn't it?'

'It's an E,' said Emma.

'And that next one is a sharp, isn't it?'

'Yes. D sharp.'

'Good, I remember that. Why don't you play it for me and I'll tell you if I remember it.'

Although 'Für Elise' was a simple piece, it had always been a favourite of Emma's. She closed her eyes and her father's proud face appeared as it so often did when she played a song from her childhood. He had loved listening to her.

'Lovely, shall I have a go now?' said Mrs Solomon, once Emma had finished.

Emma was just about to answer when there was a knock at the door.

'Who's that interrupting our lesson?' said Mrs Solomon, getting to her feet. She went to answer the door and appeared moments later with a flustered-looking Clara Clifton.

Emma got up from the piano stool. 'Is everything all right?'

Mrs Clifton bit her lip, her shoulders raised. 'Sort of. I'm so sorry to bother you, Mrs Langley. I think I need some help.'

Mrs Solomon invited her to sit down. 'I'll make some tea,' she said.

'Oh no, please don't worry. I won't be long, and my husband is waiting outside.'

The landlady raised an eyebrow. 'Your husband is waiting outside? On a freezing night like tonight? Invite him in, then he can have some tea with us too.'

Mrs Clifton's husband, Jonathan Clifton, was a well-mannered gentleman with a thick dark moustache. He kept apologising for their intrusion.

'Please don't worry,' said Emma. 'Clearly, you're worried enough about something to call here this evening. How can I help?'

'Well, I'm not sure it's something you can help with yourself,' said Mrs Clifton. She and her husband perched side-by-side on the sofa. 'However, I remember you mentioning your friend who was a news reporter and is married to a Scotland Yard detective. If possible, we'd like his advice.'

Emma felt wary about bothering James Blakely unduly. 'Why don't you explain to me what's happened?' she said.

'It's the police.' Mrs Clifton's lower lip quivered. 'They told me go to the police station today and an inspector questioned me again. And then he came to our house this evening and questioned my husband! He wanted him to provide an alibi for my whereabouts. He thinks I murdered Mrs Melbourne!' Her blue eyes grew wide and watery.

'Are you sure they think that?' asked Emma.

She nodded. 'The policeman I spoke to at the police station was kind and reassuring. But this new detective – I don't like him at all.'

'Inspector Paget,' said Mr Clifton. 'I don't like him either.'

'His manner is cold,' added Mrs Clifton, visibly shuddering. 'And he was accusing me.'

'What was he accusing you of?' asked Emma.

'Every time I told him what happened when I found Mrs Melbourne in the graveyard, he kept questioning me about it, as if he was trying to catch me out. It was as though he suspected I was lying.'

'He shouldn't be allowed to speak to my wife like that,' Mr Clifton chimed in. 'And just as Clara was telling me about it this evening, he turned up on our doorstep! And then he had the nerve to ask me all sorts of questions – what Clara had been doing two nights ago, did she know Mrs Melbourne, did I know Mrs Melbourne? The questions went on and on. It was relentless.'

'I'm worried they're going to arrest me,' said Mrs Clifton anxiously. 'And I've done nothing wrong! I suppose it's because my job is quite unusual. The police don't believe a lady would spend her time visiting disused graveyards. They seem to think it's a strange story I've made up!'

Her hands twisted in her lap and she bit her lip again. Emma felt she had to try to reassure the couple.

'I'm no expert on how the police conduct their business,' she said, 'but I've had enough experience of these things to know they like to check everything thoroughly. And it's possible to find yourself in an awkward position when you discover a body. Even though you tell the police the truth, they can continue to question it. It's quite normal for them to establish alibis for everyone who was somehow connected to Mrs Melbourne – and that includes the person who found her.' Emma paused and felt their gaze resting expectantly on her. 'I shall talk to James about it,' she added. 'He might be able to have a word with someone. I realise you're just trying to be help the police and it's not right that you feel as though you've done something wrong.'

'I just don't want to be arrested,' said Mrs Clifton. 'You hear such terrible stories, don't you? About people being forced to sign confessions.'

'Hopefully, the police investigating this case are perfectly honest,' said Emma.

'But they might not be!' said Mr Clifton. 'Mrs Melbourne's murder has attracted a lot of attention. The police are under pressure to make an arrest, aren't they? Especially as they struggle to catch anybody these days. What did they manage to do about Jack the Ripper? Nothing. So I'm worried they'll be quick to blame my wife for what happened, to save them the work of finding out who is really behind this.'

Mrs Solomon brought in the tea and offered Mr and Mrs Clifton some biscuits which seemed to calm them a little.

Emma suspected neither of them had encountered the police much in the past, and suddenly finding themselves at the centre of a murder inquiry was quite a shock.

But was it shock? Or did they feel the need to defend themselves? Emma liked Clara Clifton, but was it possible the police inspector's suspicion of her was justified?

EIGHT

Emma called on Penny the following day. She arrived just after lunchtime, hoping to catch her friend while the children were having their afternoon nap. But as she stepped into the sitting room, it was clear that peace was in short supply.

Thomas was on the sofa with a copy of *The Merry Adventures of Robin Hood*, imploring his mother to read it to him. Penny was trying to encourage Florence to remain sitting on the hearthrug with some building blocks, but the baby kept launching herself on a determined crawl towards the cat on the windowsill.

'Would you like me to read to you?' Emma asked Thomas as she sat next to him.

He gave her a bashful nod and passed her the book. She read two pages to him before he slid off the sofa and chased after Florence.

The baby seemed pleased to see her brother. He encouraged her to crawl to the hearthrug where he stacked some building blocks for her. Penny took the opportunity to join Emma on the sofa, re-pinning tendrils of hair which had fallen loose.

'Hopefully the pair of them stay there for a moment,' she said. 'And Florence will need a sleep soon so that should give us a bit of peace and quiet.'

Emma told her about the visit from Mr and Mrs Clifton the previous evening. Penny listened closely, her expression serious.

'Oh dear,' she said when Emma had finished. 'It sounds as though the police are being very thorough. Asking for her whereabouts at the exact time of the murder... I can see how that would upset Clara Clifton. But if she didn't know Mrs Melbourne, what possible motive could she have?'

Emma nodded in agreement. 'I tried to reassure her that it's normal for the police to question the person who found the body. But she seems terribly anxious. I think she's afraid they'll make her a scapegoat.'

'She wouldn't be the first,' Penny murmured. 'People do get swept up in things they had nothing to do with – especially when they don't have the means or position to defend themselves properly.'

Emma nodded. 'I've taken her at her word because she seems genuine. But part of me wonders... what if she isn't? What if she's cleverly masking something more sinister?'

Penny pursed her lips. 'That's always the difficulty, isn't it? We want to believe the best of people. But there's always the possibility we're being misled. Still, from everything you've described, she sounds more like a woman who's had the misfortune to be in the wrong place at the wrong time.'

'She and her husband asked me to speak to James,' Emma continued hesitantly. 'When I first met Mrs Clifton, I made the mistake of mentioning that I knew an inspector at Scotland Yard, and now they think he can intervene.'

'Well, I can certainly talk to him,' Penny said. 'But he can't interfere with how the investigation is being conducted.'

'That's what I thought, but thank you for talking to him,' replied Emma. 'It seems Mrs Clifton wants to get on with her work and be left alone, but she's been pulled into something beyond her control.'

'We don't always choose our battles,' said Penny softly. 'Sometimes the world chooses them for us.'

Florence knocked down the tower of building blocks and crawled off the hearthrug, heading for the cat.

Penny got to her feet. 'She can't reach Tiger on the windowsill,' she said. 'But I'm worried she'll try and Tiger will scratch her.' She positioned herself between the cat and the baby, ready to intervene.

'Do you think we should try to help Clara Clifton?' Emma asked her.

'Yes, we could,' Penny said. 'If we can gather enough information to show she had no connection to Mrs Melbourne, then perhaps the police will shift their focus elsewhere.'

Emma sat up straighter, feeling a renewed sense of determination. 'Then let's do it. Let's find out the truth.'

'Agreed.'

They exchanged a smile and Emma felt a thrill of excitement that they had a new mystery to work on. 'Where do we start?' she asked.

'There are two places we should visit. Mrs Melbourne's home and the scene of the crime. We might find someone who knew Mrs Melbourne or saw her that day.'

'And if we find a thread,' Emma said, 'we'll follow it.'

'Exactly.'

Baby Florence let out a cry, frustrated at her failed attempt to reach the cat.

'She might scratch you,' said Penny, bending down to pick up her daughter. She returned to the sofa while Florence pointed at Tiger and let out another cry of protest.

'When shall we go to Mrs Melbourne's home?' Emma asked her.

'Tomorrow morning? I'll ask Mrs Tuttle to mind the children.'

Florence pulled Penny's spectacles off her nose and flung them on the floor.

Emma gave a grimace. 'I expect you're looking forward to the break.'

'Yes, I am,' said Penny through gritted teeth. 'Very much.'

NINE

It was a drizzly morning when Emma and Penny met in Upper Belgrave Street. The row of large, stately townhouses exuded a quiet, imperious grandeur. The scent of damp stone mingled with the tang of chimney smoke.

'Number nine,' said Penny. 'That's where Mrs Melbourne lived.'

As they walked past the elegant facades, Emma noted the grand porches and polished doors. It was a world away from the soot-darkened alleys and crumbling brickwork of Soho.

'The contrast is stark, isn't it?' she murmured. 'From Belgravia to a disused graveyard in Soho. It's hard to imagine how Mrs Melbourne ended up there.'

'She was a pious lady,' said Penny, scanning the house numbers. 'Perhaps she had a link to St Anne's Church. Although I must admit, it's a long way to go for worship. There are plenty of churches around here.'

'She could have been baptised there?' suggested Emma. 'Or married, perhaps. Or maybe she had a friend buried in the churchyard.'

Penny nodded thoughtfully. 'Hopefully we'll uncover something today.'

A young man was striding towards them with purpose, his collar turned up against the damp and a notebook in his hand.

Emma's heart gave a flutter as she recognised the familiar figure – Harry Wright of the *Morning Express*. She hadn't seen him for a few weeks and had found herself hoping she would bump into him again before long.

Now that he was in front of her, his boyish handsome looks left her feeling tongue-tied. What was she going to say to him without getting bashful?

'Isn't that Harry Wright?' asked Penny, narrowing her eyes.

Emma attempted nonchalance. 'Oh... is it?' she said. Her cheeks began to warm. 'Yes, I think it is.'

Mr Wright's expression broke into a grin. 'Mrs Blakely. Mrs Langley. What a pleasure to see you both.' His tone was warm.

'Good morning, Mr Wright,' said Penny. 'I suppose we shouldn't be surprised to find you here. Reporting on Mrs Melbourne's murder, I assume?'

'Trying to,' he said, blowing out a sigh. 'But no one at number nine will say a word to me. This is the fourth morning I've turned up, and I've had no luck at all. The housekeeper, Agnes Black, has told me to stay away and never darken her doorway again. I expect you had the same problem in your Fleet Street days, Mrs Blakely.'

Penny gave a wry smile. 'Frequently. And it's understandable – they're grieving, after all. The last thing the household wants is interference. Any luck with the neighbours?'

'A little. Most are polite, but they're frosty. They don't take kindly to journalists poking around.'

'I imagine it's not an easy task,' said Emma, keen to say something. 'It must be tricky gathering facts when everyone's guarding their words.'

'Precisely.' He fixed her with his keen hazel eyes, a smile playing on his lips. 'You understand my predicament perfectly, Mrs Langley. Mr Fish still expects copy, though. Hundreds of words. And I can't just write "No one is talking to me" and hand that to him.'

Penny and Emma laughed. 'Have you learned anything useful at all?' asked Penny.

'Well,' Mr Wright said, lowering his voice, 'besides the usual – she was wealthy, devout, and charitable – I did stumble on something. There was a court case last year. She sued a doctor over an operation performed on her nephew. He'd had a riding accident and he didn't survive the surgery.'

'How awful,' said Emma.

'I wrote about it,' he said, with a little lift of pride. 'You may have read my articles on it.'

'I must have missed those,' said Emma with a smile, although her cheeks coloured slightly.

'Anyway,' he continued, 'the case caused quite a stir. But whether it has anything to do with her death is anyone's guess. I doubt the doctor took revenge – it seems far-fetched.'

'Not necessarily,' said Penny. 'People have committed murder for similar reasons. Especially if they feel their reputation has been destroyed.'

Mr Wright's expression brightened. 'That's exactly the sort of theory I'm after. The doctor had a good motive. But I've found nothing to back up the idea yet. The murderer could have been someone from her household. Perhaps one of them followed her that evening... Well, stranger things have happened. What about you?' he added. 'Are you here to ask questions too?'

'We might be,' said Penny lightly. 'Although unlike you, we don't have a professional reason to be asking.'

'So you're just loitering?' he asked, eyes twinkling. 'Once a reporter, always a reporter.'

'That's right.' She smiled. 'We've decided to take an interest in the case on behalf of Mrs Clifton. She's the lady who discovered Mrs Melbourne's body in St Anne's churchyard. Unfortunately the police seem to be questioning her quite thoroughly – perhaps a little too thoroughly.'

Mr Wright frowned. 'They think she's a suspect?'

'She's worried they think that,' said Emma. 'They've asked her husband to provide an alibi for her whereabouts on the night of the murder. Naturally, she's upset. She never expected to be drawn into something like this.'

'That's awful,' said Mr Wright. 'I'd like to speak to her – if she's willing.'

'She might be,' said Emma. 'But she's very shaken. We'll speak to her first, and let her decide. James told me Inspector Paget at C Division is leading the investigation; have you spoken to him yet?'

Mr Wright let out a dry laugh. 'Inspector Paget? He's not particularly fond of the press. The man practically growled at me when I introduced myself. I don't understand why some police officers are so resistant. Surely they realise we're trying to help? The more people who read about these awful crimes, the more likely someone will come forward with information.'

Penny nodded. 'Some officers do see the value in working with journalists. But others – especially those who've been in the job a long time – see reporters as meddlesome. They think we twist their words or get in the way.'

'Which we don't,' said Mr Wright. 'Well – most of us don't.' He tucked his notebook into his coat pocket. 'I think it's excellent you're both interested in this case. Don't think I've forgotten what you did on the Harpole mystery.'

'We just asked the right questions at the right time,' said Emma, blushing.

'And got the right answers,' replied Mr Wright. 'That's more than most people manage. If you learn anything interesting about Mrs Melbourne, you'll let me know, won't you?'

'Of course,' said Penny. 'As long as you keep us informed too.'

'I promise to.' He tipped his hat to them both. 'It was very nice to see you again.' Although his words were intended for both of them, he fixed his gaze on Emma as he spoke.

Penny tried to catch Emma's eye as Harry Wright walked away, but Emma felt too embarrassed to look at her. 'Ugh, I didn't realise it was so wet today,' she said, glancing up at the rainy sky.

Penny gave her a playful nudge with her elbow. 'Harry Wright is quite fond of you, isn't he?'

'Is he? I hadn't noticed.'

Penny laughed. 'I'm not sure I believe you.'

TEN

Emma and Penny continued along Upper Belgrave Street until they reached number nine. The imposing facade of the four-storey house showed no sign of activity. The curtains drawn across the windows seemed to echo the heavy silence from within.

'I don't think we should disturb them,' Penny said quietly. 'Not if Mr Wright's just been knocking at the door. It's probably best to leave them in peace.'

'So who shall we speak to?' asked Emma. 'The neighbours?'

'I suspect they've just been bothered by Harry Wright too. Let's see if we can find anyone interesting in the mews at the back.'

They partly retraced their steps before turning into Wilton Street, where the entrance to the mews was tucked between tall brick walls. The cobbled lane was flanked on either side by rows of stables with staff accommodation above them.

A blue-painted handcart stood in the lane, the gold lettering reading 'Beaumont's Bakery'. A boy emerged from a side gate, a large wicker basket looped over his arm.

'Excuse me,' said Penny, her tone light. 'Do you know anyone at number nine?'

The boy looked up and gave a grunt. 'Just delivered there.'

He opened a hatch at the back of the cart to replenish his

basket with fresh loaves. The warm, yeasty smell of bread made Emma's mouth water.

'Do you know the household well?' Penny asked.

'Well enough,' he replied. 'Deliver there nearly every day. Sad news about the lady who's died.'

'What did you think of her?' Penny asked gently.

The boy hesitated, narrowing his eyes. 'Why're you asking?'

'I've just moved into a house nearby,' Penny replied, adopting an innocent tone. 'It's unsettling that this sort of thing could happen so close to home.'

He shrugged. 'It didn't happen here, did it? She was found in Soho. That's where your trouble is. Not round here.'

'But it still seems so odd,' said Emma. 'She was a well-respected lady, wasn't she? Churchgoing, charitable – why would someone want to harm her?'

'Someone must have taken a dislike to her.'

Penny leaned in slightly. 'Did you ever hear anything? Ever see anything that made you think someone didn't like her?'

The boy hesitated again. 'It's not for me to say.'

'Of course not,' Penny said. 'But sometimes people hear things in passing.'

He glanced over his shoulder. 'Well... I heard she had a row with a governess at number five.'

'Really?' Emma's interest sharpened. 'What happened?'

The boy's eyes darted about nervously. 'No idea what it was about. Only that the governess left not long after. Heard she was in tears. Didn't last more than a month.'

'Did it happen recently?'

He nodded. 'A couple of weeks ago.'

'Do you remember her name?'

'Nope.' He shook his head. 'Never knew it. Didn't even see her. Just heard the other maids gossiping.'

Emma surveyed the back of the grand townhouses, imagining the kind of person who might provoke a governess's dramatic departure. 'Was it out of character for Mrs Melbourne to be involved in something like that?'

The boy shook his head. 'Couldn't say. She seemed nice enough to me. Polite, anyway. I'd best get on, I can't let this bread go cold.'

'Thank you very much for talking to us,' said Penny.

He gave a small nod and headed off for the next house with his basket.

Penny and Emma stood for a moment, watching him go.

'A governess from number five?' said Emma. 'I wonder what the argument was about. Do you think we might find someone at number five willing to talk?'

Penny gave her a confident smile. 'There's only one way to find out.'

ELEVEN

Emma and Penny returned to Upper Belgrave Street and knocked on the door of number five. It was opened by a maid with a starched apron and a wary gaze.

'I'm terribly sorry to trouble you,' said Penny, adopting an impeccable accent and serene smile. 'I'm Mrs Cumming-Bruce. I've just moved to the area and I'm in rather urgent need of a governess. A friend mentioned that number five had recently employed one. I was hoping you might recommend the agency. There are so many advertised in the newspapers, and I would much prefer a personal recommendation.'

'Well, the new governess has just joined us,' said the maid. 'She came recommended from Madame Deveraux's agency in Eccleston Street.'

'You've been so kind. Thank you,' said Penny.

Once they were safely out of earshot, Emma turned to her friend with admiration. 'That was impressive. I would never have come up with that on the spot.'

'You'd be surprised what you can do with a little confidence and a fake surname,' said Penny with a smile. 'Now let's pay Madame Deveraux a visit.'

. . .

Madame Deveraux's agency was housed in a second-floor office above a draper's shop. The elegant reception room had floral wallpaper, a vase of fresh flowers and a mahogany desk stacked with ledgers. Letters of recommendation hung in tasteful frames and a glass-fronted bookcase held volumes on education, etiquette and moral instruction.

Emma was reminded of her own governess she'd had as a child. Fortunately, she'd been a kind, friendly lady who'd always made Emma's lessons interesting.

A woman in a high-necked navy dress appeared from a doorway.

'Good morning,' she said. 'Can I help you?'

'Madame Deveraux?' said Penny, stepping forward with calm assurance.

'No. I'm her assistant, Miss Blythe.'

'Pleased to meet you, Miss Blythe. My name is Mrs Cumming-Bruce and I'm in urgent need of a governess. A friend mentioned that a woman recently employed at number five Upper Belgrave Street had come through your agency. I was hoping to learn more.'

Miss Blythe tilted her head. 'Who mentioned that to you?'

Penny gave a breezy laugh. 'Oh dear, I wish I could remember her name. I'm new to the area, you see – my husband and I have just returned from Switzerland, where he was working in finance. We only arrived last week. We spent three years in Geneva and now we've been moved back to London without much warning. So, here we are – a new home, new staff to find and no idea where to begin in Belgravia.'

Miss Blythe's gaze flickered over Penny's overcoat. Although it was good quality, it wasn't quite what a wealthy lady would wear.

'Travelling clothes,' Penny added, apologetically. 'Our belongings haven't arrived yet. I do apologise for my appearance, I'm not dressed for social calls today.'

'I see,' said Miss Blythe. 'Well, I can take down your details and see what we can do for you. How many children do you have?'

'Two,' said Penny promptly. 'Eight and ten years old. We're

looking for someone calm, sensible and kind – but firm. A well-rounded character. I hope you don't think me impertinent when I say this, but I'm interested in the governess who recently left number five Upper Belgrave Street. What's her name again?' She tapped her chin and looked up at the ceiling as she thought. 'Miss Pugh, is it?'

'Miss Jackson,' Miss Blythe corrected.

'Oh, that's right! I remember now. Please don't tell me she's been placed somewhere else?'

'No, she hasn't. Not yet, anyway.'

'Wonderful,' said Penny. 'How do we go about an introduction?'

'We need to complete your registration with us and Madame Deveraux likes to meet all our clients personally. We can do that now, if you like?'

'Unfortunately, I'm pressed for time today. I'm interviewing a potential housekeeper shortly. But I shall return tomorrow to do all that.'

'Lovely. I look forward to seeing you again tomorrow, Mrs Cumming-Bruce.'

Back out on the street, Penny gave a quiet laugh. 'That went well, don't you think?'

'Yes it did, Mrs Cumming-Bruce.'

'It's a good surname, isn't it? I much prefer it to Blakely. Now, we have a name for the governess who left number five. Miss Jackson. All we need to do next is write her a letter asking to meet.'

'But we don't know her address,' said Emma.

'We send it to her via the agency.'

'What a good idea. I'm looking forward to hearing more about her argument with Mrs Melbourne. And next, we need to visit St Anne's churchyard.'

'Yes, but not today,' said Penny. 'Mrs Tuttle can only look after the children for a few hours. But why don't we invite Clara Clifton to join us there too? She can describe the scene she found and it would be a good opportunity to meet her again.'

'And decide whether or not she's telling us the truth?' asked Emma.

'Precisely.'

TWELVE

'Miss Black?'

Agnes raised her head, feeling a sharp ache in the back of her neck. She had been kneeling for longer than she realised. Time had slipped away in the silence of the church, in the whispered prayers she had been murmuring over and over again.

As her vision refocused, she saw Reverend Underhill standing before her, leaning on his stick. His expression was gentle, his eyes filled with quiet concern.

'Would you like me to pray with you?' he asked.

She hesitated, then nodded. 'Thank you.'

His offer was welcome. In moments like these, solitude could be unbearable.

Slowly, she opened her hand. Her fingers ached from gripping the small cross so tightly that it had left angry red indentations in her palm. The reverend's gaze flickered to the marks, then he fixed her gaze again. 'How have you been keeping, Miss Black?'

She exhaled before answering. 'I don't really know. I follow my routine. We all do. The house continues on as if nothing has changed. But we all know it has. We just don't talk about it. And soon, it will come to an end, and we will have to leave.'

She got up from her kneeling position, wincing as her knees

complained. Then she sat on the pew and the reverend sat beside her.

'The house is going to Christopher Ashford, I hear.'

She nodded. Mrs Melbourne had adored her godson but he'd taken little interest in her. He'd gone away to work in India and had rarely visited. He'd barely spoken a word to the staff who had dedicated years of their lives to his godmother and the upkeep of the house. And yet, he would inherit everything.

'I couldn't tell you much about him,' she admitted. 'I know he has a home in Fitzrovia so I expect he'll sell the house. We shall have to find new places to go.'

The reverend regarded her with sympathy. 'That must be difficult for you.'

Agnes pressed her lips into a thin line, unwilling to betray just how much the uncertainty unsettled her. 'The younger members of the staff are more shaken by it,' she said. 'They aren't accustomed to change. But they're young – that's why it frightens them. At my age, I've learned to accept that such events are out of my hands.'

A small, knowing smile tugged at the reverend's lips. 'Even so, it is at times like these that faith will guide you. As the Book of Proverbs tells us, "A man's heart deviseth his way: but the Lord directeth his steps."'

'Chapter sixteen, verse nine,' Agnes responded automatically, clasping the cross in her hand once more.

'You have a great memory for scripture.'

'Yes. It brings me enormous comfort, just as it comforted Mrs Melbourne. And at times like this, I think of Psalm Thirty-Seven, verse five, "Commit thy way unto the Lord; trust also in Him; and He shall bring it to pass."'

'That is a beautiful passage,' he agreed.

For a moment, silence settled between them. The only sound was the distant creak of a wooden pew as someone shifted at the other end of the church. The candles on the altar flickered, their flames rhythmically bending and straightening.

Then, without warning, a wave of emotion surged through Agnes, sudden and suffocating. She gasped softly, startled by its force.

Memories she had fought to bury resurfaced with brutal clarity. She could see them – hear them – feel them. Things she had spent years trying to push away, to forget, now rose up, pressing against her chest, tightening her throat.

'I know Mrs Melbourne's sudden death has been difficult for you,' the reverend said gently. 'But is there something else troubling you?'

A lump formed in her throat. She blinked rapidly, willing the tears not to fall.

'I suppose the events of the past week have made me question many things,' she admitted. 'They have also made me reflect on my own actions.'

Slowly, she turned to face him.

'Do you believe in punishment, Reverend?' she asked, her voice barely above a whisper. 'Even after one has fully repented?'

His expression didn't change, but his eyes softened. 'Absolutely not. If you have prayed for your sins to be forgiven and have truly repented, then the Lord does not judge you again. You have done the right thing, Miss Black. You have reflected, you have acknowledged, and you have sought forgiveness. There is no punishment in that.'

She nodded, but her hands trembled.

She wanted to believe him. Desperately.

'Is there anything specific you would like to discuss with me?' he asked, his voice warm with encouragement. 'If something weighs on your heart, sometimes speaking it aloud can offer clarity. I can assure you, the Lord's forgiveness is infinite.'

She felt her throat tighten.

No. She couldn't say it.

She couldn't possibly tell the reverend what lay buried in the depths of her heart.

'No,' she said finally. 'Not for the time being, anyway. I shall continue to pray, and perhaps that will be enough.'

He nodded. 'Very well. Prayer is powerful, as you know, Miss Black. You should be proud of your faith. The fact you are even concerned about true repentance shows how deeply you care.'

She met his gaze, willing herself to believe him.

'Thank you, Reverend,' she said. 'You've made me feel much better.'

'I'm pleased to hear it. Shall we say some prayers now for Mrs Melbourne?'

She hesitated.

Mrs Melbourne.

She had served the woman for decades, had known every one of her moods, had endured her commands, her criticisms, her demands. And now she was gone, leaving behind nothing but questions.

And guilt.

Yes, she felt it now. Guilt. But not the kind she could confess.

She forced herself to nod. 'Yes. I would like that.'

She bowed her head as the reverend began to speak, the familiar cadence of prayer filling the quiet church.

But even as she listened, a thought pressed itself into her mind, insistent and unshakable.

What if some sins could not be washed away?

What if some things – no matter how deeply regretted – were simply unforgivable?

THIRTEEN

A tea-coloured fog hung low over the gates of St Anne's churchyard when Emma and Penny met on Wardour Street the following day.

Emma peered in through the bars of the gate. Fog curled around old, crooked headstones and the air smelled dank. She shivered and turned to Penny, 'Do we have to go in there?'

Penny peered through the gate. A sense of adventure glimmered in her eyes. 'It does look creepy! But it's just an old burial ground. Nothing to worry about.'

'I don't like old burial grounds,' replied Emma, feeling a prickle on the back of her neck.

'But here comes someone who does,' said Penny.

Clara Clifton was walking towards them from Shaftesbury Avenue. She wore a black velvet hat, a long dark overcoat and carried a large bag. She greeted them with a nervous smile.

'Thank you for agreeing to meet us here,' said Penny. 'Do you mind visiting the churchyard again?'

Mrs Clifton glanced at the gate. 'No,' she replied. 'Not at all.'

But her voice seemed to lack conviction.

'I still need to understand the job that you do,' said Penny. 'Why did you come here that morning?'

Mrs Clifton's expression brightened at the opportunity to discuss her work. 'I survey disused burial grounds for the Metropolitan Public Gardens Committee. The committee would like to clean and restore neglected graveyards and turn them into parks which everyone can enjoy.'

Penny nodded appreciatively. 'I think it's an excellent cause, Mrs Clifton.'

Emma was less sure. 'Won't it be strange?' she began. 'Enjoying a park which people are buried beneath?'

Mrs Clifton gave a knowing smile. 'You'd be surprised how many places in London are former burial grounds,' she said. 'It's believed more than 100,000 people are buried here.'

Emma and Penny exchanged a glance, raising their eyebrows at the figure.

'The burial ground was in a bad state fifty years ago,' continued Mrs Clifton. 'Apparently gravediggers complained of headaches and heart palpitations brought on by the miasma.'

Emma grimaced. 'I really don't know why or how you do this job, Mrs Clifton.'

'It's rewarding when we can put places like this to good use again,' she responded.

Penny pushed against the heavy gate and the hinges gave a groan.

Emma followed Penny and Mrs Clifton up the steps and into St Anne's churchyard. The grimy fog hid the surrounding buildings, and she felt she was entering a macabre hidden world.

She winced as her feet sank into the damp, spongy ground. The sensation reminded her she was stepping on thousands of burials. Thoughts of rotten coffin wood and bones whirled in her mind and made her nauseous. She followed Penny's route between the tombstones; some of them looked close to toppling over.

'Why did Mrs Melbourne come here?' she said. 'I can't understand it.'

'She must have been forced to,' said Penny, pulling her skirts free from brambles. 'She would never have ventured here voluntarily.'

'Forced?' said Mrs Clifton. 'You mean someone threatened her with a weapon?'

'They must have done,' said Penny.

'But why here?' questioned Emma.

'It's secluded,' said Mrs Clifton. 'I'll show you the spot where I found her.'

Emma shivered. She wanted to leave. Some churchyards held a quiet dignity, a sense of peace. But not this one. The air here felt heavy, as if something unseen lurked in the shadows between the gravestones.

Mrs Clifton stopped. 'It was her red dress that caught my eye,' she said quietly. 'An evening dress. And she was lying over there.' She pointed to a flattened patch of weeds between the headstones. 'Just staring up at the sky.' He voice quavered. 'Her skin was so white. She didn't look real.'

Emma and Penny stared at the miserable patch of ground. Emma felt her heart ache for the poor woman who'd been discarded in this bleak place. What had driven someone to attack her so brutally?

There was no sound at all except for a steady drip of water from one of the fog-obscured buildings around them.

Emma felt a wave of dizziness wash over her. She rested her hand on a tombstone to support herself, but it gave way a little under her weight. Recoiling with a gasp, she inadvertently took in more of the dank air.

It made her stomach turn.

'I'm going back to the street,' she announced.

Penny turned to her. 'Are you all right?'

'No, not really. But don't hurry – I'll wait for you by the gate.'

She didn't wait for a response. Turning, she made her way as quickly as she could across the damp, uneven ground. Back to the gate and the street.

· · ·

A short while later, the three ladies warmed themselves in a chophouse on Wardour Street. Although the freshly cooked food smelled delicious, Emma had no appetite.

'I'll just have a cup of tea,' she said glumly.

'You might feel hungry by the time the food arrives,' said Penny. 'Are you sure you don't want to order anything?'

'Quite sure.'

'I must say I was quite happy to leave that churchyard,' said Penny. 'But I think the work you do is very interesting, Mrs Clifton.'

'Please call me Clara,' she said with a smile. 'And yes, I find it very interesting. I'm determined to catalogue every disused burial ground in London. I'm an inquisitive person and I enjoy the challenges of this work. Some of the burial grounds are difficult to access and I have to request permission from people in neighbouring buildings. They're naturally suspicious, of course, so I have to pretend that I have a connection to someone buried in the graveyard. I've also encountered rude workmen and a few vicious dogs too.'

Penny grinned. 'It sounds a bit like detective work. In fact, that's what you are. A graveyard detective.'

Clara laughed.

'I can see why it's interesting,' said Emma. 'But I don't have the courage to explore graveyards. Especially on my own.'

'I never felt anxious about doing it,' said Clara. 'But that was before I found Mrs Melbourne.'

'And that's made you feel anxious now?' asked Penny.

Clara nodded. 'I'm afraid so. I'll feel better about it again, I'm sure. But for the time being... it's put me off. And with the police suspecting me... that hasn't helped at all.'

The waitress arrived with three cups of tea and Emma wrapped her hands around her cup, enjoying the heat from it.

'I don't see how the police can suspect you,' said Penny. 'They established that Mrs Melbourne died in the night and you found her the following morning. When you found her, she'd already been dead for a few hours.'

Clara nodded again, her face pale. 'Exactly. If I was the murderer then that means I attacked her at night then returned again in the day to pretend I was the person who found her. Why would I do such a thing?'

'I agree it doesn't make sense,' said Emma. She could feel her own suspicions of Clara fading now.

'I've discussed it with my husband James,' said Penny. 'As you know, he's an inspector at Scotland Yard. He's unable to intervene with the case on your behalf, Clara, because it's being investigated by C Division. But sometimes the Yard are called in to help with a murder case. Hopefully that will happen and James can get involved.'

'And in the meantime, they're going to continue suspecting me,' said Clara sadly. 'And at the committee meeting last night I had to answer a lot of questions!'

'What sort of questions?' asked Emma.

'They wanted to know if I'd visited St Anne's churchyard on the night Mrs Melbourne was killed. I had to persuade them that I'd only visited early the following morning. Some of them believed me but others... I'm not so sure. My husband Jonathan helped me try to convince them and I'm hoping we succeeded. But...' She trailed off, shaking her head. 'I'm worried they'll ask me to leave the Metropolitan Public Gardens Committee and if I have to do that then this work which I do and enjoy so much... it will be over!' Her shoulders slumped and she looked down at the table, hurriedly wiping a tear from her eye.

Emma felt a deep pang of sympathy. 'But why would your colleagues suspect you?' she asked. 'Surely they must trust you and believe what you're telling them?'

Clara nodded. 'I thought they would, but when the police are involved then I suppose people think I must have done something wrong.'

'You had no motive to murder Mrs Melbourne,' added Penny. 'You didn't even know her.'

'No,' said Clara quickly. 'That's right.' She took out her hand-kerchief and wiped her face, avoiding Emma and Penny's gaze. Was there something she wasn't telling them?

Penny continued, 'The police have been questioning you because they don't have many other suspects at the moment,' she said. 'But as they question those who knew Mrs Melbourne, I'm sure some other suspects will become apparent. Before long, the police's attention will switch from you to someone else. I know it's not nice being suspected of such a crime, but the police have no evidence you were the culprit.'

Clara sighed and took a sip of tea. 'Hopefully they'll leave me alone before long and the committee members will realise I'm innocent.'

'And hopefully you'll be able to return to your work without feeling anxious,' added Penny.

'I hope so.' Clara gave an earnest smile. 'But that could be a while yet. I can't forget the red dress and that white face.' She gave a shudder. 'It was too horrible for words.'

FOURTEEN

Lydia Jackson sat with Miss Blythe in a comfortable office at Madame Deveraux's agency. Lydia called in most days in the hope Miss Blythe would have news of a position.

'A lady was here yesterday asking for you,' said Miss Blythe as she leafed through a ledger. 'A Mrs Cumming-Bruce. She said she would come back today to fill out the necessary forms.'

Lydia felt puzzled. 'She asked for me personally? Did someone recommend me?'

'They must have done.'

After leaving her last position so abruptly, she worried potential employers wouldn't consider her.

'Mrs Cumming-Bruce and her family have just arrived from Switzerland. She has two children – eight and ten years old.'

Lydia smiled. 'That sounds good. I'm looking forward to learning more.'

Miss Blythe closed the ledger. 'I shall let you know as soon as she registers with us.'

Lydia thanked Miss Blythe and left the agency feeling hopeful. If Mrs Cumming-Bruce had a suitable position then Lydia would be able to leave her current lodgings. The lodging house was tolerable, but far from ideal. The rattling of nearby trains kept her awake late into the night and woke her again at dawn. She longed for the comfort of a proper home, preferably in a respectable part of Belgravia. And the name Cumming-Bruce suggested a family of means.

FIFTEEN

Later that day, Lydia was reading a book in her room when her landlady knocked at her door. 'A Mr Ashford is waiting in the entrance hall for you.'

Lydia felt her stomach leap and heat rushed to her face. Christopher wanted to see her again?

She prepared herself in front of the looking glass, her hands trembling as she pinned loose strands of hair into place and pinched some colour into her cheeks. Then she smoothed her plain dress, cleared her throat and made her way downstairs. Her heart pounded excitedly against her chest.

How had Christopher found her? She'd mentioned she was staying in a guest house on Buckingham Palace Road and he must have tried all the ones he could find.

As she descended the staircase, he glanced up at her from the entrance hall and gave her a broad grin. He wore a smart dark overcoat and held his top hat in his hand.

'I hope you don't mind me calling on you like this,' he said. 'We didn't get much chance to talk the other evening, and I thought... well, I wanted to see you again.'

Lydia couldn't help smiling. 'It's lovely to see you again Christopher.'

'The weather outside is awful,' he said. 'Thick fog. But if you have something warm to wear, perhaps you'd like to join me for a short walk?'

She didn't care about the weather. 'I would love to, Christopher.'

Christopher waited while Lydia fetched her coat, hat and gloves. He felt a skip of excitement in his chest – relief and happiness that she'd agreed to join him.

He hadn't stopped thinking about her since their meeting at the church service for Mrs Melbourne. He'd thought about her over the years too – even when he was married. He'd never quite loved his late wife as much as he'd loved Lydia.

Life hadn't been kind to her. He'd heard stories about what had happened, but he didn't want to mention anything just yet. She was as beautiful as he remembered, but there was a sadness in her eyes. Her clothes were sombre, whereas the Lydia he recalled had always taken care in how she presented herself. It was remarkable how his feelings for her hadn't changed, despite everything that had happened over the past twenty years.

His biggest worry when calling at the house was that she wouldn't be interested in seeing him anymore. He was uncertain how much resentment she bore him. Did she blame him for what had happened? Hopefully there was now time for them both to gain a new understanding of what had gone wrong all those years ago.

'I'm ready!' said Lydia, descending the stairs for the second time. She was wrapped up warm in a burgundy overcoat and a plain matching hat. The sort of clothing a governess wore. He couldn't resist a smile.

They left the house and walked up Buckingham Palace Road towards Hyde Park. He noticed how Lydia covered her undersized left hand as they walked. It was something she felt ashamed of. He wanted to reassure her that the deformity had never bothered him, but he knew other people could make cruel comments.

'I looked out for you when the church service had ended,' he said, 'but it was too busy, and I didn't see you. That's why I thought I'd call on you. I hope you don't mind – I know you weren't expecting me. And the weather's awful. Hardly an ideal time for a walk, is it?'

'I don't mind at all,' she replied, looking up at him with a smile. 'I'm pleased you called on me.'

'You are?'

'Very much so.'

They walked on in comfortable silence. There were so many things he wanted to say to her that he didn't know where to start.

Her shoulder brushed against his arm occasionally as they made space for passers-by on the pavement. He wanted to take her hand, just as he had many years ago. But not now. Not yet.

Everyone around them seemed to be in a hurry, carrying out their errands quickly so they could get home and out of the fog.

'I heard today there's a possibility of a new position,' said Lydia. 'Apparently, a lady asked for me by name, so I'm looking forward to finding out more.'

'That sounds promising,' he said. 'I hope it comes to something. Do you ever tire of being a governess?'

'Not really. But I don't really have any other option,' she replied. 'Because I never married, I have to work.'

'Do you regret not being married?'

A pause followed as her expression darkened. 'Why do you ask me that? We were to be married once.'

The polite facade had suddenly dropped. Now their conversation would become uneasy. But they couldn't continue avoiding discussing the past.

'You don't need to remind me,' he said, hearing the note of bitterness in his voice.

'You went away,' she said quietly.

'I had to. It was arranged that I'd work for my uncle. He had a position in the office of the Governor of Bombay.'

Lydia stopped and stared up at him. 'You had to? I thought it was your choice.'

'No. It was all arranged. Looking back, I wish I'd refused. But you'd gone and...' He ran his hand over his chin as he attempted to phrase his words. 'I wish now I'd stayed and then those awful things wouldn't have happened to you.'

'What things?'

Her response puzzled him. Didn't she know what he was referring to?

He took in a breath. 'Your disgrace.' He didn't like saying it. It was uncomfortable for him to hear. But it had to be mentioned. It had bothered him for many years.

'My disgrace?' Lydia scowled. 'What do you mean?'

'The elopement and the gentleman who deserted you,' he said.

Lydia gave an incredulous laugh. 'Elopement? There was never an elopement. And I was never deserted. Are you getting me confused with someone else?' She took a step back from him.

'No! How could I ever get you confused with someone else, Lydia? It's what I was told when I returned to England. I asked after you, and I heard all about the awful events which befell you.'

'From who?' Her brow creased with bewilderment.

'From my godmother.'

Lydia's lips tightened. 'Mrs Melbourne,' she muttered. 'So she continued to lie.'

Christopher scratched his brow, trying to make sense of their conversation. 'The elopement didn't happen?'

'No. Your godmother lied to you. And she lied to me too. She told me you chose to go away to India. She said it was all your idea.'

'It was not!' He reached for her hand, desperate for her to believe him.

'She lied to both of us,' said Lydia. 'I knew she was deceitful, but I didn't quite realise how deceitful she truly was.'

SIXTEEN

After their visit to St Anne's churchyard, Emma and Penny had decided to find out more about the doctor who Mrs Melbourne had sued the previous year.

They met outside the British Museum the following day. Before they went inside, Penny showed Emma the letter she'd drafted to Miss Jackson. It requested a meeting with her to discuss Mrs Melbourne.

'She might ignore it,' said Penny. 'But it's worth a try, don't you think?'

'Definitely.'

'Good, I'll post it once we've finished here and hopefully it will arrive at Madame Deveraux's agency in this evening's post.'

They climbed the steps of the museum and made their way to the newspaper reading room.

They settled at a long wooden table, volumes of newspapers stacked before them, and began searching through reports from the previous year.

It wasn't long before the librarian Francis Edwards stepped into the room, acknowledging them with a broad smile. He was accompanied by a monocled gentleman who he appeared to be assisting. Emma recalled how invaluable he'd been during their investigation into Lord Harpole's murder. She also remembered the lingering feelings he harboured for Penny – feelings which had endured despite the years apart and Penny's marriage. Emma felt a swell of warmth for him. He was a good man, and she hoped one day he might meet someone who could return his affections.

Once he'd helped the monocled gentleman, Francis approached them, lowering his voice to a whisper. 'Good morning. How are you both?'

'We're very well,' Penny replied in hushed tones. 'We're looking into the murder of Mrs Melbourne. She was found in St Anne's churchyard in Soho.'

'I read about that,' Francis said. 'A terrible tragedy.'

'Apparently, she sued a doctor last year,' Penny continued. 'We're searching the newspapers for more details.'

Francis glanced at the stacks of papers before them and smiled. 'I've got a few minutes to spare. Let me help. 'Do you know when the legal action took place?' he whispered.

'Unfortunately not,' said Penny. 'We only know it was last year.'

Francis adjusted his spectacles as he thought. 'It makes sense to start with the weekly newspapers. They do a good job of summarising the news for each week and once we find the date of the court case, we can look at the daily papers to get a little more detail.'

'That sounds like a good plan,' said Penny.

They followed Francis to the shelves where he pulled out a few heavy volumes. 'The *London Weekly Gazette* is a good place to start,' he said.

Penny pulled a grimace. 'Do you think so?'

Francis smiled. 'I realise you consider all publications inferior to the *Morning Express*, Penny, but this publication provides a good summary of the news. We're not reading it for its literary merit.'

Penny returned his smile. 'Very well. Let's hope it helps us.'

Francis settled beside them, scanning the headlines with practised efficiency. Emma leafed through the volume in front of her, hoping she'd be the first to find the details of Mrs Melbourne's legal case.

'Oh, what's this?' whispered Penny after a while. 'I think... no, it's not Mrs Melbourne's case.'

Emma continued working as quickly as she could. She knew this wasn't a competition but she enjoyed the challenge. But despite her hard work, Francis found the information first. 'I do believe I've found something from April last year,' he said. He cleared his throat and read aloud, '"Mrs Eleanor Melbourne of Upper Belgrave Road sued Dr Robert Lloyd, who has been prac-tising on Harley Street for several years past, for two hundred pounds damages for neglectful care of her nephew by the defen-dant."' He glanced up at them. 'Does that sound like the case you're looking for?'

'It certainly does,' said Penny. 'Thank you, Francis.'

'Good. Well let's look at the daily newspapers now and find out more detail.'

A short while later, Emma and Penny had transcribed several articles into their notebooks. Now they had the sad details of the accident, Dr Lloyd's treatment of the patient and the verdict.

'I shall carry on looking into this if you like,' said Francis. 'I can let you know what else I find.'

They whispered their thanks before taking their leave.

Once outside, able to speak freely again, Penny said, 'That was quick work, thanks to Francis. He has a remarkable ability to track down information.'

'And now we have the name of the doctor,' Emma added. 'Dr Lloyd. I'm surprised Mrs Melbourne successfully sued him. The articles suggest her nephew was in a critical condition after the accident.'

Penny nodded. 'Yes, it seems her poor nephew, Edmund, was already close to death when Dr Lloyd treated him. The doctor warned Mrs Melbourne and her sister that the surgery might not be successful and he apparently did his best to save the young man.'

'I expect Mrs Melbourne was devastated after her nephew died. Maybe she needed someone to blame.'

'Perhaps,' Penny agreed. 'I can understand her grief, but from what we've read, it seems Dr Lloyd was only trying to help.'

'And yet the court ruled against him,' Emma said. 'I can't imagine it's been easy for him to find work since then.'

Penny tucked her notebook into her bag. 'Well, there's only one way to find out.'

Emma looked at her expectantly.

'We pay him a visit at his consulting rooms on Harley Street.'

SEVENTEEN

Harley Street was a distinguished thoroughfare, its elegant rows of Georgian terraces lined with gleaming railings. The buildings exuded quiet authority, with their large sash windows and the discreet plaques which announced the physicians within. The street had long been a symbol of the capital's medical elite – a place of private consultations behind heavy doors.

Emma and Penny found number fifteen and paused to study the names engraved on the polished brass plates beside the door.

'Here he is,' said Penny, pointing. 'Dr Robert Lloyd. It says he's on the second floor.'

They stepped inside. The hallway was hushed and immaculate, the air tinged with polish and antiseptic. Their footsteps echoed softly on the polished wooden floorboards as they made their way to the second floor. When they reached Dr Lloyd's consulting rooms, they were met with disappointment. A handwritten notice was pinned to the door: "Closed until further notice".

Emma frowned. 'That's strange. I wonder if it's to do with the court case?'

'It's quite possible,' said Penny, leaning closer to inspect the message. 'If he lost his reputation over it, he may have been forced to stop working here. But we need to find out for certain.'

They descended the stairs again and found a young secretary in another office, sitting behind a dark mahogany desk.

'Excuse me,' said Penny. 'We're hoping to speak with Dr Lloyd. We saw the notice upstairs and wondered if you might know where he is?'

The woman looked up with a polite but guarded expression. 'Dr Lloyd isn't practising from this building at the present time.'

'It's rather urgent that we speak with him.'

The secretary hesitated, clearly weighing whether to disclose more. 'He's not seeing patients at all, I'm afraid.'

'We understand,' said Penny gently. 'Our visit doesn't concern a medical matter; we need to speak to him about something else.'

'He lives in Bedford Square. But I do advise caution – he's been... somewhat unwell. And understandably upset. He won't take kindly to being disturbed.'

'Thank you,' said Penny. 'We appreciate your help.'

They stepped back out into the street. The sky was overcast, the clouds heavy with unshed rain.

'"He won't take kindly to being disturbed",' said Emma. 'Do you think it's wise to visit him? If he's shut his practice after losing the case, then I doubt he'll be happy to see us.'

'No,' said Penny. 'But sometimes people who are angry want to talk. Especially if they feel wronged. And if his anger is still smouldering, he might be willing to discuss Mrs Melbourne.'

'All right. But let's tread carefully.'

The walk to Bedford Square in Bloomsbury took about twenty minutes. Each side of the square was lined with smart houses overlooking a large oval garden in the centre.

After calling at a few doors and speaking to a porter, they were finally directed to a dark brick townhouse with a red door.

'This is it,' said Penny, adjusting her gloves. 'Let's hope he's home.'

Emma drew a breath. 'And let's hope he's in a mood to talk.'

Penny lifted the heavy brass knocker and gave it three firm raps.

Dr Lloyd was at home and surprisingly pleased to see them. 'It's not every day I'm visited by two charming young ladies,' he said, settling his heavy frame into an armchair with an audible creak. 'Healthy ones, too. I see young ladies often enough – but only when something's amiss with them.'

He chuckled at his own remark and gave them both a slow, lingering smile. Emma felt her shoulders stiffen, and beside her on the sofa, she sensed Penny do the same. The doctor was a large man with a fleshy face, a drooping grey moustache, and small, close-set eyes that lingered far too long on their figures.

'Thank you for agreeing to see us, Dr Lloyd—' Emma began.

'Oh, it's no trouble at all,' he interrupted, waving a pudgy hand. 'The pleasure is all mine. What can I do for you?'

'We're friends of Mrs Melbourne's,' said Penny.

At once, the jovial expression vanished and his eyes narrowed.

'Are you, indeed?' he said bitterly. 'That surprises me. You seem far too pleasant to have been part of her circle.'

'We're helping her family sort through some of her affairs,' Penny continued. 'And it seems there's been some confusion. People remember the details of the legal action she took against you quite differently. We thought it best to come directly to the source and ask what truly happened.'

He scratched his scalp. 'Confusion, is it? What sort of confusion?'

'Oh, you know how it is,' said Penny with a light laugh. 'One person remembers one thing, someone else remembers it differently. And then, of course, there's the matter of the settlement...'

'Ah yes,' he said, his mouth twisting. 'The money. She took

plenty of it, I can assure you of that. She played on the court's emotions.'

He stared at the rug for a moment, lips compressed, before letting out a sharp sigh. 'Well,' he said, eying them both again, 'I won't bore you with every legal twist and turn – it was all rather complicated, and to be perfectly frank, much of it would go over your heads. But let's just say the outcome was driven more by emotion than fact. Logic had no place in that courtroom. Her nephew, young Edmund Melbourne, was involved in a dreadful accident. He was thrown from a horse on the Strand after it was startled by a delivery boy dropping a beer barrel outside a public house. Quite a scene, I gather. Poor Edmund suffered catastrophic injuries to the head.' He paused for a moment before continuing.

'I'd treated many members of the Melbourne family before. I was summoned and did what I could. I advised surgery but was perfectly honest with the family – there was little hope. I told them as much.'

'And yet Mrs Melbourne chose to hold you responsible?' asked Emma.

'She needed someone to blame,' he said flatly. 'That's what it came down to. Her grief needed a target. She could hardly take the delivery boy who dropped the barrel to court, could she? But me? I was a surgeon. A man with money. A professional. An easy mark.'

He reached for a cut-glass tumbler on the side table and took a sip from it.

'She sued me,' he said with a weary shake of the head. 'Despite all the years I'd cared for her family. Her late husband, Patrick Melbourne, was one of my regular patients. That counted for nothing in the end.'

Penny leaned forward. 'You said she played on the court's emotions?'

'She did,' he said, his tone sour. 'She wept. She trembled. She gave the performance of a lifetime. Her lawyer – some young man with theatrical flair – probably coached her to do it. The judge, the jury... they all fell for it. I was painted as a callous man with a scalpel, and she the heartbroken aunt.'

'Was she not genuinely distressed?' asked Penny.

'I'm sure she was,' he said. 'But grief is no excuse for vengeance. She went too far, and it cost me dearly.' His voice turned cold. 'There was something... vindictive about the way she pursued me through the courts. It wasn't just about grief – it was about the money. That's what she wanted most. My professional disgrace was, I suspect, of little consequence to her.'

'Disgrace?' Penny asked, brows raised. 'Does that mean you're no longer permitted to practise medicine?'

'Oh, I can still practise,' he replied. 'I've not been struck off. The General Medical Council has no issue with my work. But people read the newspapers, don't they? The number of patients coming to see me dropped dramatically.'

'That must have made you very angry,' Emma said gently.

His expression darkened, and he paused before replying.

'Let me ask you something, Mrs Langley,' he said. 'How would you feel, in my place?'

Emma kept her tone measured, wary of antagonising him. 'It's difficult to say. I'm not a doctor. But if I'd done everything in my power to save a young man's life, only to be dragged through the courts for my trouble... then yes, I imagine I would feel a deep sense of injustice.'

'There's your answer,' he said quietly.

'Forgive me, Dr Lloyd,' ventured Penny, 'but how did you feel when you heard of Mrs Melbourne's death?'

He was quiet for a moment. Then, with a small shrug, he said, 'It was shocking. The manner of it, I mean. Found dead in some overgrown churchyard like a vagrant. No one deserves that.'

'Did you grieve for her?'

He gave a humourless chuckle and took a sip from a glass next to him. 'No. I can't say I shed any tears. Her actions destroyed my reputation, my income, my peace of mind. I'd already lost every-thing I might have mourned for.'

There was a short silence.

'I don't know who killed her,' he added, setting the glass down. 'But I wouldn't be surprised if I'm not the only person she made an enemy of.'

He heaved himself out of his chair and began pacing the room, his hands clasped behind his back. 'I don't care to talk about this anymore. It's all in the past now. Edmund Melbourne is dead. Eleanor Melbourne is dead. And my medical practice is... struggling. But the world keeps turning, doesn't it? My days are dull, grim even, but I must say' – he ran his tongue over his lips – 'they've been rather brightened by this unexpected visit from two delightful ladies. There's something about the pair of you... You're asking me questions as though you're detectives.'

'We're not,' said Penny. 'But I was once a news reporter.'

He raised an eyebrow. 'Were you indeed? How interesting. Which newspaper?'

'The *Morning Express*.'

He gave an impressed nod. 'I read it occasionally.' Then he rubbed his hands together. 'Can I offer you a drink?'

'No, thank you,' said Penny, rising. 'We didn't plan to stay long.'

'Not staying?' His smile faded. 'That's disappointing. You come here asking questions, and now you're in such a rush to leave. Surely it's only fair I ask you some questions in return?'

Emma rose too, her heart beginning to thump. The atmosphere in the room had soured.

'No, thank you,' said Penny firmly. 'I have an appointment to meet my husband.'

'Well, what a fortunate man he must be,' Dr Lloyd said smoothly, then turned his gaze to Emma, looking her up and down. 'And you, Mrs Langley – does your husband know how lucky he is?'

Emma's smile was tight. 'Yes. I'm quite sure he does. Thank you for your time, Dr Lloyd.'

'Oh, the pleasure has been entirely mine,' he said, his tone syrupy. 'If you ever have further questions about the case – or wish to learn a little more about legal proceedings – I'd be more than happy to see you again. And should either of you require a physician... well, my rates are very reasonable.' He leaned forward and held out a hand for them to shake. Emma reluctantly shook it, recoiling at his sweaty palm.

Penny had already made for the door. 'That won't be necessary,' she said briskly. 'Thank you for seeing us, Dr Lloyd.'

They didn't wait for him to reply. With Emma close behind, Penny opened the door and stepped out into the corridor. They left the house quickly, neither speaking until they were out on the street.

Penny exhaled sharply. 'Ugh. I think I'd have preferred him to be furious with us rather than... whatever that was.'

Emma pulled on her gloves with trembling fingers. 'He was horrid. I don't want to see him again.'

'No,' said Penny. 'But he certainly gave us something to think about. He has a very clear motive – he lost both his livelihood and reputation because of that case. He tried to appear indifferent, but I don't believe it for a moment. He's still angry, and hiding it badly.'

'Do you think we should tell the police?' asked Emma.

'Yes. If Inspector Paget is paying attention then he'll have considered Dr Lloyd already. The case was covered in the newspapers, after all. But if not, then he needs to.'

'They'll need to confirm his whereabouts on the night of the murder,' Emma said. 'And see if he had any connection to St Anne's churchyard. That part still puzzles me.'

'Me too,' said Penny. 'But one thing's for sure, I don't intend to ask him about it. Do you?'

Emma shivered. 'Absolutely not. I think we've spent quite enough time in his company.'

EIGHTEEN

Dr Robert Lloyd poured himself another brandy after the two ladies had left. It was disappointing that he hadn't been able to persuade them to stay and have a drink with him. Visitors were few and far between these days. Ever since the court case, people had been avoiding him – as though his misfortune were contagious.

He crossed the room, drink in hand, and stood by the window, staring out over Bedford Square. He could see the two women walking towards Tottenham Court Road. Their silhouettes grew smaller as they moved further away.

He took a slow sip, the brandy burning his throat.

Had he said too much?

He often did when he was in the company of women. That had always been his weakness. He wasn't sure why – perhaps it was a need to impress, or simply the fact that he enjoyed their company more than he should. It had been so long since he'd had any pleasant conversation. He turned the glass in his hands, frowning.

They had described themselves as friends of Mrs Melbourne, but he doubted it. He couldn't imagine two well-mannered young ladies willingly associating with someone as repugnant as her.

So who were they? If they'd been close to the Melbourne

family then they would have attended the court case. But he was fairly certain he hadn't seen either of them before.

He swallowed the rest of his drink and immediately poured another. The sound of the liquid splashing into the glass filled the silence of the room. He returned to his armchair and sank into it, trying to recall exactly what he'd said to his visitors.

Lately, the brandy had become his only true companion. It helped him push everything else aside – the memories, the shame, the weight of his ruined reputation. But the trouble was, it also muddled his thinking. Even though the ladies had only just left, his recollection of the conversation was already hazy.

It was important not to speak too freely – not now Mrs Melbourne was dead.

The police would come, of course. It was inevitable. After all, it made perfect sense for them to question him. He had been Mrs Melbourne's adversary, the man she had dragged through the courts, humiliated and ruined.

So why hadn't they come yet?

That was the troubling part. Perhaps they had a long list of adversaries to question. The waiting was worse than the accusation itself. Perhaps he could find a reason to approach them and find out what they knew?

He rubbed his temple and exhaled heavily. It was such a shame the ladies had left. It had been good to speak with someone, even if their interest in him had been impersonal. Now, he was alone again, trapped with nothing but his own thoughts.

And he hated being alone with his own thoughts.

There was no way to silence them, no matter how much he drank. And he had to be careful – he had seen what brandy had done to his father. It was easy to let it take hold, to let it cloud everything, to let it drag him under.

Still, he hoped the women would return. If they didn't, perhaps he could find them himself. He needed to ensure they had the right impression of him.

What had they said their names were? He frowned. He would forget if he wasn't careful.

Reaching into his jacket pocket, he took out his pen and pocket diary. Flipping through the pages, his eyes skimmed past old appointments, now nothing more than fading ink and vague memories. How busy he had once been. How sought after.

Now, his days were empty. And so were his pockets.

That woman had ruined him.

He pressed the pen to the page and wrote: *Mrs Langley and Mrs Blakely*. Two pleasant ladies. And two names to remember.

NINETEEN

Vine Street police station was a large, bustling establishment, tucked away behind Regent Street and Piccadilly. Emma and Penny were shown to a wood-panelled waiting room where faded police notices about thieves and pickpockets were pinned to a board above the fireplace.

Inspector Paget joined them a few moments later. He was a tall, lean-limbed man with a wispy moustache. He'd barely taken a few strides before he slowed and narrowed his eyes at Penny.

'Miss Green, isn't it?' His voice carried a note of suspicion. 'A reporter for the *Morning Express*. I was told Mrs Blakely and Mrs Langley were here to see me. Not you, Miss Green.'

Penny straightened. 'My name is Mrs Blakely now, Inspector,' she said coolly. 'I married Chief Inspector Blakely of Scotland Yard.'

Paget's expression flickered with recognition. 'Ah. That's where I've heard the name. I thought it sounded familiar. So, you're no longer a news reporter, then?'

'No.'

Penny turned to Emma. 'Inspector Paget and I have met a few times before, particularly when I was reporting on the murder of Augustus Forster.'

'That's right,' said the inspector. 'And I can't deny that – on that occasion – you were helpful. But why are you here now?' He remained standing and folded his arms.

'My friend Mrs Langley and I would like to speak with you about the murder of Mrs Melbourne,' Penny replied. 'We understand you've been questioning a friend of ours, Mrs Clara Clifton.'

Paget studied her for a moment. 'She's a friend of yours, is she? I see.'

'She's concerned that you suspect her of the murder.'

Paget exhaled sharply. 'She discovered the body, Mrs Blakely. I don't need to explain to you why that makes her a person of interest.'

'We believe she's innocent,' Emma interjected.

'I'm sure you do. And she probably is. She seems a perfectly nice lady – although why she chooses to wander around graveyards, I really don't know. You're bound to get into trouble doing that sort of thing. It's hardly a sensible pastime for a respectable woman. I told her as such.'

Emma frowned. 'But you're not convinced of her innocence?'

Paget shrugged. 'Not entirely, no. That's why I had to establish an alibi for her – and unfortunately, it isn't perfect.'

'Why not?' asked Penny.

'Because her alibi is her husband. Naturally, he'd say she was with him that night, wouldn't he? He's hardly going to let his wife be dragged into a murder investigation. This is exactly why I told her she'd be better off avoiding graveyards. You find yourself in all sorts of trouble that way.'

Penny exchanged an exasperated glance with Emma. It was becoming clear why Mrs Clifton felt so uneasy about the inspector's attitude. He'd already decided she was a suspicious person based on her job.

'Perhaps there's someone else to consider, aside from Mrs Clifton,' Penny suggested.

Paget furrowed his brow. 'If you've come here to give me advice, Mrs Blakely, I'm not interested. I recall you dished out quite enough of that in your days as a reporter. Now that you're a wife, I would suggest it's uncalled for.'

Penny smiled tightly. 'This isn't advice, Inspector. I merely wish to bring someone to your attention. Do you know who Dr Lloyd is?'

Paget opened his mouth as if to respond, then hesitated. 'The name is familiar,' he said at last.

Emma wasn't convinced he'd heard the name at all.

'Dr Lloyd was sued by Mrs Melbourne last year,' Penny explained. 'As a result, he was forced to close his practice. Mrs Langley and I have spoken with him, and we can see how deeply the loss of his profession has affected him. He seems angry about it, and resentful. Perhaps he sought revenge on Mrs Melbourne?'

Paget pursed his lips and nodded, as though giving the matter some thought. 'There are many people to speak to in this investigation, Mrs Blakely,' he said. 'I'm certain that either I or one of my men will speak to Dr Lloyd in due course.'

Penny smiled. 'Of course, Inspector. Thank you for taking the time to see us. I know you're a busy man.'

'I am.'

'So, will you leave Mrs Clifton alone now?'

'I'm not promising you anything, Mrs Blakely. This is my investigation. And I'm not obliged to share my thoughts with you or Mrs Langley. I trust you appreciate that.' He checked his pocket watch. 'Now, if you excuse me, I must be on my way.'

Penny sighed once they'd left the police station. 'Well, we did what we could. We told him about Dr Lloyd so it will be interesting to see if he interviews him.'

'He didn't write anything down that we told him, did he?' said Emma.

'Of course not,' Penny said dryly. 'That would be an admission that we were actually being helpful.'

The rain which had been holding off all day finally began to fall as they walked along Regent Street. The sky was darkening and warm lights glimmered in the shops and restaurants.

'So we've spoken to Dr Lloyd and established he has a motive for murdering Mrs Melbourne,' said Emma. 'Who else can we speak to?'

'There's Miss Jackson if she agrees to meet with us.'

'And if she doesn't?'

'We might have to impose ourselves on her,' replied Penny with a smile. 'But I'm hoping that our polite letter writing will be enough.'

Emma recalled the memorial service for Mrs Melbourne and the people she'd seen there. 'We could speak to the housekeeper, Agnes Black,' she said. 'And there's the reverend to consider too. From the way he spoke about Mrs Melbourne during the service, I get the impression he knew her well. I'd like to hear his personal thoughts about what's happened. Shall we call on him at St Peter's tomorrow?'

TWENTY

Lydia rested on her bed that evening, reading a book. Her room was a cramped space which was sparsely furnished, but her small collection of books offered some solace.

She was immersed in the story when her landlady disturbed her with a sharp knock. 'There's a lady downstairs to see you,' she called through the closed door.

Downstairs in the hallway stood Miss Blythe from Madame Deveraux's agency. She greeted Lydia with a polite smile and handed her an envelope. 'This arrived for you in this evening's post. As my route home takes me past your address, I thought I'd deliver it to you.'

'Thank you,' said Lydia. 'I appreciate you taking the time to drop it in to me.'

'It's no problem at all.' Miss Blythe gave another dry smile and turned to leave.

'I don't suppose you've heard anything more from Mrs Cumming-Bruce?' Lydia called after her.

'Oh.' She pulled a thoughtful expression. 'I haven't. She said she'd return, didn't she?'

'Never mind,' said Lydia, her heart sinking a little. 'But thank you again for this letter.'

Once Miss Blythe had left, Lydia went up to her room and examined the envelope in her hand. She didn't recognise the handwriting on the front, although the postmark indicated it had been sent from central London. She hesitated for a moment, turning the envelope over in her hands, before tearing it open. The paper was thin, the ink slightly smudged, as though it had been written in haste.

She sat down on her bed, opened the envelope and pulled out the letter.

Dear Miss Jackson,

My name is Penny Blakely and my friend Mrs Emma Langley and I would be grateful for the opportunity to speak with you at your earliest convenience about Mrs Melbourne.

We are making inquiries on behalf of a friend of ours, Mrs Clara Clifton. She is the lady who discovered Mrs Melbourne in the churchyard and is now, regrettably, being considered a suspect by the police. We are trying to better understand Mrs Melbourne's circumstances and would deeply appreciate any insights you might be able to offer. If you would be willing to meet with us, please do reply at your convenience.

Yours sincerely,
Mrs Blakely and Mrs Langley

Lydia let the letter fall into her lap. She stared at it for a moment before picking it up again, rereading the lines.

Mrs Clara Clifton – a suspect? The name meant nothing to her, and yet the whole thing felt unsettling. Why would the police suspect the person who'd merely found the body? And what business was it of these two women to get involved?

She tossed the letter aside and reached for her book, hoping to lose herself in its pages. But her eyes drifted over the same paragraph again and again, the words blurring, their meaning refusing to settle. Her thoughts kept returning to the letter.

Why had they written to her, of all people? How had they even known of her connection to Mrs Melbourne?

The truth was, she didn't want to talk about Mrs Melbourne. She had spent years trying to forget her. To shut away the past like a locked box. The idea of unsealing it, of inviting strangers into that part of her life, was not appealing.

And yet...

Something about the letter lingered. It was carefully polite, as if Mrs Blakely had anticipated resistance. Was it possible the two women were trying to investigate the death themselves? Was that even allowed?

Surely it was a matter for the police, not two women making inquiries on a friend's behalf. And still, curiosity tugged at her. If these women knew enough to contact her, what else did they know?

Lydia sighed and set the book down. Perhaps she would meet them after all, if only to satisfy her own curiosity rather than theirs.

TWENTY-ONE

'I forgot Mrs Tuttle has the day off today,' said Penny as Emma met her outside St Peter's church in Belgravia the following morning.

Penny stood with the large perambulator, baby Florence gurgling inside. Thomas peeked through the railings at the church.

'I'm sure the reverend won't mind you bringing the children with you,' said Emma. 'Families are always welcome to church, aren't they?'

'I hope so.'

Inside the church, Reverend Underhill was speaking to a well-dressed elderly lady. Penny pushed the perambulator down the aisle and Emma followed behind, holding Thomas's hand. They seated themselves on a pew at the front of the church. Thomas sat next to Emma and swung his legs, kicking the pew with his heels.

'Thomas!' hissed Penny. 'You mustn't kick your legs like that!'

He stopped but Emma sensed he was soon going to get bored.

The reverend joined them as soon as he'd finished his conversation. He had a friendly round face and thinning white hair.

'Have we met before?' he asked them, leaning on his stick. He wore a long black frock coat and his distinctive white collar.

'No,' said Penny. 'Although Mrs Langley here attended the service you held for Mrs Melbourne the day after her death.'

'Ah yes. That was very well attended. You must forgive me for not remembering your face, Mrs Langley.'

'You knew Mrs Melbourne well?' asked Emma.

'Oh yes. I considered her a friend.' He ran a hand over his chin. 'I'm quite new to this parish and she was one of the first parishioners to invite me into her home. I never knew her to miss a Sunday service. In fact, she prayed here most days. Her faith was the foundation of her life, she told me it strengthened her enormously after her husband passed.'

Thomas got down from the pew. 'I want to go over there,' he whispered to Emma as he pointed at the altar.

'All right then, but you mustn't touch anything. Just look.' She could see how the altar would look appealing to a young child with its ornate table, colourful screen and bright candles.

Thomas took some steps forward to look at it and the reverend acknowledged him with a smile.

Everyone speaks highly of Mrs Melbourne,' said Penny. 'She was a charitable lady.'

'She was.' He nodded. 'Many charitable causes benefited from her devotion. And like all of us...' He hesitated before continuing. 'She had her burdens. The loss of her husband was one, certainly. But she also had flaws, and those flaws shaped her.' He raised his eyes to the ceiling. 'Isaiah, chapter sixty-four, verse eight tells us, "But now, O Lord, thou art our father; we are the clay, and thou our potter; and we all are the work of thy hand."' He lowered his gaze again. 'We are all imperfect vessels, you see, shaped by hardship and experience. But the tragedy of the world is that some allow their flaws to fester into hatred. Someone believed they were wronged by Mrs Melbourne – and in their mind, they deemed the punishment to be death.' His expression darkened. 'The murderer will face judgement.'

Penny gave a polite nod. 'It's reassuring to know the murderer will face divine punishment,' she said. 'But it's also important they're caught and held accountable here on Earth, too.'

The reverend's gaze was steady. 'Oh, they will be. God ensures justice prevails.' He sat down next to Emma and rested his stick next to him.

Penny's brow furrowed. 'But that doesn't mean we can sit back and wait for justice to happen. We have to put in the effort to find the truth – otherwise, the person responsible might get away with it.'

Reverend Underhill sighed, rubbing his fingers together as if in contemplation. 'Yes, of course. I have no doubt the police will work tirelessly to uncover the truth. But I must admit... as a man of faith, I've found it difficult to contain my anger over this. Scripture tells us to seek understanding, to have compassion, but I...' He shook his head, his voice thick with emotion. 'I have struggled.'

He looked over at the altar as though searching for reassurance. Penny shifted slightly in her seat. She was clearly growing impatient with him.

'There have been moments over these past few days where my faith has wavered, however briefly. This tragedy has tested me deeply, making me question why the Lord allows such things to happen. But when those doubts creep in, I remind myself of Romans, chapter five, verses three to four: "Tribulation worketh—"'

'Did Mrs Melbourne have any connection to St Anne's church in Soho?' Penny interrupted.

The reverend stared at her for a moment, surprised by her interjection. 'Yes,' he said eventually. 'She was married there. In the 1840s, I believe. So it's dreadfully sad and poignant that she died there.'

Emma and Penny exchanged a glance; finally they'd discovered Mrs Melbourne's connection to the place of her death.

'Is that why she went to that churchyard that night, do you think?' Emma asked the reverend.

'She sometimes prayed in St Anne's because the church was an important place for her. But why she was there that night...' He shook his head. 'I just don't know.'

Thomas had finished looking at the altar and he returned to the pew, pouting when he saw the reverend had taken his place. His eyes moved to the walking stick which leaned again the pew and he picked it up.

'I'll have that, young boy,' said the reverend sharply, moving forward. He took the stick from Thomas and rested it across his lap.

'Come and sit with me,' Penny implored her son. Thomas jutted his chin and shuffled up to the perambulator.

Penny kept an eye on him as she addressed Reverend Underhill again. 'Mrs Melbourne must have confided in you a great deal. Did she ever mention any concerns? Anyone she feared?'

'No, she never spoke of feeling threatened. There was, of course, the matter with the doctor.' He frowned. 'I imagine he wasn't pleased about being sued. But she did what she felt was right. She was deeply devoted to her nephew, and she believed Dr Lloyd had failed him.'

'The lawsuit effectively ended his career,' Penny pointed out. 'That would be more than enough to fuel resentment.'

The reverend pursed his lips. 'Perhaps. But would a man of medicine – someone sworn to save lives – truly be capable of taking one in such a brutal manner? I struggle to believe it. And besides, I know the man. Not terribly well, I should add. But I see him occasionally at the club.'

'You're members of the same club?'

'Yes. The Athenaeum. I refuse to believe Dr Lloyd would have harmed Mrs Melbourne in any way. If it's the case, however, I imagine the police will determine it soon enough.' He took in a breath and raised his voice a little. 'Let's remind ourselves that judgement belongs to God. As Revelation tells us, "he shall have his part in the lake which burneth with fire and brimstone!"'

Emma and Penny exchanged another glance. The certainty in his tone left no room for argument.

TWENTY-TWO

Lydia Jackson sat at her small desk, a pen in her hand. She dipped her pen into the inkpot, and began to write, "Dear Mrs Blakely and Mrs Langley". As she composed her reply, unpleasant memories of Eleanor Melbourne returned.

'My butterfly brooch is missing, Miss Jackson.' Mrs Melbourne's eyes regarded her with a steely, cold gaze.

It felt like a confrontation. Lydia straightened where she stood, her hands clasped tightly. She knew the brooch well. It was a delicate piece, with gold gilded wings dusted with tiny diamonds. The butterfly's body was formed by two luminous pearls cradling a deep ruby. Mrs Melbourne wore it often. It was one of her favourites.

'I'm very sorry to hear that,' Lydia said carefully. 'Do you remember when you last wore it?'

'I wore it to dinner two nights ago,' Mrs Melbourne replied. Her tone was clipped, measured. 'But this isn't a case of misplacing it. I always return it to the same compartment in my jewellery box. It's not there now. It's been taken.'

Lydia took in a breath. 'You believe it's been stolen?'

'Yes. And I believe I know by whom.'

The following silence seemed to stretch unnaturally long.

Mrs Melbourne sighed, then folded her hands in her lap with slow precision. 'This isn't easy for me to say, Miss Jackson. I have spoken to all the household staff. You were seen entering my bedroom yesterday afternoon.'

Lydia felt her stomach drop. 'No,' she said, her voice barely above a whisper. 'Mrs Melbourne, that's not true. I haven't been anywhere near your room.'

Her employer's expression remained neutral. 'That's not what I've been told.'

'Who said that?' Lydia demanded. Her face flushed with heat. 'Please – tell me who made that accusation.'

'That would be improper,' Mrs Melbourne replied coolly. 'But it was not said lightly.'

'They're lying,' Lydia said, her voice firm now. 'I haven't stolen anything from you. I would never—'

'My staff do not lie to me, Miss Jackson.' Mrs Melbourne rose slowly from her chair, as if ending the conversation. 'I suggest you return the brooch quietly. There's no need to involve the authorities – unless you force my hand.'

Lydia stood rooted to the spot, stunned by the injustice of it all. 'I don't have your brooch,' she said. 'I didn't go into your room, and I certainly didn't steal from you. If you call the police, they can search my room, and they won't find it there. And if they speak to everyone in the house they might find out who planted this lie. Because that's what it is, Mrs Melbourne. A lie. And I believe the person who told it is the one you should suspect.'

She could feel herself trembling. A cold silence grew between them. She glared at Mrs Melbourne, her heart thudding with disbelief, but the older woman looked away, unmoved.

'It won't be that straightforward, Miss Jackson,' she said. 'And besides, I believe it's for the best that you leave my employment now.'

'Leave?' Lydia's voice cracked. Her thoughts turned instantly to Mrs Melbourne's niece, Catherine. Bright, sensitive Catherine, with her eager questions and her quiet confidence. 'But what about Miss Catherine? What will she think?'

'I shall tell her,' Mrs Melbourne said, brushing imaginary lint from her sleeve, 'that her governess was a thief.'

'You can't.' Lydia's voice rose. Tears welled in her eyes, blurring the image of the woman before her. 'She trusts me. She looks up to me. You know she does.'

'My decision is final,' said Mrs Melbourne without a flicker of remorse. 'You may pack your things. And you can expect the police to pay you a visit.' She looked her up and down, her eyes lingering for a moment on Lydia's undersized left hand.

Lydia stood in stunned silence, her mind spinning. Her career – her future – was being dismantled by a single lie. She brought to mind the faces of the household staff, wondering who'd betrayed her. Her suspicion settled on Miss Black. There had always been a chill between them, an unspoken animosity. Could she have lied to get rid of her?

Tears spilled down Lydia's cheeks, and she pressed her lips together tightly, refusing to let a sob escape. There was no use arguing. Mrs Melbourne's mind was fixed.

Lydia turned and left. Upstairs in her room, she packed her belongings with trembling hands. Ten minutes later, she returned to the parlour.

'May I say goodbye to Miss Catherine?'

Mrs Melbourne didn't look up. Her voice was clipped, final. 'No. You may not.'

And that was that.

Lydia stepped out of the house and did not look back. She never returned.

The police never came. No questions were asked. No brooch was recovered – or if it was, no one told her. The incident faded like smoke, disappearing as swiftly as it had arrived. And with time, the truth dawned more clearly than ever: Mrs Melbourne had invented the theft to remove her.

She wanted her gone. And not just from the household.

She wanted to separate Lydia from her precious godson – Christopher Ashford.

Twenty years hadn't dulled the pain. Lydia felt a tightness in her chest as she recalled her departure from Mrs Melbourne's home. How had her charge, Catherine, reacted when she'd been told her governess was gone? Lydia imagined she'd been upset and angry at her. She would have felt let down. Had she carried those feelings into adulthood? Lydia would never know. And she'd never have the chance to explain herself to Catherine.

At least she could explain everything to Christopher now. But would it make any difference? Had too much time passed and too many opportunities been missed?

Lydia signed the letter, folded it and put it into an envelope. Mrs Melbourne was gone now. And her death gave Lydia a chance to mend some of the damage she'd caused.

TWENTY-THREE

'I can't say this is the best meeting place,' said Penny the following morning. She and Emma stood by the bookstand in Victoria railway station. It was busy and noisy. Travellers and porters bustled past. The place echoed with the rumble of trolleys, hiss of steam and regular shrills from the guards' whistles.

'Why did Miss Jackson suggest we meet here?' asked Emma.

Penny examined the letter in her hand. 'Her address is on Buckingham Palace Road which is close by. I suppose Victoria station is convenient for her.'

'And I suppose a busy place feels like a safe place to meet two strangers,' said Emma, glancing around.

'She signed the letter Lydia Jackson,' added Penny. 'So we know her full name now.'

As Penny spoke, Emma noticed a woman approaching them. She looked about forty and wore a burgundy hat and coat.

'Mrs Blakely?' she said. 'Mrs Langley?'

Her honey-blonde hair was pinned neatly and she peered out with cautious eyes beneath her hat. Her porcelain skin was ghostly pale and her shoulders tense. Emma suspected she was nervous.

'Yes, that's right,' said Penny with a warm, friendly smile. She and Emma introduced themselves and attempted to put Miss Jackson at ease.

Shall we talk over a cup of tea in the station dining rooms?' suggested Emma.

Miss Jackson agreed.

The tea in the dining rooms was strong. Emma added more milk than usual but her tea stubbornly remained a deep brown as she stirred it with her teaspoon.

'You want to speak to me about Eleanor Melbourne,' said Miss Jackson. 'May I ask why?'

Penny told her about Clara Clifton and how she and Emma were keen to prove to the police that she couldn't be a suspect. Emma quietly knew this had become little more than an excuse to investigate the murder, but hopefully Miss Jackson would be convinced by it.

'Well I'm sorry to waste your time, but I don't think I can tell you anything which can help you,' said Miss Jackson. 'I knew her many years ago, but it's a time I'd rather forget about.'

'Did something unpleasant happen?' ventured Penny.

'Not particularly.' Lydia's voice lacked conviction. 'It was just a position I didn't enjoy.'

'You were her governess?'

Miss Jackson's gaze sharpened. 'How did you know that?'

'We made some inquiries,' said Penny.

'Why?'

'Because we wanted to talk to you. We found out you were hired by Madame Deveraux's agency—'

'Just a moment,' interrupted Miss Jackson. 'Are you anything to do with Mrs Cumming-Bruce? She called in at the agency to ask about me but never returned.'

Penny looked down at her tea and cleared her throat. 'Erm, yes. That was me.'

Miss Jackson stared at her for a moment. Emma felt the silence grow uncomfortable.

'I got my hopes up about that,' said the governess. 'I thought it could lead to a new position.'

Penny met her gaze. 'I apologise if my visit gave you false hope,' she said.

Miss Jackson took a sip of tea, wincing because it was too hot to drink yet.

'You mentioned you knew Mrs Melbourne years ago,' ventured Penny. 'Do you mind telling us about that?'

Miss Jackson replaced her teacup. 'I was a governess to her young niece for a while. Mrs Melbourne's sister was in poor health for a few years and so the niece – Catherine – lived with her for a few years. I then left the position and never saw her again.'

'You worked at number five Upper Belgrave Road, is that correct?' asked Penny.

Miss Jackson's eyes narrowed. 'How do you know that?'

'We spoke with someone locally,' Penny replied. 'And I tend to find things out – I was a news reporter once.'

The governess sat back in her chair, her eyebrows raised. 'A news reporter?' She shook her head. 'Then I have no chance.'

Her words were puzzling. 'What do you mean by that?' asked Penny.

'I don't know... I didn't mean to say it.' Miss Jackson leaned forward again. 'I took a position with the Brockhurst family at number five a few months ago. I knew their home was on the same street as Mrs Melbourne, but I tried not to think about that. I really liked the family and their children – they were delightful. At the time I hoped Mrs Melbourne had moved away from the area. Or if she hadn't, then I felt certain I wouldn't encounter her.'

'But you did,' said Penny.

Miss Jackson nodded. 'I'm not going to bother asking how you know that; you used to be a reporter so I imagine you found out easily enough. Unfortunately, it transpired Mr and Mrs Brockhurst were quite friendly with Mrs Melbourne. When I realised it, I had to prepare myself for the likelihood of seeing her again. At first, it was manageable. She visited the house a few times and we exchanged brief pleasantries. I thought that would be the extent of it.' She paused and took a sip of tea. 'And then... one day, she turned on me. We found ourselves alone for a moment in the hallway and she said something deeply personal. Looking back, I wish I had ignored it, but I couldn't. Her words were calculated to wound, and they did.'

She glanced down and self-consciously covered her twisted left hand with her other.

Emma and Penny remained silent, leaving her to talk.

'After that, I gave my notice to the Brockhursts, with great regret. I hate to leave a position so suddenly because it's not fair on the children.' Her voice choked. 'I can only hope the Brockhurst children are happy with their new governess.'

'What did Mrs Melbourne say to you?' asked Penny, softly.

'I'm not going to say,' Miss Jackson's voice sharpened. 'I won't go into any more detail, I'm afraid. It was personal, and I'd rather keep it private.'

Emma watched her closely. Her lower lip and hands trembled. Whatever Mrs Melbourne had said had struck her deeply. The governess inhaled sharply and straightened her shoulders. 'That's all there is to it.'

She glanced towards the door, as if keen to escape the conversation.

'So how did you feel when you heard Mrs Melbourne was dead?' asked Penny.

'I was shocked... but I can't pretend I miss her. In fact, I would like to return to the Brockhursts, but they have a new governess now so it's not possible.'

'We didn't know Eleanor Melbourne,' said Emma. 'But we've heard she was a pious, generous lady.'

Miss Jackson gave an embittered smile. 'Yes. That's what she wanted everyone to believe.'

'It wasn't true?'

'She was very good at acting a part.' She finished her tea and put on her gloves, readying herself to leave.

'And her godson inherits her estate,' Penny said. Emma could sense she was keen to keep the governess talking. 'Is he upset about his godmother's death?'

Miss Jackson paused for a second, then got up from her chair, avoiding Penny's gaze. 'You'd have to ask him that, Mrs Blakely.'

'His name is Christopher Ashford, is that right?'

'I believe so.' Miss Jackson put on her coat and hat. 'Forgive me for leaving so promptly, but I don't enjoy talking about Mrs Melbourne. There's only so much...'

'It's fine,' said Penny. 'We understand. Thank you for meeting with us.'

The governess gave a nod and left.

'Goodness,' said Penny as they watched Miss Jackson dash through the dining room door. 'She really didn't like Mrs Melbourne, did she?'

'No,' Emma replied. 'And from what she's told us, Mrs Melbourne had an unpleasant side to her. It's frustrating she won't tell us what Mrs Melbourne said to her, but I suppose it's personal.'

'That could be a reason,' said Penny. 'Or perhaps Miss Jackson won't tell us because it could incriminate her in Mrs Melbourne's murder? Something must have passed between them when she worked for her many years ago. She was clearly concerned about encountering her again when she began working for the Brockhurst family. Miss Jackson is deliberately keeping something back, and I think it's something which could be a motive for murdering Mrs Melbourne.'

Emma drained her teacup as she gave this some thought. 'She had to leave a job she loved because of Mrs Melbourne. Just like Dr Lloyd.'

'Yes!' Penny's eyes glinted with excitement. 'They both have the same motive, don't they? The loss of a profession and the loss of income. It could make someone very resentful indeed.'

TWENTY-FOUR

Clara Clifton paused by the railings and glanced around her. A gentleman was passing by, tapping his stick on the ground as he walked. Then a hansom cab dashed past, no doubt using the road as a shortcut to avoid busy Old Street.

Once she was sure no one would notice her, Clara took off her overcoat, folded it then draped it over the top of the spiked railings. She dropped her bag on the other side and placed one foot on the wall, pushed between a pair of railings. She then gripped the top of the railings either side of her coat and made one last check around her. There was still no one about. In a swift movement, she pulled herself over the fence. She had to rest on top of it as she swung her legs over, but her overcoat and corset offered her protection from the spikes.

It was a risky but well-practised move, and she always felt a sense of accomplishment when she managed to get into a cold, closed burial ground.

She was in St Luke's churchyard. A damp, untidy place strewn with rubbish and overgrown with ivy. The church had two grave-yards, and one had already been laid out as a public garden. But this one – closer to the church – was in need of restoration.

Cautiously, she made her way between the sunken headstones;

the ground was uneven and there was always a worry it would give way beneath her feet. She'd heard of it happening when burials were only just beneath the surface.

She prayed she wouldn't catch a glimpse of bright-coloured fabric again. She was trying her best to forget about the discovery of Mrs Melbourne's body, but this quiet, neglected churchyard was serving as a reminder.

She took in a breath to calm herself and pulled her notebook from her bag. It was always helpful to read what George Walker had written about London's burial grounds in 1839. She turned to the page where she'd copied down his notes about St Luke's:

The grave digger assured me, that he had often experienced the effects of the effluvia arising from the coffins, to an alarming extent, a frequent occurrence when coming suddenly upon a fresh grave, where the body had been kept too long before interment; then the effluvium would penetrate through a foot and a half or two feet of earth, and frequently produced nausea and loathing of food.

It was unpleasant to read, but Clara had learned to have a strong stomach for these details.

She turned to a new page in her notebook, rested it on a nearby lichen-covered tomb and made some observations. Thankfully, St Luke's churchyard had been closed to burials some years ago so effluvia were no longer a problem. Unless... she gave the air a cautious sniff. There was a hint of something unpleasant. A faint odour of neglect and decay.

Clara shivered, losing her enthusiasm for exploring the rest of the burial ground. She had seen all she wanted to. And – as usual – she would make a recommendation to the Metropolitan Public Gardens Committee that this disused burial ground was repurposed into a pleasant public garden. Just like the other churchyard close by.

There was a risk they wouldn't listen to her. Although the police hadn't spoken to her for a few days, some of the committee members were still being cool towards her. For the time being, she had to continue with her work and hope that her visits and reports would make a difference.

She finished making her notes and put her notebook back in her bag. As she made her way back to the fence, she wondered how Mrs Blakely and Mrs Langley were progressing with their investigation. Had they discovered yet how Mrs Melbourne had ended up in St Anne's churchyard?

A pang of guilt accompanied her thoughts. Mrs Blakely and Mrs Langley appeared to be friendly, honest ladies. How could she have lied to them?

It was only a small lie. But it still mattered. She'd still been dishonest. She'd told them she'd never seen Mrs Melbourne before and didn't know her.

But that wasn't quite true.

She had.

And so had the Metropolitan Public Gardens Committee.

TWENTY-FIVE

Christopher Ashford's townhouse stood on Fitzroy Street in Fitzrovia. It was a four-storey Georgian terrace with tall sash windows and a fan-shaped window over the door.

'It's a smart house,' said Penny. 'But not as smart as the house he's now inherited in Belgravia. I wonder if he'll move there now?'

'We could ask him,' said Emma.

'Yes, we could. And while we're speaking to him, we need to remind ourselves how well he's benefited from his godmother's death.'

Emma gave her a wry smile. 'Are you considering him to be a suspect before you've even met him?'

'No. That would be unfair, wouldn't it?' Penny returned her smile. 'Let's hope he's happy to talk to us.'

Mr Ashford was a gentleman in his mid-forties, his features still bearing the remnants of youthful handsomeness despite the lines etched into his face. He welcomed Emma and Penny in his drawing room furnished with deep mahogany furniture, embroidered cushions and silk curtains. Paintings of Indian landscapes adorned the walls: rolling hills under hazy skies, bustling markets and serene riverbanks. A striking image of the Taj Mahal held pride of place above the fireplace.

But it was another painting which caught Emma's attention. A tender portrait of a woman cradling a very young baby. The brush-strokes captured an intimacy that made her pause.

Mr Ashford noticed her gaze lingering on it. His voice was measured but held a quiet sorrow. 'My late wife and child,' he said. 'I commissioned it after their deaths.'

Emma reeled slightly from the unexpected revelation. 'Oh goodness, I'm so sorry to hear that. It must have been an incredibly difficult time for you. What a beautiful way to remember them.'

He nodded. 'Yes, it brings me comfort. The artist worked from photographs taken of my wife. I think he captured her beautifully.'

A moment of silence followed before Penny gestured towards the other paintings. 'Do you have a connection to India?'

'Yes, I lived there for twenty years, in Bombay. I was a bachelor for a long time but eventually I married. My wife was the daughter of a British consul. We were married for two years, but she died shortly after the birth of our daughter last year. Our daughter lived a few more days, but...'

Emma felt a lump in her throat as his voice cracked with sorrow.

'I no longer had the heart to stay there,' he continued, his eyes shining with tears. 'So I returned to London last autumn.' He looked away and took a moment to compose himself before he turned back. 'Anyway,' his face brightened, 'I shan't bore you with the details of my grief. How can I help you?'

'We're friends of Clara Clifton,' said Penny. 'The lady who discovered your godmother's body in St Anne's churchyard. We promised her that we would look into the murder because, at present, the police suspect her.'

His brow furrowed. 'Do they? That's troubling. I've not met Mrs Clifton, but from what I've heard, she's a well-respected lady. I can't imagine she had any involvement in my godmother's death.'

'She didn't know her at all,' Penny said. 'But the police have to consider all possibilities. Mrs Langley and I are sure she's innocent. We both have experience solving cases like this.'

Mr Ashford raised an eyebrow, intrigued. 'Do you now? That's rather impressive. If you believe the police are on the wrong track and you think you can uncover the truth, then I'll do whatever I can to help.'

He leaned forward in his chair.

'Were you close to your godmother?' Penny asked.

'I was when I was younger. My mother passed away when I was a boy, and my father was often busy with work. Mrs Melbourne took a keen interest in my upbringing. She never had children of her own, so I believe she saw me – and her nephew Edmund – as sons. She was particularly fond of Edmund.'

'Edmund died after an accident, is that right?' said Penny.

'Yes.' He ran a hand through his hair. 'It was awfully sad. Then my godmother sued the doctor who treated him.' He shook his head. 'I believe Dr Lloyd did everything in his power to save him, but my godmother... she saw things differently. She needed someone to blame, and the doctor was an easy target. I was in India at the time and read all about it in the newspapers. I never agreed with the court case, and I was astonished when she won. The whole thing was unnecessary and, in my opinion, unfair.'

'Can you think of anyone who would have wanted to harm her?' asked Penny.

He exhaled and leaned back slightly, contemplating the question. 'I want to help, so I'll speak plainly. My godmother was... complicated. There were two sides to her. Publicly, she was charitable, generous, a pillar of the community. She donated money and supported good causes. Many charities flourished under her patronage. But privately...' He hesitated before continuing. 'She was rather different. She had strong opinions – very strong opinions – on how others should behave. She liked to exert control over people. She was not a woman who took kindly to disobedience or opposition.'

His voice lowered slightly. 'She wasn't an easy woman to be

around. She had a way of making people feel as though they owed her something, even when they didn't. She could be harsh and judgemental. But as controlling as she was, I still can't fathom why anyone would go so far as to murder her. She had her faults and she made enemies, but to be left like that, in the cold and darkness of a graveyard... it's a horrifying thought. Whoever did this – whoever had such hatred for her – it must have been deeply personal.'

Silence settled over the room.

At last, Penny spoke. 'Apparently your godmother had a disagreement recently, with a lady who once worked for her as a governess. Miss Lydia Jackson. Do you know her?'

'Miss Jackson?' His brow raised and his eyes were wide. 'I think I met her once or twice... in the distant past.' He smiled. 'Very distant past. It must be twenty years since Miss Jackson worked for her.'

'Do you know anything about a disagreement between them?'

'No, I'm afraid not. But as I've said, my godmother wasn't an easy woman to be around.'

'And she left everything to you in her will,' said Emma.

'Yes.' He ran his hand through his hair again. 'That was quite a surprise. Actually... perhaps it wasn't. She considered Edmund and me to be sons of hers. And with Edmund no longer around... I suppose I've become the beneficiary. Sadly, there's no one else.'

Was he secretly pleased he'd inherited a large fortune? Emma wanted to ask him but reasoned the question would be impolite.

'Is there anything else I can help you with?' he asked them. 'I've told you what I know but I don't think any of it's particularly useful, I'm afraid.'

'No, I think that's all,' said Penny. 'Thank you for your honesty, Mr Ashford.'

He nodded, still looking troubled. 'I can only hope the murderer is caught soon. And the police are taking their time over this. I think it's admirable that you're taking it upon yourselves to look into it. If there's anything else I can do to assist you, please don't hesitate to ask.'

Once outside on the street, Emma and Penny headed south towards Oxford Street.

'What a pleasant, polite gentleman,' said Emma.

'He is,' replied Penny. 'But possibly a little too pleasant and polite? I like him, but we can't ignore the fact he benefits so much from his godmother's death.'

'But why murder her if he's the beneficiary? The estate was always going to pass to him eventually,' said Emma.

'Perhaps he needed the money? And, from the way he spoke, he doesn't appear to have been particularly fond of his wealthy godmother.'

TWENTY-SIX

Christopher Ashford watched from the window as the two ladies headed in the direction of Oxford Street. He liked them. They were clearly intelligent and he had admiration for anyone who took matters into their own hands.

But he hadn't enjoyed answering their questions. He'd chosen his words carefully, but there'd been little use in pretending he held much fondness for his late godmother. Though hopefully he'd persuaded them he was much too nice to have harmed her himself. He'd become a rich man since his godmother's death. Would they believe he wanted her dead?

But thankfully, the two ladies didn't know the full story. They didn't know about him and Lydia. The discovery that she'd gone had been one of the worst days of his life.

His breath quickened at the memory. His gaze shifted from the two women up to the rooftops and low grey clouds above. The scene played in his mind again, just as it had so many times before. The pain returned, as if he'd received a punch to the stomach. His mouth felt dry as he recalled the conversation in that stifling parlour. He could feel the gnawing disbelief again, the suffocating helplessness.

His godmother had answered his questions with a self-satisfied smile playing on her lips.

'Where's Lydia?' he'd asked.

'I had to let her go, I'm afraid,' she'd replied. 'She stole from me.'

'She stole from you?' he had echoed, scarcely able to believe it.

'I'm sorry, Christopher. I know it's hard for you to hear. But Miss Jackson isn't the sort of girl you imagine her to be.'

'I know exactly who Miss Jackson is,' he'd said, his voice firm. 'And I know she would never steal from you. This has to be some dreadful misunderstanding. What are you saying she took?'

'My butterfly brooch.' Her tone had been casual, almost bored. 'You remember it – the one with the diamond wings.'

Of course he remembered it. She'd worn it often, sometimes even boastfully.

'And you think Miss Jackson took that?' he'd said incredulously. 'What would she possibly want with it?'

'She could sell it, of course. It's worth a small fortune.'

He recalled how he'd locked his gaze with hers, struggling to make sense of her explanation. 'If Miss Jackson were in need, she would have mentioned it. She wouldn't risk her position, her reputation, for a piece of jewellery.'

His godmother had given a dismissive sniff. 'You'd be surprised what people will do when they're desperate.'

His stomach had begun to twist then, a slow and sickening churn of dread. 'There's more, isn't there?'

'There is.' She had given a theatrical sigh, as though burdened by her own righteousness. 'I discovered why she left her last position. She had an affair with the father of her pupils. A married man.'

He remembered how he'd closed his eyes, trying to protect himself from the words. When he'd opened them, his voice had sounded different. Choked. Hoarse. 'That isn't true.'

'And how would you know?' she'd retorted. 'Miss Jackson was hardly going to confess it to you. You were blinded by her, Christopher. I understand – it's easy to be misled when someone is young and charming.'

He'd wiped his brow, struggling to comprehend it all. The truth was that Lydia had captured his heart completely. And this was the moment he'd discovered Mrs Melbourne had known it all along.

'I won't deny our feelings for each other,' he'd said carefully. 'But we were discreet. How could you possibly know?'

'A friend confided in me,' she'd said. 'A very reliable source. I made inquiries of my own, and what I found only confirmed it.'

Which friend had it been? He'd held his breath as he'd waited for more explanation.

'Shortly after that, my brooch vanished,' she'd continued. 'And one of the servants told me Miss Jackson had been seen entering my room. When I questioned her, she denied everything. But I'm afraid, Christopher, she deceived us both.'

'I need to speak to her.'

'That won't be possible. She's already left London. She packed her things and departed quickly. Quite ashamed, I think.'

He recalled how his fists had clenched, his jaw and neck tightened. His godmother's nonchalance had been infuriating.

'If I were you, I'd put it all behind you. Focus on your future. My brother's offer in India is a rare opportunity. It will open doors for you that Lydia Jackson never could.' Her voice dropped, silken and poisonous. 'Don't waste your time on girls like her, Christopher. Women can be terribly manipulative. The sweeter they seem, the more dangerous they often are.'

'But not Lydia,' he'd whispered. He'd detested the sense of weakness which had washed over him like tepid water. He'd felt powerless. His godmother had been pulling the strings. And he knew she had done this deliberately. To separate them.

She had succeeded.

Christopher took in a breath and turned away from the window. The memory couldn't be allowed to control his emotions any longer.

He was growing weary of the polite formalities, of having to feign sorrow for a woman he had long since resented. People spoke of his godmother with admiration, offering him their sympathies as if they expected him to be grieving. But why should he?

For reasons he never fully understood, she'd always claimed to be fond of him. But had she truly cared for him? Or had her so-called affection been nothing more than a convenient excuse to manipulate his life?

Whenever someone expressed their condolences, he felt an almost unbearable urge to tell them the truth – that his godmother's influence had not been one of kindness, but of control. That she had meddled, schemed and dictated, forcing him down paths he never wanted to take. But speaking openly about such things would only invite trouble.

Only Lydia knew the truth. She had been a victim of Mrs Melbourne's interference too. They had both suffered under her relentless need to orchestrate the lives of others, enduring her lies, her manipulations, her ruthless determination to shape their futures to her liking.

And now it was over.

But at what cost?

How many years had been lost because Mrs Melbourne had insisted on having her own way? How many opportunities had slipped through their fingers because she'd forced them to conform to her desires rather than their own?

She had left him everything, and he knew she would have expected him to be grateful. The money, the house, the possessions – they were meant to be some final, magnanimous gift. But he couldn't see them that way. The inheritance felt less like a legacy and more like an apology, an attempt to make amends for the years she had stolen from him.

But it was too late for apologies.

No amount of money could buy back lost time.

Not all the wealth in the world.

TWENTY-SEVEN

Emma and Penny invited Clara Clifton to their next lunch at the ladies' dining room in Café Monico, Piccadilly Circus. The atmosphere was warm and lively. The gentle clatter of china and low murmur of conversation created a pleasant backdrop as they took their seats.

'We did our best to persuade Inspector Paget that you're completely innocent of Mrs Melbourne's murder,' Penny said, setting down her gloves. 'But he's a difficult man to deal with.'

Clara sighed. 'I can imagine. Thank you for trying.'

'He even blamed you making yourself suspicious by visiting disused graveyards,' Penny continued. 'Quite astonishing, isn't it? He clearly doesn't think it's the sort of thing a lady should be doing.'

Clara gave a knowing smile. 'I've heard plenty of remarks about my interests. And I expect you have too, Penny.'

Penny nodded. 'Indeed. But we both know the only thing to do is ignore them and carry on. I suspect that's why he's being so difficult with you – he simply doesn't understand the work you're doing.'

They told Clara about Dr Lloyd, Miss Jackson and Mr Ashford – three people they now believed were worthy of suspicion.

'I didn't realise Mrs Melbourne had fallen out with so many people,' Clara said. 'I've only heard kind things about her.'

'That's what we discovered at first,' Emma said. 'But the more people we speak to, the more we realise Mrs Melbourne wasn't quite as perfect as we first believed.' She paused and smiled. 'Then again, no one is, are they?'

'I suppose not.' Clara broke off a piece of bread and spread butter on it. Emma noticed she'd been struggling to meet her gaze since they'd sat down at the table. As if something was bothering her. 'I must admit,' continued Clara, 'whenever I hear about someone being exceptionally pious and charitable, I find myself wondering what their less admirable traits might be.'

The waiter arrived to take their order. Clara glanced at the menu. 'What would you recommend?'

'I'm afraid we always order the same thing,' Emma admitted. 'Consommé au riz followed by saumon grillé.'

Clara smiled. 'Then I shall try it too.'

The waiter looked amused as he noted their identical orders before retreating.

Emma reached into her bag and pulled out the *Morning Express*. She had read an article that morning which she was keen to show them.

'I've found someone else we can speak to about Mrs Melbourne,' she said. 'Did you see this morning's paper?'

Penny shook her head. 'I'd like to be able to read the newspaper every morning, but I rarely get the chance. I'm usually too busy cleaning up bread crusts and spilled milk at breakfast.'

'Goodness,' Clara said. 'Your husband sounds like hard work.'

Emma and Penny laughed.

Emma unfolded the newspaper and turned to the relevant page.

Tribute Paid to Mrs Melbourne

Mrs Margaret Harwell, chairlady of the St James's Diocesan Home for Penitents in Fulham, has paid tribute to the late Mrs Melbourne, who was tragically found murdered in St Anne's Churchyard, Soho, last week.

'On behalf of the charity, I would like to offer our deepest condolences to Mrs Melbourne's family,' she said. 'Mrs Melbourne's untimely death has come as a great shock to us. We would like her to be remembered as a kind, generous lady who devoted a great deal of time and money to our worthy cause.

'Mrs Melbourne dedicated many years of her life to helping those who were less fortunate than herself. Her tireless work for the St James's Home provided countless fallen women with the valuable skills needed to work in service. Mrs Melbourne's enthusiasm and generosity will be sorely missed by all of us here at the charity.'

Clara broke off another piece of bread. 'Well, I suppose it's good that she helped the charity. The St James's Diocesan Home for Penitents. Is that a home for unmarried mothers?'

'Yes, I think so,' said Penny. She turned to Emma. 'Can you remind me of the name of the lady who paid tribute to her?'

'Mrs Harwell,' said Emma.

'Of course!' Penny's eyes brightened. 'We've heard that name before. Isn't that the name of the lady Mrs Melbourne had dinner with on the evening of her death?'

'Yes! I'd forgotten her name until you reminded me of it just now. We need to speak to her.'

'We do. She might have some insight into who might have wanted to harm Mrs Melbourne.'

Clara seemed quiet and thoughtful for a moment. Then she pinched her brow, as if she had a headache.

'Is everything all right?' Emma asked her.

Clara nodded but pursed her lips and kept her eyes on her bread plate.

'What's wrong?' asked Penny.

'Oh...' Clara pulled at her ear lobe. 'I'm sorry. I...' She looked up at them and sighed. 'I haven't been very truthful with you.'

Emma's heart sank. What had Clara been hiding?

She said nothing. And neither did Penny.

Clara took in a breath and continued. 'When I said I didn't know Mrs Melbourne... I had to say it! The police were questioning me about her and I knew that if I admitted that I had—'

'Just a moment,' interrupted Penny. 'You did know her?'

Clara gave a tearful nod.

'Oh no.' Penny slumped back in her chair. 'Emma and I have been telling everyone the police are wrong to suspect you and that we're trying to find out the truth and all along you've been lying to us!'

'Not intentionally!' Clara's eyes darted frantically as a tear rolled down her face and she wiped it away. 'I didn't know her very well, I met her a few times. That was all. But I was too scared to tell anyone as I thought I'd be arrested!'

Emma and Penny exchanged a glance. Penny was scowling deeply, clearly annoyed that she'd been misled.

'So please explain it all to us now,' implored Emma. 'Tell us the truth.'

Clara let out a shaky breath. 'It was when you mentioned the charity just then... Mrs Melbourne approached the Metropolitan Public Gardens Committee and asked to join the board. She said she could donate a lot of money to our cause. Thankfully, the chairman said they would invite her to a meeting and then everyone could decide whether or not they wanted to admit her. I attended the meeting myself and it was... oh, she made such a nuisance of herself.'

'In what way?' queried Penny.

'She dominated the conversation and told everyone how they should be doing things. She kept talking about how much money she had, but in return for her funding she wanted complete control. Fortunately the chairman found her insufferable and wasn't tempted by the large amount of money she was offering. She wasn't happy the committee turned down her offer and she turned up to a second meeting unannounced.' Clara shuddered. 'That was awful too. Eventually the chairman was quite rude to her and the committee didn't hear from her again.'

'So you didn't know her personally?' asked Penny.

Clara shook her head. 'No. Although...'

'Although what?' asked Emma.

'She called on me one day.'

Emma caught her breath. 'She called on you? Why didn't you tell us this?'

Clara sat back a little, biting her lip. 'I wanted to but I worried that...'

'It's all right,' said Penny, reaching out and resting a hand on her arm. 'You don't have to explain. You're telling us now and that's all that matters.'

Emma felt a snap of irritation. How could Penny suddenly be so calm with Clara? She hadn't been completely truthful with them.

Clara took in a breath and continued, 'She called on me and told me she'd read some of my reports. She said they were verbose and long-winded and told me I should make them more concise. She said concise reports would help the members of the Metropolitan Public Gardens Committee make better use of their time.'

'How rude of her!' commented Penny.

'This was shortly after the first meeting,' said Clara. 'I tried to defend myself but she was just so... domineering and superior.' She shook her head. 'So I just had to listen to her and once she'd said all she wanted to, she left again.'

'It sounds like that was all you could have done,' said Penny.

'And I didn't tell anyone this because it makes me look suspicious, doesn't it?' said Clara. 'I met Mrs Melbourne a few times but I didn't know her. And although she was mean to me, I could never have harmed her. Not like the person who murdered her in the churchyard. And when I found her that morning... I didn't recognise her immediately. She looked so different...' She trailed off. 'Then the police told me who she was and I realised.' Her brow furrowed and her eyes widened. 'I'm so sorry I didn't tell you sooner, I was so scared the police would find out and... that would be it, wouldn't it? They would arrest me immediately. And this is why some members of the committee don't believe me. I told the chairman about Mrs Melbourne's visit and I think some people still believe I murdered her out of revenge. But I didn't!'

Emma felt persuaded by her. Although it was annoying she hadn't been forthcoming from the outset, Emma now understood her reasons why.

Penny placed her hand on top of Clara's. 'Thank you for being honest with us,' she said. 'Now that you've explained it, it makes sense. You only met us recently and it takes a little time to know who to trust. For the time being we can keep this between ourselves.'

'You won't tell the police?' asked Clara anxiously.

Penny shook her head. 'Not right now. There are other people they need to look at.'

Clara took a handkerchief from her bag and wiped her eyes. 'Thank you for being so understanding. The longer I kept that from you, the worse I felt.'

TWENTY-EIGHT

Emma and Penny travelled to Fulham the following morning beneath a leaden sky. A damp chill clung to the air, and a fine mist blurred the outlines of chimneys and rooftops.

'Do you find it a little odd that Clara didn't immediately tell us she knew Mrs Melbourne?' said Penny as they left the bustle of the railway station.

'Yes, a little,' replied Emma. She thought back to the moment she'd found Clara upset on the bench in St James's Square. 'When I first met her, I asked her if she knew who the dead woman was and she told me she didn't.' She couldn't help feeling a little wounded that Clara had lied. 'I suppose she didn't know who I was then,' she reasoned. 'She didn't know if she could trust me. And, as she explained to us, she was scared the police would find out she knew Mrs Melbourne.'

Penny nodded. 'I can understand her reasoning. And I suppose we should be pleased she's told us the truth now. Or what she claims is the truth.' She paused, thoughtful. 'You can never be completely sure, can you?'

After leaving the high street behind, they followed a quieter road that passed Fulham Palace – the ancient riverside residence of the Bishop of London. The grand building stood solemnly in the grey light, its silhouette softened by the drifting fog. Beyond it, the surrounding farmland and marshes stretched down towards the Thames, ghostly and desolate in the morning haze. Across the road, a row of freshly built houses stood stiffly in a line. Scaffolding creaked in the breeze, but no labourers were in sight – the dreary weather had evidently driven them away.

Eventually a large rambling building came into view. It was set back from the road and a faded sign announced it was the place they'd come to visit: *St James's Diocesan Home for Penitents.*

'I feel terribly sorry for any young woman who has to spend time here,' said Penny. She and Emma walked down the gravelled drive, their footsteps crunching in the silence.

A young sombre-faced woman wearing a plain cotton dress and apron answered the door. Emma guessed she was one of the unfortunate penitents.

The entrance hall was austere but clean with a wooden floor and framed notices on the wall. Some were lists of rules while others were Biblical quotes. Emma read one as they passed: "The Lord is merciful and gracious, slow to anger, and plenteous in mercy."

They followed the young woman along a corridor which smelled of antiseptic and boiled vegetables. Emma heard someone talking beyond one of the doors and the scrape of a chair beyond another. Then, from an upper floor, came a distant wail. Penny reached for Emma's arm, her eyes filled with concern. The wailing was a chorus of young babies crying.

Emma imagined them lying in rows of cots in a cold, spartan dormitory. All wrapped in identical blankets and separated from their mothers. A heavy, sickening sensation weighed inside her and tears pricked her eyes. Penny gripped her arm tight and emitted a quiet, stricken gasp.

They had managed to recover themselves a little by the time they paused by a polished oak door. 'Come in!' came the commanding voice after the young woman had knocked. She left them as Emma and Penny stepped into an office where a stocky, bespectacled woman sat behind a desk. Her wavy grey hair was pinned back in a sensible style. She wore a well-tailored woollen dress, its deep blue fabric trimmed with black velvet. Her matching hat sat at a perfect angle, secured with an ornate silver hatpin.

Organised piles of paperwork were laid out across the desk. Shelves were crammed with ledgers and neatly tied stacks of pamphlets.

'Mrs Harwell?' asked Penny.

The woman set down her pen and removed her spectacles, greeting them with a polite but reserved smile.

'How can I help you, ladies?'

'We'd like to speak with you about Mrs Melbourne, if we may,' Penny said, stepping forward. 'We read your tribute to her in the *Morning Express* newspaper.'

Mrs Harwell folded her hands neatly on the desk. 'Did you? Well, it's nice that they printed it.'

She gestured for them to sit on the chairs opposite her.

'I'm a former news reporter,' Penny explained as she sat down. 'And this is my friend, Mrs Langley. We're investigating Mrs Melbourne's murder.'

Mrs Harwell removed her glasses and regarded them carefully. 'Investigating? I would have thought that was the police's job.'

'It is,' Penny agreed. 'But they suspect a friend of ours may have been responsible. We're quite sure she wasn't, so we've decided to do some investigating on her behalf. We've both done this sort of thing before.'

'Oh, have you? And what exactly does that make you? Lady detectives?'

Penny gave a small smile. 'If you like.'

Mrs Harwell leaned back slightly, studying them. 'Well, I don't know why you've come to me. I can't imagine what help I could possibly be.'

'But you knew Mrs Melbourne?'

'Of course. She did a great deal of work for this organisation.'

'Then you must be terribly shocked by what happened,' Penny prompted.

Mrs Harwell pursed her lips. 'Oh yes, very shocking. Murder always is, isn't it? It really isn't the sort of thing that should happen to anybody.'

Her words seemed impersonal and Emma couldn't imagine her shedding any tears for Mrs Melbourne.

'You had dinner with her that night,' ventured Penny.

'I did.' Mrs Harwell's response was curt and guarded.

'When did you last see her?'

'When she got into a hansom cab outside the restaurant. We got into separate cabs and went our separate ways.'

'Did she mention she was planning to go to Soho?'

Mrs Harwell sighed. 'I've gone through this with the police. Why are you asking me the sort of questions a police detective asks?'

'I'm just wondering what Mrs Melbourne's last movements were.'

'She got in a cab and that was the last time I saw her.' She steepled her fingers. 'There really is nothing else to it.'

'Did Mrs Melbourne mention any disagreements with anyone?' Penny asked.

Mrs Harwell hesitated, then shook her head. 'No. There was that business with the doctor a little while ago. She sued him after her nephew's death. And she was successful, as I understand it. But beyond that, I don't know of any conflicts.'

'Can you think of anyone who might have wanted to harm her?' Emma asked.

Mrs Harwell shook her head. 'Well, no, of course not. If I could, I would have told the police.

'We suspect she arranged to meet someone in the graveyard,' Penny said.

Mrs Harwell let out a dry laugh. 'Do you? Well, I can't see why anyone would want to arrange a meeting in a graveyard. Especially not that one. I've walked past it a few times, and it's dreadfully unkempt.'

Emma observed her carefully. Her responses were too measured, too controlled.

'How long did you know Mrs Melbourne?' Penny asked.

'About ten years, I suppose. She did some good work for this charity for a long time. She'll be greatly missed.'

'Was she a personal friend?' Penny inquired.

Mrs Harwell hesitated. 'No, not a personal friend. But we got along well because we shared a common cause – we were both determined to help those in need.' She smoothed a piece of paper on her desk before continuing. 'In some ways, we were similar. We were both widows, both women of independent means, both wanting to use our positions to help others. It's a natural thing to do when one is widowed, I think. It gives life a sense of purpose.'

'How long have you been involved in charitable works?' Emma asked.

Mrs Harwell's expression softened slightly. 'As long as I can remember. I have worked here for decades. And since my husband's death five years ago, I have put even more of my time into good works. I needed something to occupy me, something meaningful. There are many women like me who do nothing at all. They spend their days attending social gatherings, exchanging idle gossip. And to be honest with you, I find that sort of existence incredibly dull.' She leaned forward slightly, her tone taking on a note of conviction. 'All that sitting about, discussing trivial matters, passing judgement on others – it never suited me. I spent years playing the role of a dutiful wife, standing beside my husband at every function, smiling and offering polite conversation to people I hardly knew. I made them feel at ease, I played my part well. But now, at last, I have found something truly fulfilling. No longer do I have to flatter the powerful and privileged. Instead, I use my influence to help those who are overlooked, the ones society so easily forgets.'

'Unmarried mothers,' said Penny.

'Yes. Society is very keen to ostracise them and forget about them. But they're young and have many years ahead of them. With the right intervention, these girls can be encouraged to follow a respectable path. Our role here at St James's is to offer them moral guidance – not companionship. The girls are not here for leisure. They are here to correct their behaviour before re-entering society And if they're lucky, no one else will ever learn of their disgrace.'

'And the babies?' asked Penny. A lump came to Emma's throat as she thought again of them lying in rows.

'They're adopted by respectable families where they can grow into healthy children, free from the sin and shame of their birth.'

Penny frowned. 'But surely it must be difficult for the mothers?'

'Of course it is. But that's the nature of it. The girls are young and unmarried, with no ability to care for a child. Adoption spares the baby a life of hardship and gives the mother a chance to rebuild her life. They're expected to forget and move on.'

Penny's heart ached at the coldness of the words. Forget? How could anyone forget a child they'd carried and birthed?

Mrs Harwell glanced at the clock on the wall. 'Now, ladies, if you'll excuse me, I have work to do. She gestured at the papers on her desk.

'Of course.' Emma and Penny rose from their seats. 'Thank you for your time, Mrs Harwell.'

Low mist hung over the long drive as Emma and Penny walked back to the railway station.

'Mrs Harwell says she and Mrs Melbourne got into two sepa-rate hansom cabs,' said Penny. 'Do you believe her?'

'I think I do,' said Emma. 'And it's possible her account is supported by staff at the restaurant. Perhaps a waiter or doorman hailed the cabs for the two ladies and helped them get in.'

'That's a good point.'

'And besides, what motive could Mrs Harwell have for murdering her friend?'

'Nothing immediately comes to mind,' said Penny. 'But she didn't let anything slip about her relationship with Mrs Melbourne, did she?'

'No,' said Emma. 'And despite the notice she had published in the *Morning Express*, she doesn't seem particularly upset about her death.'

TWENTY-NINE

After the two ladies had left, Mrs Harwell sat back in her chair with a weary sigh. She removed her spectacles, dropping them onto the desk with a soft clatter, and pressed her fingers to the bridge of her nose.

She had never wanted to publish that tribute to Mrs Melbourne in the newspaper. But it had been expected of her. If she hadn't, people would have questioned why, and questions – particularly about Mrs Melbourne – were something she had no desire to invite. And now, despite her careful efforts, two ladies had come asking them anyway.

Amateur detectives. She could see it in their eyes – their curiosity, their determination. They were intelligent, certainly, but it wasn't the sort of thing well-bred ladies ought to be concerning themselves with.

She exhaled sharply, shaking her head.

No, she wasn't sorry that Mrs Melbourne was dead. If anything, she was relieved. First her husband, and now Mrs Melbourne – the two people who'd wielded power over her choices were finally gone.

She had expected to feel freer. Lighter.

But she didn't.

Instead, a heavy weight pressed upon her chest. A creeping unease.

Her secrets should have died with Mrs Melbourne.

But what if they hadn't?

What if Mrs Melbourne had told someone?

Or worse – what if she had written something down?

A knock at the door disturbed her. She sighed, irritated that she was struggling to get any work done.

'Come in!' she said, putting on her spectacles again.

John Curtis stepped into the room. He'd worked for her husband for years and she didn't feel particularly pleased to see him now. He was a grey-suited fellow with hair and a moustache of the same colour. There was nothing especially disagreeable about him, but his presence carried an unwelcome weight. He reminded her of her husband.

'It's a pleasure to see you again, Mrs Harwell,' he said, holding out his hand. 'It's been a long while hasn't it?'

'It certainly has, Mr Curtis.' She took his hand briefly before gesturing towards the chair opposite her. 'Please, do sit.'

'I'm here to extend an invitation to you,' he said, settling into his seat. 'We're holding a ceremony at our newly built offices in Holborn.'

'Ah. You've moved in, then?'

'We move in next week.' His voice was thick with pride. 'They're very grand offices, Mrs Harwell. I know you'll be most impressed when you see them.'

She had no desire to visit, but she offered the expected response – a polite smile and a nod.

'And,' he continued, pulling an envelope from his pocket, 'I have the pleasure of inviting you to the unveiling of a plaque dedicated to your late husband.'

She accepted the envelope without enthusiasm, glancing down at it before placing it on her desk. 'A plaque?'

'Of course. If not for his leadership, the company would never have been able to afford such an ambitious expansion. Without him, we simply wouldn't be where we are today.'

'No, I suppose not.'

'The ceremony is scheduled for the sixteenth of July. Would you be able to attend?'

She hesitated, although she knew full well she had no pressing engagements then. 'It's a few months away. I shall read the invitation properly and send your secretary my response.'

'Excellent.' He rubbed his hands together, pleased. 'I should add, the decision to honour him was unanimous. The plaque will be placed in the entrance hall – everyone who visits the building will see it. A fitting tribute to a truly dedicated man.'

Dedicated.

A fitting word, certainly.

Dedicated to his work. Dedicated to the company. Dedicated to ensuring his name would live on in stone and bronze.

But never dedicated to her.

She kept her expression neutral, although inwardly, she marvelled at how effortlessly her husband had fooled them all. John Curtis, like the rest of them, had been taken in by the illusion – her husband's carefully curated persona, his impeccable reputation as a fair, intelligent, hardworking gentleman.

None of them had known what he was truly like.

And none of them ever would.

'It's a shame he never lived to see the new headquarters,' Mr Curtis added, shaking his head. 'In hindsight, he worked himself too hard. The strain on his heart, well... it caught up with him, didn't it?'

'Oh, absolutely,' she said smoothly.

It was fortunate that no one had ever questioned it.

'It just goes to show,' Mr Curtis continued, 'none of us truly know when our time is up. Mr Harwell certainly made the most of every day – what he achieved in his lifetime was remarkable.'

'Yes,' she agreed, 'he was very... accomplished.'

Accomplished at deception. Accomplished at control. Accomplished at ensuring no one ever saw the cracks beneath the surface.

She felt an unwelcome tightness in her chest, a familiar but well-buried resentment stirring. But she had learned long ago how to keep her composure.

Instead, she glanced at the papers on her desk, a subtle but unmistakable cue that their conversation had run its course.

Mr Curtis took the hint and pushed himself up from his chair. 'I can see you're busy, Mrs Harwell. I'll leave you to it. I look forward to seeing you at the unveiling.'

'Thank you for the invitation,' she said, rising as well.

He glanced around the room, taking in the surroundings. 'And I must say, you work as tirelessly as your husband did.' He smiled. 'You and your husband were very alike, weren't you?'

She held his gaze, willing her smile to stay in place.

'Absolutely.'

And she ushered him towards the door before he could see the lie in her eyes.

THIRTY

Emma had a piano lesson to teach after the trip to Fulham. Penny decided to visit Francis Edwards at the reading room to see if he'd found out anything more about Dr Lloyd.

She always enjoyed a reason to visit the reading room; it was a place she'd spent a lot of time in when researching for her news reports. The vast domed space, with its towering bookshelves and the quiet scholars at work, was a familiar comfort to her. When she arrived, she scanned the room and soon spotted Francis on the upper gallery, assisting a lady with locating a book.

As he descended the wrought-iron staircase, he caught sight of her and gave a brief nod before retrieving a small stack of papers from the central desk. When he reached her, he spoke in a low whisper.

'It's probably best if we talk outside, Penny. I can already sense the disapproving glares of those trying to concentrate.'

Penny smiled. 'Of course.'

They left the reading room and went to the nearby Roman Gallery, finding a bench beneath one of the tall windows. The statues of ancient emperors and philosophers stared impassively as visitors wandered through.

Francis set the papers on his lap and tapped the top sheet. 'As you'll see, I've managed to uncover some rather interesting details about Dr Lloyd. He hasn't exactly had a perfect career.'

He glanced down at the notes before continuing. 'Eight years ago, he was summoned to appear before the General Medical Council. He was accused of knowingly allowing an unqualified individual to practise medicine under his name – essentially providing cover for a man with no medical qualifications. He enabled him to carry out treatments at his surgery as though he were a fully licensed doctor.'

Penny's eyebrows rose. 'That's astonishing. He was willing to let a gentleman without training treat patients?'

Francis nodded. 'It would seem so. When confronted, Dr Lloyd expressed deep regret for his actions. He insisted it was a lapse in judgement and claimed he'd trusted the man far more than he should have. He received a formal admonishment from the General Medical Council.'

He lifted another sheet. 'But that wasn't the only time he faced professional misconduct allegations. Four years ago, he was fined three pounds for issuing a false death certificate.'

Penny leaned forward. 'A false certificate? What were the circumstances?'

'A woman was brought to his surgery in a critical condition and was attended to by his medical assistant – another man of dubious qualifications, from what I can gather. The patient died shortly afterwards, reportedly of heart failure. Dr Lloyd signed the death certificate without ever examining her himself. He simply accepted his assistant's word and made it official.'

Penny exhaled. 'That's careless at best. At worst, it's dangerously negligent.'

Francis pushed his spectacles up his nose. 'Precisely. And while neither of these offences were enough to have him struck off the register, they raise questions about his integrity. It suggests a pattern of recklessness. Cutting corners where he shouldn't, turning a blind eye when it suits him.'

Penny gave this some thought. 'Perhaps Mrs Melbourne had

reason to sue him after all. Perhaps he could have done more for her nephew.' She took the papers from him and leafed through them. 'I appreciate all of this, Francis. You've been an enormous help.'

'It's no problem at all. I enjoy researching things like this.'

She rested the papers on her lap and folded her hands on top of them. 'And how are you settling back into life in England?'

He gave a dry chuckle. 'I think I'll feel a little better about my decision to return when the weather improves. Right now, I find myself longing for the Mediterranean climate.'

Penny smiled. 'I don't blame you. Perhaps you'd like to join us for dinner again one evening?'

He hesitated. 'That would be nice,' he said, but Penny detected reluctance.

She tilted her head. 'Would it really be nice, Francis? Or are you saying that just to be courteous?'

He let out a soft sigh, his gaze flickering away. 'No, it would be nice.' Then, after a pause, he admitted, 'It's just... I don't think your husband likes me very much.'

Penny gave a quiet laugh. 'That's not true! I know he likes you.'

Francis turned to her, looking unconvinced. 'Are you sure? Perhaps it's not outright dislike. Perhaps I'm just... not his favourite person.'

Penny's amusement faded slightly. 'What are you trying to say, Francis?'

He hesitated, rubbing his brow as though trying to find the right words. 'Please don't take offence, Penny. I had a wonderful time when I last had dinner with you, James and the delightful Mrs Langley. But surely you recall that James and I had a disagreement about Sir Francis Drake? I know it was only a small, irrelevant disagreement, but I fear we are the sort of men who will never quite see eye-to-eye.' He gave another small sigh, shaking his head. 'I wish I could explain this better. I suppose... there's a history between us. And that history makes it difficult. It's not that I don't want to get along with James. In fact, I would very much like to.

But I suspect he – understandably – sees me as a complication in his life rather than a friend. I can hardly blame him for that. I think, perhaps... he worries that I still have feelings for you.'

The statement lingered between them for a moment. Penny felt a strange pang of guilt, even though she'd long since made her choice. She had married James. She had built a life with him. But that didn't change the past – or the fact that Francis had once been part of it.

She gave a slow sigh. 'I understand what you're saying. And I can understand why you might find it a little... awkward. But, Francis... I truly hoped that by now you might have found someone else who...'

She trailed off, uncertain how to phrase it without sounding patronising.

Francis gave a tight smile. 'You hoped I would have fallen in love with someone else by now?'

She nodded, gritting her teeth with discomfort.

He looked down at his hands. 'So did I.'

Another brief silence stretched between them. Penny cleared her throat, determined to lighten the mood. 'Maybe I could make dinner a larger gathering – something less formal. In fact, I could invite Clara Clifton too. You'd be interested in meeting her. She visits and catalogues disused graveyards.'

Francis looked intrigued. 'Really? That does sound fascinating. I once came across a book from fifty years ago about the state of London's graveyards. An updated account is certainly overdue. I should be very interested in meeting her.'

Penny smiled. 'Then it's settled. We'll arrange something soon. In the meantime, thank you again for all your help, Francis. It truly means a lot.'

Francis nodded, but as Penny walked away, she couldn't shake the feeling that, no matter how much time had passed, there were some things between them that would never quite be resolved.

THIRTY-ONE

Penny called in at the *Morning Express* offices to hand in her latest article. Edgar Fish, the editor, sat at his desk, his usual air of jovial amusement somewhat muted. He glanced up from a stack of proofs, waved her in and gestured to the chair opposite him.

She noted the faint crease of concern on his brow. He was often quick with a quip or a sarcastic remark, but today he merely picked up his pencil and tapped it against the desk.

Penny set her article in front of him. 'I've written about ways in which mothers can make use of their spare time,' she said.

Edgar's eyebrows raised. 'Spare time?' He leaned back in his chair. 'From what I recall from your previous articles, Mrs Blakely, mothers don't have any spare time.'

'They don't have much,' she admitted. 'But I've been wondering whether my tone has been a little too... well, pessimistic at times. I thought it might be useful to provide some ideas for those rare moments when a mother does find herself with time on her hands.'

Edgar nodded thoughtfully and picked up the article. 'Let's see what you've come up with, then.'

He began reading aloud, '"Friendships are important at this time. They offer a good opportunity to discuss concerns with other mothers. Although I believe these matters should also be discussed with one's husband, he is not always in the mood to hear them when he returns home after a long and strenuous day at work.'"

Edgar nodded and lowered the page. 'Now, that's something I can agree with. After a day spent dealing with printers, reporters and the endless chaos of a newsroom, my evening conversation preferences lean towards the monosyllabic. On the other hand, dear Mrs Fish is an enthusiastic conversationalist. She meets with her friends regularly and I encourage her to do so more often. It means she can unburden herself to them rather than me.' He resumed his reading. '"Making an arrangement to meet with friends once a week for afternoon tea or lunch, if time allows, will provide opportunities for conversation with someone other than a small child. Consider also a walk in the park or countryside. Or joining a library. Books bring such enjoyment, allowing the reader to immerse themselves in another world."' Edgar let out a short laugh. 'Reading books. Now that's an interesting one. Mrs Fish refuses to read. She claims books are boring.'

'Perhaps she hasn't found the right ones yet,' Penny suggested.

'Perhaps. But I fear her patience for fiction is rather limited. Maybe I should send her to the library and see if anything sparks her interest.' He tapped his fingers against the desk. 'There are a few more ideas you could include in this article. What about philanthropy?'

Penny hesitated. 'I deliberately left that out.'

'Why?'

'Because philanthropy is already expected of women. Motherhood is an act of constant giving, Edgar. Every waking moment is devoted to someone else's needs. My goal is to suggest ways for a mother to enrich herself – for her own joy, not out of duty or for charitable causes.'

Edgar considered this, nodding slowly. 'That's an interesting point. You know, I rather like that perspective. It's refreshing.'

But even as Penny spoke, she couldn't help but think of Mrs Melbourne. The woman's life had revolved around charitable work, yet what had it truly meant to her? Had her generosity been entirely selfless, or had it served as a way to control others?

Edgar placed Penny's article on his desk and rubbed his temple. Although he seemed happy with the article, something was bothering him. Penny's stomach tensed. Was he about to tell her that the *Morning Express* no longer wanted her articles?

'Is there something wrong?' she asked, keeping her voice light but firm.

'Not wrong but... There's something else I need to speak to you about.' He shifted the piles of papers on his desk. 'It's here somewhere.'

Penny clasped her hands in her lap, waiting. Finally, he pulled out a single sheet of paper, folded neatly in half.

'An anonymous letter,' he said. 'It arrived here yesterday. We get plenty of them, of course. You know as well as I do, Mrs Blakely, how much nonsense gets sent to every newspaper. But this one is different.' He hesitated. 'It's addressed to you. And, I suspect, you won't like what it has to say.' He slid it across the desk. 'It was delivered here, I imagine, because the sender didn't know your home address. Which, once you've read it, you might find rather reassuring.'

Penny unfolded the letter.

Dear Mrs Blakely and Mrs Langley,

Your preoccupation with the death of Mrs Melbourne is both unusual and strange. Why two respectable ladies should wish to spend their time on something so macabre, I cannot fathom.

It is neglectful of Detective Inspector James Blakely, a respected officer at Scotland Yard, to allow his wife to behave in such an undignified way. Perhaps I should remind you that you are a wife and a mother, and that is where your focus must lie.

And as for Mrs Langley, a recently widowed lady – occupying herself with this unpleasant task is disrespectful to the memory of her late husband. If he were still alive, I doubt very much she would be conducting herself in this way.

The pair of you should be putting your time to much better use. For you, Mrs Blakely, that means motherhood and loyalty to your husband. For Mrs Langley, it means following the example of the widowed Mrs Melbourne – helping those less fortunate and doing good in society.

I ask you this, Mrs Blakely: what will your children think when they are old enough to understand what you are doing? They will undoubtedly be ashamed that their mother gave more importance to amateur detective work than to raising them. They will learn that they meant so little to her that she pursued a pointless yet dangerous exercise, driven purely by her own vanity.

I trust you will make the right decision and put a stop to this needless prying.

Penny's grip on the letter tightened. The paper crinkled slightly under her fingers.

She had received plenty of letters from displeased readers before – snide remarks, patronising suggestions and thinly veiled insults. But this was different.

This was personal.

It passed judgement on who she was – a mother. A wife. Someone who was meant to protect and nurture her children.

And that was exactly where the writer had struck.

A deep, uncomfortable chill spread through her chest. The words 'what will your children think' echoed in her mind. Whoever had written this letter hadn't just wanted to unnerve her. They had wanted to wound her.

And it had worked.

For the first time, she felt tempted to stop.

She blinked quickly, willing away the dampness in her eyes before Edgar could notice. Tossing the letter onto his desk, she exhaled slowly.

Edgar allowed a respectful pause before speaking.

'I'm sorry, Mrs Blakely.' His voice was uncharacteristically gentle. 'I didn't want to show you that letter. But I knew you'd be far more annoyed with me if I hadn't.'

Penny straightened her back. 'I would have been.' Her voice was firm now. She wouldn't give whoever had written the letter the satisfaction of upsetting her. She met Edgar's gaze. 'Thank you for showing it to me. But I can't stop now,' she said. 'And I don't think Mrs Langley will, either.'

Edgar studied her carefully, then sighed. 'And if it becomes more dangerous?'

Penny met his gaze. 'We'll decide for ourselves when to stop. But I won't be told what to do by an anonymous coward.'

Emma sat in the parlour that evening updating her notes on her pupils' progress. The twins were doing well but Beth was learning quicker than her sister, Harriet. She was good enough to begin learning Debussy's 'Clair de Lune', but Emma knew Harriet would feel resentful about this. She was yet to complete Bach's 'Minuet in G Major'.

As she pondered on how to manage this conflict, her thoughts were interrupted by a knock at the door. From the moment she saw Penny on the doorstep, she sensed something was bothering her. 'Is everything all right?' she asked.

'There's something I need to show you.' Penny pulled a letter from her bag and handed it to Emma once they were seated in the parlour. 'This was sent to the *Morning Express* offices.'

Emma took it with hesitant fingers and opened it. The moment her eyes scanned the first few lines, her stomach twisted into a tight knot. She paused halfway down the page, feeling a chill creep over her skin.

'This is horrible,' she murmured, gripping the paper. 'Who wrote this?'

'I don't know,' said Penny. 'Have you read all of it?'

Emma swallowed, suddenly reluctant. 'Not yet. I'm not sure I want to.'

Still, she forced herself to continue reading. The words were laced with calculated cruelty. But it was the mention of Penny's children that made her wince. She exhaled sharply, tossing the letter to the side.

'How?' she said, her voice trembling. 'How do they know all these things about us? They mention I'm recently widowed.' She turned to Penny. 'Is this someone who knows us?'

'It can't be someone we know well,' she replied. 'They'll have asked around and found what they could about us.'

Emma felt nauseous. 'But that's a horrible thought!'

'Yes, it is.' She rested a hand on Emma's lap. 'They want to upset us and it's working. It's their way of attacking us and they're doing so because of our actions, not who we are.'

'We can't let them stop us.' Emma clasped her arms in an effort to comfort herself. 'And the things they write about are ridiculous. They clearly have no idea my late husband was a scoundrel. I couldn't care less what he would have thought.' She rested her hand on Penny's. 'But what they wrote about you... that was vile.'

She noticed Penny's eyes were damp behind her spectacles. She sighed and blinked the tears away. 'It's not the first letter I've received like this,' she admitted, her voice steady but subdued. 'When I was a reporter, I regularly received hate mail. Some were even sent by James's fiancée.'

Emma startled. 'James had a fiancée?'

Penny gave a small nod. 'Her name was Charlotte. And, looking back, I do feel a bit sorry for her now. She and James were engaged before he met me. When our paths crossed... well, everything changed. She even tried to sue him for breach of promise.'

Emma's mouth fell open. 'Goodness. I had no idea.'

'It was an ordeal,' Penny admitted. 'And yes, Charlotte wrote me a fair number of unpleasant letters. Nothing as vicious as this one, but still rather cruel. And, to be fair, I could understand why she was angry. One might even argue that I deserved it at the time.'

'But not this time,' Emma said firmly. 'This is different.'

Penny pressed her lips together. 'No, in some ways, it's the same. The intent behind it is the same – it's designed to hurt, to shake us. But the crucial difference is that I believe the person who wrote this is the murderer.'

Emma felt a prickling sensation run down her spine. She swallowed hard. 'You really think so?'

'Why else would they be so desperate to make us stop? I know what disapproval looks like. Some people find our investigations improper, unconventional. But this letter goes beyond disapproval – it's calculated malice. Someone is afraid of what we might uncover.'

Emma's gaze drifted to the discarded letter by her side. 'If they think sending us a nasty letter will make us cower, they're sorely mistaken.' She picked it up and examined it again, looking closely at the handwriting. It was elegant: slanted and tidy with decorative loops on the letters. The ink appeared to have flowed with ease, the words swiftly and confidently covering the page.

'Do you recognise this handwriting?' Emma asked Penny.

'No.'

'I don't think it's disguised,' continued Emma. 'The letters are even and consistent. This could be someone's usual handwriting.'

Penny peered at the letter. 'That's a good observation,' she said. 'If the author of this letter had tried to disguise their handwriting, it would appear clumsier and less consistent.'

Emma ran her eyes over the words, trying not to let their meaning upset her. 'And this person seems well-educated, don't they? There are no spelling mistakes and their language is quite eloquent.'

Penny nodded. 'Someone quite clever and confident in how they express themselves. That gives us an idea of the sort of person we're looking for. It's likely we'll receive more letters from them if we continue investigating this case.' She took off her spectacles and wiped them with her cuff. 'Are you sure you're all right, Emma? I've received letters like this before, but you haven't. Mr Fish was hesitant to show it to me at first, and I hesitated to show it to you. But I think it's important that we remain honest with each other. After everything you've been through, I know you can handle a few rude, cowardly words.'

Emma gave a small smile. 'Yes, well. Just as long as—'

She hesitated, feeling a shiver of unease.

Penny frowned slightly. 'As long as what?'

'As long as no one tries to harm us.' She inhaled slowly. 'I keep thinking about what happened to James – not long ago, he ended up in hospital because of his work. I really hope that doesn't happen to us. But, Penny, it is a possibility, isn't it?'

A shadow crossed Penny's face. She paused before responding. 'There's no denying that what we're doing carries risks,' she admitted. 'But I've always believed it's worth it.'

'But is it? I can't forget how injured James was in that attack...' She trailed off, recalling the harrowing sight of James lying unconscious in a hospital bed.

'I know,' Penny squeezed her hand as if reading her thoughts. 'But we need to carry on. Just look at Inspector Paget – what has he accomplished? No progress has been made in the police investigation. We have to do this, Emma, for Clara's sake.'

Emma nodded slowly, knowing Penny was right.

'She suffered when she found Mrs Melbourne's body in the graveyard,' Penny continued. 'And now she's suffering under the suspicion of the police. We need to find out who did this. We've done it before, and we can do it again. And one thing is clear – we're dealing with someone very dangerous.'

Emma exhaled. 'The sort of person who stabs a defenceless woman in a churchyard.'

Penny nodded. 'Yes. And the sort of person who is now watching us.'

THIRTY-TWO

Detective Inspector Paget checked his pocket watch the following morning as he took his seat in the dingy interview room. 'I'm afraid I don't have long, Dr Lloyd. Will this be quick?'

Robert Lloyd bristled at the words. He loathed being told others were short on time, particularly when he was the one doing the talking. Time, after all, was something he believed should be offered freely to a man of his standing. He crossed his legs slowly, deliberately, and gave the inspector a cold smile.

'I must say, I'm rather surprised you haven't called on me before now,' he said. 'Given the public interest in the court case, I'd have thought I'd feature higher up on your list of persons to speak to.'

Paget opened the file on the table. 'My men are working through their inquiries, Dr Lloyd. I'm quite sure someone would have reached you in due course. But since you've contacted me directly, I'm happy to hear what you have to say – provided it's relevant to the investigation.'

Robert leaned forward slightly. 'You do realise who I am, don't you? I was the man Mrs Melbourne sued last year. It was all over the papers.'

'Yes,' said Paget, glancing at the file. 'I'm familiar with the case.'

'Then perhaps you'd like to hear my side of it.'

Paget frowned. 'Your side of the court case?'

'It's important context,' said Robert, voice lowering as though confiding something of great significance. 'It might help you better understand the sort of woman Eleanor Melbourne truly was.'

The inspector flicked another glance at his watch. 'If you could give me the bare bones of it, Doctor, I'll take some notes.'

'Bare bones?' Robert echoed, incredulous. 'Inspector, if the police are content with skeletons instead of substance, it's little wonder cases remain unsolved.'

Paget offered a tired smile. 'We value detail when it's useful. But a concise account will help me know what questions to ask.'

Robert gave a slow, theatrical sigh and began. He told the story of Edmund Melbourne's accident on the Strand and the injuries sustained. He explained how he, as a long-serving family doctor, had been summoned and, despite warning the family of the risks, had attempted a cranial operation that ultimately failed. The young man had died. The family, overcome with grief, had needed someone to blame. That someone had been him.

'She turned the entire courtroom against me,' he said. 'With her tears and tragic silences and appeals to justice. She knew exactly what she was doing.'

Paget jotted a few notes. 'Yes, I recall the case now. Unfortunate for all involved.'

'Unfortunate?' Robert repeated, his voice rising a fraction. 'It was ruinous. My practice never recovered. Patients stopped coming. I had to close my rooms in Harley Street.'

The inspector tapped the tip of his pencil against his papers. 'That must have been difficult.'

There was a pause. Then Robert gave a short, dry laugh. 'Some people might suggest I was a suspect in her murder.'

Paget looked up sharply. 'You speak as if you want to be considered one.'

'Of course not,' Robert snapped. 'I'm merely saying it wouldn't be unreasonable for someone to suspect me. And yet, until now, no one from the police has come knocking.'

'You have an alibi, I take it?'

'I do,' Robert said at once. 'I was playing whist at my club until nearly midnight. Plenty of witnesses.'

Paget made a note. 'Very good. So although the lawsuit was no doubt upsetting, you didn't murder Mrs Melbourne in a fit of revenge.'

'No,' said Robert tightly. He tugged at his jacket cuffs. 'But I did expect the police to show some interest. Frankly, I'm concerned about the way this investigation is being conducted.'

'Oh?' Paget folded his arms. 'And why is that?'

'Because it seems... complacent. Surely your pathologist has reviewed the nature of her wound?'

'He has,' said Paget. 'Single stab wound by an unusually long, thin bladed weapon. Death by exsanguination and cardiac arrest.'

'I see,' said Robert thoughtfully. 'If I could examine the post-mortem report, I might offer a more seasoned interpretation. Perhaps identify something your man has missed.'

Paget's eyes narrowed. 'You want to see the report?'

'I do. Not for payment. Out of interest. Professional curiosity.'

'I'm afraid that won't be possible. The post-mortem report is confidential, and our pathologist is more than qualified. I don't believe a second opinion is necessary.'

Robert clenched his jaw. 'I have decades of experience, Inspector.'

'I'm sure you do, Doctor. And if I find myself needing a medical consultation, I'll know where to find you.'

Robert sat back, irritated. He didn't like being dismissed – certainly not by a man who clearly didn't grasp the depth of his expertise. He wanted to read the report, not just out of curiosity but out of something darker. He wanted to see the precise angle of the blade, the depth of the wound, the manner of death in all its cold finality.

He wanted to know, without doubt, that Eleanor Melbourne had suffered.

Paget closed the file slowly. 'Unless there's anything else, Dr Lloyd...?'

'No,' Robert muttered. 'That's all.'

Paget stood. 'Then thank you for your time.'

Robert remained seated. But as the door closed behind the inspector, he allowed himself a slight smile.

There was more to be said. Just not yet.

THIRTY-THREE

Paraffin splashed across the hearthrug, its stench sharp, oily, and suffocating. With shallow breaths and trembling hands, the arsonist flung the can aside and snatched the matchbox from the mantelpiece. Their fingers fumbled, clumsy with anticipation, as they drew out a single match.

Then – a pause. A final look around the room. No farewell, no sentiment. Just the quiet thrill of destruction. It felt clean. It felt like freedom.

They glanced at the closed door – their escape. The fire would take hold quickly. The chimney was blocked; the smoke would choke the room in seconds. They'd have to move the instant the flames caught. Holding their breath, they struck the match.

It snapped in two. Useless. It dropped to the floor.

Too fast. Too forceful.

Time was slipping away, but panic would ruin everything. A second match was chosen.

Lighter now. Calmer. A bead of sweat slid down their temple.

The second match sparked, fizzled – and died. Another strike, then another. Nothing. With a muttered curse, it too was discarded.

The paraffin stank. Thick and nauseating, it swamped the senses.

The third match had to work. Not too heavy, not too light. Controlled. Measured. Like lighting a candle in the dark.

This time the match rasped and flared to life, a flicker of gold dancing in the draught before it touched the rug. A moment's hesitation. Then—

The heat was immediate.

No time to falter now. A wall of fire surged up. The door blurred behind the smoke. It was too much, too fast.

Eyes burning, lungs tightening, they staggered towards escape.

THIRTY-FOUR

'What's this then?' said Mrs Solomon. She peered closely at the piece of music on the piano stand. '"Prelude in C Major" by J S Bach.'

'Yes,' said Emma. 'Have you learned this piece before?'

Mrs Solomon shrugged. 'I can't remember.'

'I'll play it for you,' said Emma. As she began to play the lilting melody, Mrs Solomon clapped her hands in glee.

'I know this one!' she said. 'It's a well-known tune.'

Emma stopped playing. 'Did you learn it when you were younger?'

Mrs Solomon bit her lip as she thought. 'I might have done... it was a long time ago. I can't really remember.'

'Well we can learn it now. Let's begin with the right hand. Your thumb needs to rest on E.'

'E?' Mrs Solomon looked up and down the keyboard. 'Which one is that again?'

Emma forced a smile and pointed it out to her. This was the fourth lesson with her landlady and she didn't seem to remember much from one lesson to the next. Emma had reminded her she needed to practise between lessons but she hadn't heard her doing any.

A knock at the door interrupted them.

'Would you mind answering it, Mrs Langley?' said Mrs Solomon. 'I need to make sure I can remember where E is.'

Penny was at the door. Her eyes were wide behind her spectacles and her face was flushed. A hansom cab waited in the street behind her. 'There's a fire!' she said before Emma could ask anything. 'Mrs Melbourne's house!'

Emma startled. 'Is it serious?'

Penny gave a vehement nod. 'Have you got time to go there now?'

'Yes!' Emma reasoned Mrs Solomon wouldn't mind.

The cab took them to Eaton Square. On the way, Penny explained how she'd heard the news. 'James sent me a telegram,' she said. 'He must have heard about it from his colleagues or been working in the area.'

'Blimey,' exclaimed the cab driver. 'That's a large one.' Black smoke billowed from Upper Belgrave Street. A crowd of people prevented the cab from getting any closer. 'That lovely big house,' he added, 'all gone up in smoke.'

They paid the driver and joined the crowd. Emma's throat felt tight with worry. 'I hope everyone got out safely,' she said.

They made their way through the crowd to where teams of firemen were battling the blaze with hosepipes. As they got closer to the fire, Emma could feel the heat from the blaze.

Three red fire engines were parked in the street; the horses had been unshackled and taken away to safety. One of the engines was steam-powered with a large copper boiler on the back.

'Goodness,' said Penny. 'There's very little of the place left.'

Orange flames roared through the shell of the house, licking at the charred remains within. The lower windows glowed like furnaces, their panes shattered and blackened, framing the inferno inside. Above, the upper storeys had been devoured – only a few scorched timbers jutted skywards, silhouetted against the smoky sky.

Emma's eyes watered from the heat and smoke. She turned away, blinking, and surveyed the other onlookers. They stared at the fiery ruin, their expressions a mix of shock and grim fascination. Among them, Emma spotted a familiar face. She nudged Penny lightly with her elbow.

'That's Agnes Black the housekeeper over there. I met her at the service for Mrs Melbourne.'

The housekeeper stood apart from the small crowd, her face drawn and ashen. Her hands were clasped in front of her, gripping the fabric of her shawl tightly, as though holding herself together. Her gaze was locked onto the inferno in front of her.

'We should speak to her,' said Penny.

They approached carefully. Miss Black remained oblivious to their presence, seemingly lost in her own thoughts.

'Miss Black?' Emma ventured gently. 'I'm so sorry about what's happened.'

The housekeeper flinched slightly, as if pulled from a trance. She turned to them with a slow, unfocused stare, her brow creased in confusion. Then, recognition flickered in her weary eyes.

'You...' she murmured. 'I remember now. I saw you at the church.'

'That's right. You look as though you're in shock.'

Miss Black gave a small, brittle nod before turning back to the fire, her lips pressing into a thin line.

'Everything is gone,' she said weakly. 'Everything. I don't know what we're going to do. The staff... we all lived there. Our rooms, our belongings. All of it – up in smoke.'

Her voice wavered, and she swallowed hard, as though forcing herself to keep some semblance of composure.

Emma felt a pang of sympathy. It wasn't just a place of work that had been lost – it had been a home, a livelihood, a life.

Emma touched the housekeeper's arm. 'This is my friend, Mrs Penny Blakely. Would you like to find somewhere for a cup of tea?'

For a moment, Miss Black didn't respond. She stood there, shoulders hunched, eyes still trained on the fire as though waiting for it to reveal some answer, some explanation. Then, after a long pause, she gave a slight, almost imperceptible nod. 'I'd rather get something stronger.'

THIRTY-FIVE

Agnes Black led Emma and Penny past St Peter's Church in Eaton Square to an establishment called The Plumber's Arms in Lower Belgrave Street.

Inside, the atmosphere was thick with the scent of ale and pipe smoke. The interior was dark wood with large decorative mirrors and well-worn brass fixtures. A group of uniformed soldiers stood at the bar engaged in lively conversation.

Emma cast a quick glance around. They were the only women present.

Miss Black sank heavily into a wooden bench seat, exhaling as though the events of the day had finally caught up with her. There was a gauntness to her face, accentuated by her sharp features.

A barmaid, a round-faced woman with a crisp white apron, approached their table, her brow furrowed with concern. 'Are you all right, Miss Black? I heard about the fire.' She shook her head. 'First Mrs Melbourne's death, and now this.'

Miss Black wiped her brow. 'I don't even know what to think anymore.'

'The usual, is it?'

The housekeeper gave a weary nod.

Emma and Penny ordered a glass of sherry each, then settled into the seats opposite Miss Black.

'Was anyone hurt?' Emma asked.

Miss Black shook her head. 'No. We were lucky, everyone got out in time.'

'Do you know how the fire started?' Penny pressed.

'No.' Her answer was clipped.

'Who discovered it?'

'The stable boy from the mews. He saw smoke coming from the back of the house and hammered on the door. I thought I would have smelled the burning, but the air is always thick with coal smoke these days. It's hard to tell.' She sighed. 'If it weren't for the boy, it could have been much worse. But once the fire took hold, there was no stopping it. It spread so quickly. And now... now there's nothing left.'

Emma tried to imagine the depth of that loss – the suddenness of it, the complete upheaval. It reminded her, in a way, of when her husband had deserted her at Liverpool Street station. That dizzying sensation of the ground vanishing beneath her feet. 'Do you have somewhere to stay?' she asked.

Miss Black nodded. 'A local lady has already offered to put us up in her lodging house in Ebury Street, it's not too far from here. The others have gone there already but I felt the need to stay and watch... I don't know why. Perhaps I'm hoping it's all a bad dream which I'll wake from at any moment.'

The barmaid brought the drinks to their table. Miss Black picked hers up and took a large gulp.

'I suppose we'll all have to find new positions now. It's not something I imagined having to do at my age.' She let out a bitter laugh, shaking her head. 'I was quite content where I was. But I suppose these things are out of our hands, aren't they?'

Penny took a sip of her sherry before asking, 'How long did you work for Mrs Melbourne?'

'Thirty years. I started as a scullery maid when I was sixteen, back when Mr Melbourne was still alive. I worked my way up through the household.'

'You must have had a good relationship with her, to have stayed so long.'

Miss Black gave a small shrug. 'The position suited me well enough. I did my job, and Mrs Melbourne had no reason to complain. She valued loyalty and liked to keep the same staff around her. She wasn't one for change – she liked familiarity, routine.'

'We've heard conflicting opinions about her,' Penny said carefully. 'Many people described her as kind and generous, but others suggested she could be... difficult company in private.'

Miss Black's lips pressed into a thin line. 'I'd say that's fair.'

'How did you get on with her?' asked Penny.

'I worked for her and carried out my duties as she expected me to.' She shrugged again. 'That was the extent of it.'

Emma noticed she kept her reply succinct. She clearly didn't want to share her personal opinion of her employer.

'Can you think of anyone who might have wanted to harm her?'

The housekeeper exhaled sharply, rubbing at her temple. 'I've been asked that question more times than I can count. The police have pestered me about it. And I've told them the same thing I'll tell you – I don't know. Whoever did it must be some kind of monster.'

Her gaze dropped to her glass, her fingers tightening around it. 'I don't understand why she went to that churchyard. Why was she there, of all places? It makes no sense.'

'Apparently she was married there,' said Emma. 'And occasionally went to services.'

Silence settled between them, heavy and uneasy. Penny turned her glass between her fingers, deep in thought. Emma, watching Miss Black's face, had the distinct feeling that the housekeeper knew – or suspected – more than she was letting on.

THIRTY-SIX

Christopher Ashford's maid led Lydia Jackson to his study. The scent of wood polish lingered in the air and the walls were lined with bookshelves. It was a comfortable room with two armchairs and a smart, baize-topped desk. A fire burned low in the grate, casting shifting shadows across the furniture.

As soon as Christopher saw her, he abruptly rose from his chair with a smile. His greying hair was slightly tousled, as though he'd been running his fingers through it absentmindedly. A cup of tea sat half-finished on a nearby side table.

'Lydia,' he said with a note of surprise. 'What brings you here?'

She took a step towards him. 'I heard about the fire! I'm so sorry.'

He gestured for her to sit in the chair opposite him. He sank down into his own chair wearily. The firelight flickered over his features, accentuating the sharpness of his cheekbones. 'It was quite unexpected. The fire brigade think it started in a fireplace – perhaps a stray cinder or something of the sort. Either way, the entire house is gone.'

'How awful. It was your home.'

He rubbed the back of his neck. 'I suppose it was. Although I only lived there for a short while when I was young. Perhaps it's for the best.'

Lydia frowned. 'What makes you say that? It was a beautiful house, Christopher. And in Belgravia, no less. You'll rebuild it, won't you?'

'Yes, I suppose so.' He let out a slow breath. 'I need to speak with the insurance company. Rebuilding it makes the most sense, and then, I imagine, I'll sell it. But I haven't thought that far ahead yet.'

His eyes met hers. 'Thank you for coming, Lydia. It's thoughtful of you.'

'I wanted to see how you are. I was worried you'd be terribly upset.'

'I don't think I'm upset.' He leaned back and stretched out his legs. 'These past few weeks have been... strange. I suppose I always knew I would inherit Mrs Melbourne's estate – she held me in high regard for reasons I never fully understood. I assume it was because she had no son of her own. But for her to die the way she did... and then the fire...' He trailed off, shaking his head. 'It's all rather a lot to take in.'

'And the things inside the house?' she asked. 'Surely there were items of sentimental value?'

Christopher gave a half-smile. 'Sentimental to my godmother, certainly. But for me? I don't think so. If anything, I feel guilty that I don't feel more... affected by it. Instead, I'm seeing it as an inconvenience – a mess to be sorted.'

Lydia lowered her eyes to the ornate oriental rug beneath her feet, its vibrant patterns illuminated by the firelight. 'I can't help but think it's all rather tragic,' she said. 'All those things lost in the fire, and yet... no one seems to care.'

'Why do you say that? Do you expect me to be more troubled?'

Lydia met his gaze. 'No. I didn't expect anything from you. I just find it... sad. Mrs Melbourne lived for sixty-five years, and yet... I don't think anyone truly mourns her. She's gone, and the world carries on as if nothing of significance has happened.'

Christopher leaned forward, his elbows resting on his knees, his hands loosely clasped. 'You're right, Lydia. I don't think there's a single person who is truly grieving for her. We acknowledge her absence, yes. But real sorrow?' He shook his head. 'I don't believe anyone feels it. And I feel guilty that I'm not upset enough. Does that sound terrible?'

Lydia offered a small, knowing smile. 'No, Christopher. It doesn't.'

He studied her for a moment before nodding thoughtfully. 'Now that I understand the full extent of who she was, I realise the only person she ever truly served was herself.'

Lydia nodded in agreement. 'That's exactly how I feel about her. When I left her employment twenty years ago I wasn't sorry that I'd never see her again. And then... when I did see her again... it was awful.'

Christopher's brow furrowed. 'You haven't told me much about that meeting.'

She lowered her gaze, staring at the cuff of her sleeve. 'I haven't told anyone about it, Christopher. It's humiliating.'

'It only felt humiliating because she wanted you to feel that way.'

She lifted her eyes to his and gave a small nod. 'Yes, that's right.'

'But truly, there's nothing for you to be ashamed of. If her words were designed to hurt, then she should have felt ashamed about it – not you.'

Lydia looked away again, focusing on the fire in the grate. 'I'll talk about it when I'm ready, Christopher. But not yet. We've only just got to know each other again.'

'And I'm glad we have, Lydia.' His voice was soft.

She felt warmth spread through her chest, an unfamiliar but not unwelcome sensation. 'Good.' She smiled. 'I'm happy you feel that way.'

She rose and wandered over to the window. It was late afternoon and the light was fading. The window had a view of the small garden with its ivy-covered brick walls and a bare-branched tree.

'You have a nice view from here,' she said. 'It's peaceful. And I can see snowdrops.' Her heart lifted at the sight of the small white flowers beneath the tree. 'The first sign of spring.'

'Yes. It's good to see something growing in the midst of all this.'

She turned to him again. 'I met with two women the other day. Mrs Blakely and Mrs Langley. They say they're investigating Mrs Melbourne's death.'

'They called here too.'

Lydia returned to the armchair. 'They did? Why are they asking so many questions?'

Christopher sighed, rubbing the bridge of his nose. 'They fancy themselves as lady detectives I think.'

'But why ask us? Do you think they suspect us?'

He shrugged. 'No. They're just gathering information. Trying to piece everything together.'

'I hope they don't find out too much.'

Christopher studied her carefully, his gaze unreadable. 'Is there something to find out?'

Lydia gripped the arms of her chair. 'We both know what your godmother did to us, Christopher. And there were times when I wished I'd...'

'What?'

She pushed the dark thoughts from her mind. 'It doesn't matter. Things have changed. She's gone now.'

His gaze remained steady. 'Yes. She's gone.'

THIRTY-SEVEN

The following day, Emma finished teaching a piano lesson in Victoria. As she left the house, she hesitated for a moment. Mrs Melbourne's former home was only a ten-minute walk away. She couldn't shake the thought of it. Had there been any new discoveries about how the fire had started?

On impulse, she headed in the direction of Upper Belgrave Street.

Although she'd witnessed the fire, its ruins were still shocking. Where number nine had once stood, there was only charred rubble – still wet from the firemen's hoses. Blackened beams rose jaggedly from the ruins like broken bones. A layer of soot covered the pavement and blackened the puddles of water. The acrid scent of burned wood lingered in the air.

The neighbouring buildings, although streaked with soot, remained intact. Among the onlookers, a young man picked his way over the ruins, occasionally pausing to inspect something. Was he searching for something valuable? A trinket overlooked in the ashes? Emma could only hope that Miss Black and the other household staff had been able to salvage something before scavengers got here. But looking at the sheer devastation before her, she doubted much had survived the blaze.

'It's a sorry mess, isn't it?'

Emma started slightly at the voice at her shoulder. She turned to see Harry Wright standing beside her, hands in his pockets, his expression half-curious, half-concerned. His usual smile played at the corners of his lips, but his eyes were serious.

She returned his smile, but only just. She didn't want him to think she was too pleased to see him – although she couldn't ignore the little somersault her heart gave at the sight of him.

'It's a terrible mess,' she agreed, turning back to the ruin. 'I wonder if they've discovered how it started yet?'

'Someone did it deliberately, I expect,' Harry said matter-of-factly.

Emma glanced at him. 'What makes you say that?'

'Destroying evidence,' he replied. 'Someone inside that house could have been responsible for Mrs Melbourne's murder.'

Emma felt a chill settle over her. 'Do you have any idea who?'

'Not yet. I need to learn more about the people who worked in the household. But it's not easy. None of them wanted to speak to me after her death. And now, with the house burned to the ground, I doubt they'll be any more forthcoming.'

Emma told him about their conversation with Miss Black the previous day. Harry listened intently, nodding occasionally.

'Do you think Miss Black could have started it?' Emma asked.

He shrugged. 'It's possible. Maybe she was trying to get rid of evidence. Maybe she was the murderer?'

Emma pondered this. 'She was reluctant to tell us exactly what she thought of Mrs Melbourne. But she worked for her for thirty years so the two clearly found a way to get along with one another. Why would she kill someone she depended on for employment?'

'People do foolish things when emotions run high,' Mr Wright said. 'Maybe Mrs Melbourne threatened to dismiss her, or maybe there was some other grudge she never spoke about. If she did it, she's keeping her reasons well hidden. But I still believe someone in that house was responsible.'

He glanced at the ruins again. 'One of them sent Mrs Melbourne a note, luring her to that churchyard.'

'Do you know that for sure?'

'No. But it's what I believe.'

'It must have been a very persuasive note,' said Emma. 'I can't think of any reason why she would have agreed to go that place late at night.'

'Perhaps the note offered her information,' said Mr Wright. 'Or money, maybe. Or something else valuable.'

Emma frowned. 'But neither money, a valuable item nor a note was found with her body.'

'Because the person who lured her there never intended to give it to her,' Harry pointed out. 'They used it to bait her.'

Emma nodded, her mind working through the possibilities. 'That makes sense. So now all you have to do, Mr Wright, is work out who that person was.'

He chuckled. 'Yes. That's the tricky part, isn't it? But I'll let you know as soon as I make progress. And will you do the same?'

Emma smiled. 'Of course. At the moment, I feel like we've got few ideas. There's so much left to uncover.'

'There certainly is.'

They turned back to the ruins, watching as the young man continued his search.

'I don't know why he's bothering,' Mr Wright muttered. 'If there was anything valuable left, it's long gone by now.'

Emma's gaze lingered on the rubble. 'Isn't it remarkable,' she said, 'how someone's entire life can be reduced to this?'

'What do you mean?'

'Within a matter of days, Mrs Melbourne is gone. Her home is gone. It's as if someone wanted to erase all traces of her existence.'

Mr Wright stroked his chin as he thought. 'Yes, that's what someone has tried to do. But they failed, of course. Everything she did or said has lived on. Somewhere, there's a murderer carrying their secret. And no matter what they do, they won't be able to erase her completely.'

Emma took a step closer to the ruins, wrinkling her nose at the sharp burned scent. The destruction was uneven – some objects had been reduced to blackened husks, while others had miraculously survived. Half a chair still bore traces of its plush upholstery, standing amid the wreckage. Scattered bricks, jagged stones, and splintered timber lay in chaotic heaps. A table leg jutted out awkwardly and a portion of what had once been a polished door leaned against it.

Among the charred remnants, Emma spotted something.

'Look,' she said, stooping to pick up an object near her feet. 'It's a book. And it's almost completely intact.'

The pages were swollen with water, stuck together in a sodden mass, but the cover had survived. She wiped some of the soot away with her sleeve.

'*Pride and Prejudice*,' read Mr Wright. 'Jane Austen. A fine choice.'

Emma glanced at him. 'You've read Jane Austen?'

'Yes. I've read all of them,' he replied. 'It's a shame she didn't write more. Had she lived longer, then she would have, I'm sure.'

Emma smiled. 'Jane Austen is a favourite of mine too.'

'Is she?'

They held each other's gaze for a moment, then Emma turned away as she felt the heat in her face. She could feel him watching her as she tossed the soggy book back to the pile of rubble. 'I didn't expect a newspaper reporter to be well-versed in Austen's works.'

'Ah, but you forget – I make my living from words,' he said with a grin. 'And besides, she understood people. I think a journalist can learn a lot from her.'

Emma turned back to the debris. Now that she was looking more closely, other objects began to stand out – a few fragments of china, a tarnished candlestick, and what appeared to be a section of patterned rug. But something else caught her eye.

A wooden box, half-buried in a pile of rubble.

'Over there,' she said, pointing. 'Do you see that? It looks like a box. And it seems intact.'

Harry followed her gaze. 'Interesting. It must have been protected from the worst of the fire.'

Emma's pulse quickened. 'I wonder what's inside?'

'There's only one way to find out.' He glanced around before lowering his voice. 'We could pull it out and have a look.'

Emma hesitated. 'Wouldn't that be stealing?'

Mr Wright gave a secretive smile and leaned closer. 'Possibly. But who does all this belong to now? Christopher Ashford, isn't it? If we find anything valuable, we'll hand it to him. But there's no harm in taking a quick look first.'

Emma surveyed the street. A few onlookers lingered, casting occasional glances at the ruins. Only an elderly woman nearby seemed to be watching them with any interest.

She bit her lip, then made a decision. 'I'm going to get it.'

Mr Wright grinned. 'That's the spirit. Shall I fetch it for you?'

Emma shook her head, feeling a surge of determination. 'No, I can manage.'

She stepped forward, carefully navigating the debris.

'Be careful,' Mr Wright warned. 'There's a basement under all this. You don't want to fall through.'

She nodded, placing her feet cautiously on what seemed to be stable pieces of debris. The damp, burned stench filled her nostrils as she moved closer to the box. A heavy panel of charred wood – perhaps once part of a table – rested partially over it.

She reached out, gripped the box and gave it a gentle tug. It didn't budge.

Frowning, she pulled harder, and at last, it came free with a sudden jolt. The table panel above it shifted dangerously. She stepped back quickly, wary of it collapsing onto her. But in her haste, she failed to check her footing.

Her foot slipped between two loose bricks.

'Ouch!' she cried as her leg scraped against something rough. She felt her stocking rip.

'Mrs Langley!' Mr Wright was beside her in an instant. 'Give me your hand.'

She reached out, and he grasped her firmly, steadying her as she clambered back over the rubble.

She stumbled as she stepped down, nearly falling forward – straight into him.

For a moment, they were inches apart. She held her breath, staring up into his dark eyes. Time seemed to slow.

Then she quickly stepped back, embarrassed at how much she had enjoyed being so close to him.

Mr Wright released her hand. 'Well done,' he said. 'You got it.'

She looked down at the charred box in her hands. 'Yes, I did.'

It looked like a stationery box. Its surface had gilt detailing in delicate, vine-like patterns. The lid had ornate brass embellishments and a monogram with the letters 'EJM'. Mrs Melbourne's initials?

'Now, let's find out what's inside.'

It felt quite heavy and as Emma turned it in her hands, some grubby water trickled out from beneath the lid. Emma became aware of the elderly woman still watching them.

Mr Wright turned to her with an easy smile. 'Don't worry, madam,' he called out. 'I'm a reporter for the *Morning Express*. We've just noticed this box in the rubble and realise it could be valuable. We're going to make sure it's returned to Mr Christopher Ashford – the rightful owner of this... ruin.'

The woman gave them a long, scrutinising look, then turned and walked away.

THIRTY-EIGHT

Emma and Mr Wright carried the waterlogged stationery box to Belgrave Square where they could find a bench to sit on. Drops of murky water trickled as they walked. A large drop flicked onto Emma's skirts, darkening the fabric with an unsightly stain.

'Did you hurt yourself when you slipped?' Mr Wright asked.

'Only a little bit,' she replied. The scrape on her leg stung as her skirts brushed against the raw skin, aggravating the pain. But she couldn't inspect it now. Not in public. And certainly not in front of Mr Wright. She would tend to it when she was safely home, away from prying eyes.

They reached the square and found an empty bench beneath the bare branches of a winter-stripped tree. A chilly breeze rustled through, making Emma shiver as she set the box down between them.

'Well, let's hope we've found something interesting,' Mr Wright said, rubbing his hands together in anticipation.

'Or something entirely mundane,' Emma countered, eyeing the battered box. 'Given the state of it, anything inside is likely to be ruined beyond recognition.'

Still, she couldn't deny the thrill of curiosity as she prised open the latch and lifted the lid.

The interior was lined with once-opulent red velvet, now sodden and stained with grimy water. Nestled inside was a thick pile of papers, clumped together in a damp, dishevelled mass. There was also a pot of ink and a pen.

'Oh dear,' Mr Wright muttered, peering in at the wet contents. 'That doesn't look very promising.'

Emma sighed. 'No, it doesn't.'

'I don't think there's any need to hand this over to Mr Ashford, I shouldn't think he'll miss it at all.'

Emma removed her gloves and gingerly lifted the soggy bundle, feeling the cold moisture seep into her fingertips. The papers, stuck together by water, were fragile. Emma attempted to peel two sheets apart but the soft edges tore with the faintest effort.

Faint traces of ink swirled on some of the pages, although most of the writing had bled away into an unreadable blur. The entire pile appeared ruined.

Emma bit her lip. 'Do you think anything can be salvaged?'

Mr Wright leaned closer, assessing the damage. 'It's hard to say. But maybe something deeper inside the pile can be retrieved. I want to know what these papers say!'

Emma nodded. 'So do I! I'll have to dry them carefully. If there's anything legible, I'll find it.'

Mr Wright grinned. 'You're a determined lady, Mrs Langley.'

'I prefer to think of it as patience,' she corrected, a smile tugging at her lips.

'Patience is a trait I admire,' he said. 'I wish I had some of it myself.'

'It's all very well being patient, but I suspect we'll uncover nothing more than household accounts or a list of servants' wages. But I have to try.'

'Well, if you do find something thrilling – perhaps a scandalous secret or the answer to all our questions – promise me I'll be the first to know.'

Emma laughed. 'Very well, Mr Wright. If I uncover anything intriguing, you'll be the first to hear of it.'

He leaned back against the bench, his expression amused. 'Good. Now, how about I buy you a cup of tea after your rescue of a waterlogged stationery box?'

Emma felt an excitable flutter in her stomach. A cup of tea with Mr Wright? Would it be appropriate? She hesitated for a second but knew she wanted to spend a little more time with him. 'All right then. But not for long.'

'Not for long?'

'No. I want to try and rescue these papers.'

THIRTY-NINE

Emma could feel herself still smiling as she arrived at the British Museum. Harry Wright was good company and they'd found lots to talk about. It had been difficult to pull herself away from their conversation but she didn't want to appear too keen on him. And she certainly didn't want anyone questioning her respectability.

She'd reasoned a librarian might know what to do with water-damaged papers, so she'd called at the museum hoping to find Francis Edwards in the reading room. Fortunately she didn't have to wait long for him to take his break for lunch. He suggested they examine the box and its papers in the manuscript room.

'Goodness,' he said when Emma opened the box. 'This is a soggy mess, isn't it? What is it?'

Emma told him how she'd retrieved the box from the ruins of Mrs Melbourne's house. 'Can the papers be recovered?' she asked.

Francis rubbed his chin. 'Possibly. But we're going to need an awful lot of blotting paper. I can use some of the museum's supply but not too much, I'm afraid. We'll have to buy the rest.'

'I can do that,' said Emma.

'And we'll need a lot of space.' Francis glanced around him. 'Not in here, but there may be some space in the sorting room.'

· · ·

The sorting room was a long narrow room lined with shelves and with tables running through the centre. Francis cleared one of them, moving ancient-looking clay pots, a marble bust and a pile of weathered-looking books.

'Let's begin by laying out the pieces of paper on the blotting paper.' Slowly and carefully, he peeled off the top sheet of paper. Emma held her breath as he did so, certain it would tear.

Cautiously, Francis lay down the sodden piece of paper onto a sheet of blotting paper. Emma worked on lifting the next sheet of paper, her fingers fumbling as she did so.

'Carefully does it,' said Francis.

She felt a sense of accomplishment as she successfully laid the soaked paper onto the blotting paper. 'Most of the ink has washed away,' she said despondently.

'It appears so,' replied Francis. 'But all is not lost. Let's wait for the paper to dry; we might be pleasantly surprised. All this could take a while though. Once the blotting paper has absorbed all it can, it will need to be replaced.'

'I'll go and buy some more now,' said Emma.

A pear-shaped man with heavy jowls strolled up to the table. 'What's going on here then, Edwards?'

'This lady has recovered some important documents; I believe they may relate to the Napoleonic Wars,' replied Francis.

'Is that so? Where did she find them?'

'In the flooded basement of a house in Chelsea,' said Francis without missing a beat. 'The house once belonged to Sir James Blakely.'

Emma bit her lip, trying to hide her mirth.

'Sir James Blakely?' said the gentleman. 'Who was he then?'

Francis paused and gave him a puzzled glance. 'You've not heard of him, Graves? He famously tutored William Pitt the Younger.'

'Oh. Yes, I recall now. Well, good luck with it, hopefully you can retrieve something from that mess, Edwards.'

He strolled away and Francis gave Emma a playful wink. 'I don't like Mr Graves very much,' he whispered.

FORTY

Emma opened her notebook that evening, tapping the end of her pencil thoughtfully against the page. She and Penny had spoken to many people about Mrs Melbourne, yet there was an undeniable similarity in all their responses – an elusive restraint, as if they were all holding something back. No one had spoken about her with warmth or enthusiasm, but neither had they expressed outright dislike. It was as if they had collectively agreed on a stance of careful indifference, and that, to Emma, was strange.

Among everyone they had spoken to, only Christopher Ashford had shown any real keenness to see justice done. And yet, even with him, Emma felt sure there was something unsaid, something lurking beneath his measured words and composed demeanour.

She wrote Dr Lloyd's name in her notebook. He remained the most obvious suspect – his career had crumbled after Mrs Melbourne successfully sued him, and with his livelihood in tatters, he had reason to hate her. But Mrs Melbourne had willingly gone to meet someone in the churchyard that night. Would she have agreed to a meeting with Dr Lloyd after ruining him in court? It seemed unlikely. Unless, of course, he had tricked her, sending a message in someone else's name.

Then there was Lydia Jackson, the governess. Her abrupt departure from the Brockhurst household following an argument with Mrs Melbourne was telling. Emma had no doubt that Lydia was concealing something, but why? What had been so terrible about the argument that she refused to speak of it? If it was trivial, she would have said so. But her silence suggested it was something more.

And then there was Mrs Harwell – a figure Emma couldn't quite make sense of. Apart from the hansom cab driver, she had been the last person to see Mrs Melbourne alive. She had spoken of her friend's charitable work with a surprising lack of sentiment, as if it were merely a duty to acknowledge her contributions rather than a true loss to grieve. She had claimed to be shocked by the murder, but had she really shown it? Emma had expected some sign of distress, some flicker of emotion in her voice or her expression. But Mrs Harwell's eyes had remained dry.

Could it be that Mrs Melbourne had simply been too unlikable for anyone to truly mourn her? Perhaps Mrs Harwell had maintained their friendship not out of genuine fondness, but because Mrs Melbourne's wealth and influence had been useful to the charity. If that were the case, was she grateful for Mrs Melbourne's financial contributions? Or had she been quietly resentful, tolerating her for the sake of the cause?

Emma turned to the next name on her list: Christopher Ashford. He had inherited everything. With her beloved nephew gone, Mrs Melbourne had named Mr Ashford as the sole beneficiary in her will. Had he killed her, knowing he would soon be in possession of her wealth? Perhaps she had threatened to change her will, and he'd wanted to stop her from doing so. Or maybe, after returning from India, he'd found himself in need of money more urgently than he cared to admit.

The fire that had destroyed the house was also troubling. Emma imagined Mr Ashford must be devastated by its destruction – but what if the fire had been deliberate? Had someone set it ablaze out of jealousy, furious that he had inherited it? Or was the fire meant to conceal something? Evidence, perhaps?

Finally, there was Agnes Black, the housekeeper. She had worked for Mrs Melbourne for thirty years, yet Emma had not seen her exhibit any genuine grief. It was the loss of the house that had devastated her – not the loss of her employer. Perhaps she had merely endured Mrs Melbourne because of the stability she provided, rather than out of any true loyalty or affection.

Emma sat back, tapping the pencil against her notebook once more.

How tragic it was that no one had shed a tear.

The suspects were all different – Dr Lloyd, Lydia Jackson, Mrs Harwell, Christopher Ashford, and Agnes Black – but none had appeared to have cared for Mrs Melbourne in life. And it seemed that, in death, no one truly cared what had happened to her either.

FORTY-ONE

'Goodness what a lot of paper,' said Penny as Emma and Francis showed her the sheets drying in the British Museum sorting room the following day. Emma had sent her a telegram early that morning informing her she had something interesting to show her.

'Unfortunately much of the ink has been washed away,' said Emma. 'But we might be able to retrieve something.' She lifted up a dried sheet of paper which was now as stiff as a board. It was stained with pale blue ink and just a few letters were decipherable.

Penny bit her lip as she peered at it. 'Goodness,' she said. 'Do you really think you'll be able to find something useful?'

Her tone seemed a little defeated which Emma thought unusual for Penny. Was something bothering her?

'It might be possible to read some words,' said Francis. 'But it could prove tricky.'

'I agree,' said Emma. 'In fact Mr Wright commented that—'

'Mr Wright?' Penny gave her a puzzled look. 'Why do you mention him?'

Emma cleared her throat, a little embarrassed. 'Ah yes, I haven't told you about that yet. I happened to bump into him when I was at the ruins of the house...' She felt herself blushing. 'Between us we agreed it would be all right to retrieve the box and give it to Christopher Ashford as it's rightfully his now. But he helped me when I slipped—'

'Did he?' Penny gave a teasing smile.

'Yes and we looked at the papers together, or... what was left of them as they were absolutely dripping wet as you can imagine. He wasn't hopeful I would find anything useful and perhaps he was right.'

'Maybe. You and Mr Wright seem to get on quite well.'

'We just happened to be in the same place at the same time.' Blushing again, she avoided Penny's gaze and pretended to examine another stiff sheet of paper. 'And we had a cup of tea together afterwards.'

'A cup of tea?' Penny grinned. 'And how was that?'

'Fine,' responded Emma, trying to ignore the butterflies in her stomach.

'Just fine?'

They exchanged a glance and Emma gave a bashful laugh. 'It was just a cup of tea. And anyway, I don't want to dwell on it too much because it's just a distraction.'

'Very well,' said Penny, clearly sensing Emma's embarrassed discomfort. 'Let's see what we can decipher from these papers. Thank you for helping dry them, Francis.'

'Oh it was no trouble at all. I should get back to the reading room now, but let me know if you need any help.'

Emma and Penny painstakingly examined each paper, transcribing every discernible word into Emma's notebook.

After an hour they paused from their work. Emma had a look at what she'd written so far. It wasn't much.

Had they become too caught up in this investigation? It had seemed such a promising find when she and Mr Wright had pulled the stationery box from the ruins of Mrs Melbourne's house. He'd shared her enthusiasm at first, but even he had given up on the contents when they turned out to be nothing but a ruined stack of papers. Now, looking at the few words in her notebook, she had to admit he might have been right.

Penny seemed to read her thoughts. 'What's wrong?' she asked.

'I think we could be wasting our time. These papers aren't telling us anything. And poor Francis spent so long helping me get everything dry.'

'He likes helping,' said Penny. 'And he understands that sometimes investigative work ends up in a dead end. So don't worry about Francis.' She peered over Emma's shoulder at the notebook. 'What have we got so far?'

Emma read out the notes. '"Margaret Harwell, church, yesterday I wrote, Arthur Thornwood."'

'Arthur Thornwood?' asked Penny.

'I don't know. But the name came up three times.'

'What we need to do now is ask around and find out who knows who Arthur Thornwood is.'

'Maybe Christopher Ashford will know?' suggested Emma. 'I need to give him the stationery box so perhaps I can ask him.'

'Yes, that's a good idea. I'll come with you. Shall we call on him tomorrow? Meanwhile...' Penny rubbed her temple. 'What could the other words mean?' She sighed and gestured at the papers they hadn't looked at yet. 'And there's more to go through.'

Once again, Penny seemed a little subdued. 'Is everything all right?' Emma asked her.

She smiled and gave Emma's arm an encouraging squeeze. 'Fine. Let's carry on with our work. We don't want to give up on it.'

They worked for another hour and Emma felt relieved once they'd finished with the last sheet of paper. She placed it on top of the neat stack they'd made of dry, crispy paper.

'So what have we got now?' asked Penny, peering at Emma's notebook. 'If there's the smallest clue hidden within these words, we have to find it.'

Emma read them out. '"Remember me, pretend, Ashford, Dr Lloyd, I knew him, Africa, money, God's forgiveness, stole, perhaps, I realise, truth, secret."'

'That's all?' said Penny. Her expression lacked enthusiasm, as if she'd been expecting something more.

'I'm afraid so. There were a few other words like "the" and "of" and so on, but I didn't think it was worth writing them down.'

'It's interesting three suspects are mentioned,' said Penny. 'Mrs Harwell, Mr Ashford and Dr Lloyd. The doctor is mentioned twice, in fact.'

Emma nodded. 'Hopefully we can make a little more sense of it when we've given it more thought. Let's put everything back in the box. The papers are of little use to Mr Ashford but I suppose we should give them to him.'

Penny gathered up the papers and Emma opened the box so she could put them in. Once the task was done, Penny's expression grew pensive again.

'What is it?' Emma asked.

'What is what?'

'You don't seem your usual self.'

'Don't I? I feel fine...' Penny sighed. 'I'm trying to feel fine, but actually I'm not. I told myself I would refuse to allow these letters to bother me, but...'

Emma now realised what was bothering her friend. 'You've received another letter?'

Penny nodded. She reached into her bag, took out an envelope and handed it to Emma. 'It was put through the letterbox. They know where I live.'

Emma felt a cold prickle on the back of her neck.

The envelope had just a few words on it: 'Mrs Blakely, St John's Wood.'

Emma pulled out the letter.

Dear Mrs Blakely,

I hope you received my previous letter. I must confess I'm puzzled why you continue to investigate matters which are better left alone.

I have already warned you. Kindly understand that I do not enjoy repeating myself. Ignoring my advice is not only foolish – it is dangerous.

I will give you the benefit of the doubt and assume you missed my first letter. To be sure there is no further misunderstanding, I am now writing to you directly, at the place where you live.

'We have to find out who this is,' said Emma, her stomach in knots. 'They can't torment you like this. When did this letter arrive?'

'This morning while I was out with the children, I took them for a walk on Primrose Hill. Mrs Tuttle was out doing some errands.'

Emma shuddered. Had the person been watching the house and waited until everyone had left before delivering the letter? She chose not to voice this, wary of worrying Penny even more.

'I have the other letter with me,' Penny said, taking it from her bag. 'Let's compare the handwriting on them both.'

They stood side-by-side, examining the two letters. 'The same paper, the same ink and the same hand,' said Emma. 'I'm still convinced this is someone's genuine handwriting.'

'If we could obtain another example of their handwriting, we could prove they wrote these letters,' said Penny. 'But that seems rather impossible, doesn't it? We'd need to be certain about our suspect first...' She trailed off, her expression despondent.

Emma knew Penny was more upset than she was letting on. 'Is all this worth it?' she asked.

Penny turned to her, surprised by the directness of her question. 'Worth it? Of course it's worth it. I never give up on an investigation.'

'But that doesn't mean you have to keep going with this one. These letters are horrible. And what if this person doesn't stop at writing letters? What if they turn up at your door or mine? With a weapon?' She shuddered. 'We've seen what they did to Mrs Melbourne, they could do the same to – '

'No,' said Penny. 'We can't allow ourselves to think like that. It would stop our work.'

'But perhaps that's the sensible thing to do? After all, Mrs Melbourne wasn't even well-liked, was she? Is it really worth our while putting our loved ones at risk for someone like her?'

Penny closed her eyes for a moment, as if willing the thought away.

A pause followed and Emma knew her friend would be thinking about her husband and children.

Eventually Penny recovered herself. 'What you're saying makes sense, Emma. And if you want to stop working on this, I really wouldn't resent you for making that decision. It would probably be a sensible choice. And... I hate to admit it, but there is a risk. However, the fact remains that Mrs Melbourne's murderer is at large. A person who is dangerous and may well strike again. I believe there's a lot we can do to find that person. We've done it before and I know we can do it again. We've already made good progress and we can't let these letters scare us off. The letters bother me and sometimes I feel afraid, but...' She turned to Emma. 'How would we feel if we stopped now and walked away?'

Emma imagined it. An uncomfortable sense of failure. The sinking disappointment of not having tried her hardest. 'I don't want to stop,' she said. 'I think it's wrong the killer is out there still, enjoying their freedom.'

Penny nodded. 'Then we continue.'

FORTY-TWO

Emma and Penny travelled by omnibus to Fitzrovia and made their way to Fitzroy Street. It was a cold, cloudless day and the afternoon air was crisp, carrying the scent of coal smoke. Emma held Mrs Melbourne's stationery box under her arm.

As they approached Mr Ashford's house, the door swung open, and a man stepped out onto the street. A woman followed, her head slightly bowed as she adjusted her gloves.

Penny tapped Emma's arm and they stopped. 'Look,' whispered Penny. 'That's him.'

The couple were walking away from them. Emma fixed her gaze on the tall figure of Christopher Ashford. He strolled along with an air of easy confidence, his dark overcoat buttoned against the chill. But it was his companion who caught her interest next. 'So it is,' she whispered. 'And... is that Lydia Jackson?'

Penny nodded. 'Yes, I think it is. Why are they meeting? Neither of them suggested to us they knew each other well.'

'Maybe they don't?' said Emma.

Penny gave a little gasp as she spoke. 'I say they do! Look! She's just taken his arm!'

Emma inhaled sharply. 'Well, that's rather intimate, isn't it?'

Penny's brows lifted. 'It is. And yet, neither of them mentioned the other when we spoke to them.'

'Do you think we should follow them?' Emma asked.

'Yes. Let's see where they're going.'

Moving with careful discretion, they followed at a distance. The couple didn't appear to be in a hurry, their pace leisurely as they made their way towards Fitzroy Square. They paused on the corner and Mr Ashford tilted his head as if listening intently to what Miss Jackson was saying. Then he turned to her and both their faces were in profile for a moment.

'They're both smiling,' said Emma. 'They seem quite fond of each other.' Her mind raced, trying to recall every detail of her encounters with both Mr Ashford and Miss Jackson. Had there been any hint – any mention at all – that they were acquainted? Nothing came to mind.

In Fitzroy Square, the couple strolled around the central garden. The wrought-iron railings surrounded a neatly kept green space, the bare branches of trees swaying slightly in the breeze. It was a quiet, secluded place. Mr Ashford lowered his head, as if relating something quietly to Miss Jackson. Her step faltered a little and then she gave a laugh which carried to Emma and Penny on the breeze. She demurely placed a gloved hand over her mouth, as if embarrassed she'd made such a noise.

'I wonder what they're finding so amusing,' said Penny. 'It would be interesting to know, wouldn't it? They're obviously very comfortable in each other's company. I almost feel we should approach them and ask outright about their relationship. But I don't suppose they'd take kindly to that, would they?'

'No, I don't think they would. Especially if they have something to hide.'

They continued walking, careful not to draw attention to themselves, but keeping their distance as they observed. Mr Ashford and Miss Jackson lingered in the square, seemingly in no rush to be anywhere.

'They look like a couple who've known each other well for some time,' said Penny.

Emma bit her lip, her thoughts turning over. 'Which begs the question – why keep it a secret? He's a widower, and she's a spinster. Surely there's no reason for them to keep their relationship hidden?'

'I agree. There must be something more to it.'

Mr Ashford and Miss Jackson were moving a little faster now and there was no longer laughter. Miss Jackson removed her hand from his arm and the couple stopped and turned to face each other.

Emma and Penny halted by a lamp post, making sure they didn't get close enough to be spotted. 'The conversation seems a little more serious now,' whispered Penny. 'Confrontational even. I wonder why the mood changed so quickly?'

Miss Jackson turned away and walked on ahead of her companion, as if angered by something.

'Oh dear,' said Emma. She seems upset. She watched Mr Ashford catch up with her. After a brief conversation, the pair walked together again.

'That's what happens in the early days of love,' said Penny, wistfully. 'All the emotions are intensified. One moment everything is perfect and the next it's awful. Then it's perfect again.' She turned to Emma and smiled. 'It's just as well it doesn't stay that way, isn't it? It can be exhausting.'

Emma nodded but said nothing. She thought she'd been in love with her late husband but had come to realise he'd manipulated her. She turned her gaze back to Mr Ashford and Miss Jackson. 'Maybe someone who worked in Mrs Melbourne's household will be able to tell us more about them,' she said. 'Perhaps the housekeeper? Miss Black.'

'Yes, she might know something,' replied Penny. 'In the meantime, I'm worried we could be spotted by Mr Ashford and Miss Jackson if we hang about here much longer. Shall we find somewhere for a cup of tea? And after that, let's try calling on Mr Ashford again. Hopefully he'll have returned home from his walk.'

FORTY-THREE

A short while later, Christopher Ashford received Emma and Penny with his usual easy manner.

'How nice to see you both again,' he said, his gaze drifting to the object in Emma's arms. 'And what's that you've brought with you?'

Emma stepped forward, holding out the box. 'I don't know if you recognise it,' she said. 'It's your godmother's stationery box.'

His brow furrowed slightly as he took it from her. 'Is it indeed? And how did you come by it?'

Emma hesitated, suddenly self-conscious about how it might look – that she had taken it upon herself to claim an item from the ruins of his godmother's home.

'I hope you don't mind,' she said carefully, 'but I spotted it among the rubble.' His fingers traced the initials EJM, his expression unreadable. Emma felt the need to explain further. 'I was teaching a piano lesson nearby and happened to pass the house. I couldn't help stopping to look at the devastation – it's dreadful to see a home reduced to ruins. That's when I saw this, and I thought... well, it seemed precious, so I retrieved it.'

Christopher regarded her for a moment before nodding. 'I see.'

His fingers tightened slightly on the box. 'Was there anything inside?'

Emma cleared her throat. 'Only some very sodden papers, I'm afraid. The fire brigade soaked everything when they put out the flames. I dried them out as best I could – I hope you don't mind. I thought there might be something important among them, but there was nothing legible. I put them back in the box for you, though I imagine they won't be of much use.'

For the briefest moment, a shadow flickered across Christopher's face, so fleeting that Emma might have imagined it. She shifted from one foot to the other, suddenly uneasy. Although she was returning the box to him, she suspected he was silently questioning why she'd taken it in the first place.

Sensing the tension, Penny spoke up. 'We were terribly sorry to hear about the fire. It must have been an awful shock.'

Christopher exhaled, placing the box down on a side table. He gestured for them to sit and he did the same. 'I didn't have any great personal attachment to the house,' he said. 'Even though my godmother lived there for many years. Still, it's upsetting. So many of her personal belongings are gone. The fact that you found this box is rather fortunate, really. I went down there myself but didn't see it.'

'Did any of the staff manage to salvage anything?' Emma asked.

He nodded. 'Apparently, Miss Black and some of the others recovered what they could, but from what I hear, there wasn't much left intact.' He ran a hand through his hair. 'To be honest, I don't feel as if I've lost anything personally. But it is, of course, a dreadful nuisance to deal with. In fact, my life has become unexpectedly busy over the past week or so.' He gave them a wry smile. 'I'm planning to rebuild the house, but it won't be my godmother's home anymore. Just a house – one that someone else can make their own.'

'Do you think you might live there yourself?' Penny asked gently.

'I don't think so. I'm quite happy here. Belgravia is an exclusive address but that sort of thing doesn't interest me.'

A maid entered with a tray of tea, setting it down before them. Penny waited for her to leave before she turned to Christopher. 'Do you know anyone called Arthur Thornwood?'

He looked thoughtful for a moment. 'No. Never heard of him. Why do you ask?'

'His name is mentioned in some of the papers in the stationery box.'

'I don't know him at all. He could be the local greengrocer for all I know.' He leaned forward in his chair and poured out the tea. Emma thought he was a little more irritable than before. Was it possible he was annoyed she'd taken his godmother's stationery box from the ruins of the house?

'Do the police still suspect your friend Mrs Clifton?' he asked, handing Penny a cup of tea.

'Yes,' Penny answered swiftly, as if to remind him that their continued investigations were justified.

Mr Ashford sighed. 'I find it difficult to believe she had anything to do with it. In fact... the more I think about it, the more I'm convinced Dr Lloyd was involved.'

He handed Emma a cup of tea. 'The doctor who Mrs Melbourne sued?' she asked.

'Absolutely. I was reluctant to consider it at first, but now it seems the most plausible explanation. He had the strongest reason to resent her.' He shook his head. 'What I can't fathom is how he convinced her to meet him in that graveyard.'

'Yes,' Penny mused. 'That's the great mystery, isn't it?'

He took a sip of his tea, then set the cup down with a quiet clink. 'I can only hope the police find the answers soon.'

Penny exchanged a glance with Emma before saying, 'Mrs Langley and I saw you earlier in Fitzroy Square. You were with Miss Jackson, weren't you?'

Christopher's hand stilled on the handle of his teacup. A pause followed and Emma held her breath. She sensed Christopher was assessing Penny's words carefully.

'Yes,' he said at last. 'It was Miss Jackson. Have you met her?'

'We have,' Penny said lightly. 'We were curious about an argument between her and Mrs Melbourne, so we sought her out.'

'I see.' Christopher leaned back in his chair. 'I knew Miss Jackson many years ago, when she was briefly a governess to Mrs Melbourne's niece. We hadn't seen each other in years, but I suppose... her death has brought us together again.'

Emma studied him, trying to read beneath his carefully neutral expression. He gave nothing away.

'Not in a romantic sense, of course,' Christopher added quickly, as if anticipating their thoughts. 'But we share a common experience – we both knew Mrs Melbourne. Frankly, I was surprised to see Miss Jackson again at all. I assumed she'd left London. So yes, it's been good to see her again.'

His smile was polite, but Emma couldn't ignore the feeling that there was something he wasn't saying.

FORTY-FOUR

After his visitors had left, Christopher Ashford sat down and opened his godmother's stationery box. The hinges creaked slightly, the wood swollen from water damage. Inside, as Mrs Langley had described, was a pile of dried, crumpled papers, their ink blurred beyond recognition. A small pot of ink sat in one corner, its label ruined, and beside it lay an old pen.

He lifted a few sheets, turning them over in his hands. Most of the writing had faded into obscurity, leaving only a few scattered words visible. Nothing of significance. Nothing worth keeping. He let the brittle papers drop back into the box with a quiet sigh. This was little more than debris now, a relic of no value to him.

Closing the lid, he ran his hand over the wood, noting the stains from smoke and water. It had once been a handsome piece, but now? It wasn't worth keeping. And yet, something nagged at him.

Why had Mrs Langley gone to such lengths to retrieve it?

If she had simply picked it up in passing, that was almost understandable. But she had taken the time to dry the papers, to sift through them, to bring the box here personally. What had she been looking for? A damning clue hidden among the pages?

He frowned, drumming his fingers against the lid of the box.

He wished now that he had questioned them more directly. Instead, he had let their polite words wash over him without pressing them on their true intentions. He wouldn't make that mistake again.

Then there was their unexpected question about Lydia.

That had caught him off guard. He had no objection to people knowing they had rekindled their acquaintance – it was hardly scandalous. But how had Mrs Langley and Mrs Blakely come to see them together? Had they been watching him? And why had they felt the need to ask?

Something about the two ladies' quiet persistence unsettled him. They had a way of asking questions that seemed harmless on the surface, but which hinted at something sharper beneath.

He would have to be careful with Mrs Langley and Mrs Blakely.

More than that – he would have to warn Lydia.

The less they told those two women, the better.

FORTY-FIVE

Emma and Penny made their way to Ebury Street. After making some inquiries, they found the lodging house where Miss Black and the other former members of Mrs Melbourne's household had taken refuge.

It was a scruffy building with grimy windows and a door which was in need of a lick of paint.

Miss Black's expression was unreadable when she answered the door.' We can speak downstairs in the parlour,' she said, leading the way. She didn't seem particularly pleased to see them, but nor did she turn them away. There was a strange indifference about her, and Emma couldn't shake the feeling that she smelled faintly of drink.

The parlour was furnished with dark wood panelling giving the room a sombre, oppressive feel. The flickering gas lamp threw Miss Black's gaunt features into sharp relief.

'How are you, Miss Black?' Emma asked.

'I've been better,' she replied tersely. 'I'm applying for positions at the moment. I've got an interview for a new post tomorrow.'

'That's excellent news,' Emma said brightly, although Miss Black's expression remained as grim as ever.

Penny wasted no time in steering the conversation towards the matter that had brought them here. 'I noticed Miss Lydia Jackson and Christopher Ashford together,' she said. 'Did they know each other well?'

The housekeeper gave a slow exhale. 'Yes, they did. A long time ago. I believe there was a romantic liaison between them. Completely inappropriate, of course. She's a governess, and he's a gentleman. You saw them together again, did you?'

'We did,' Penny confirmed. 'They were walking near Mr Ashford's home in Fitzrovia.'

The housekeeper gave a tut of disapproval. 'I'm surprised he's spending any time with her at all after her disgrace.'

Emma startled. 'Disgrace?'

Miss Black turned her sharp eyes on her. 'She stole from Mrs Melbourne.'

Emma exchanged a quick glance with Penny. Miss Jackson had been reserved – perhaps even curt – when they'd spoken, but a thief? That seemed unlike her.

'What did she steal?' Emma asked.

'A valuable brooch which belonged to Mrs Melbourne. It went missing after Miss Jackson was seen in her room.'

'And that was the end of her employment?' asked Penny.

Miss Black nodded. 'Dismissed immediately.'

'Well, that's certainly an unfortunate story,' Penny said. 'Miss Jackson didn't mention any of that when we spoke with her.'

A dry smile played at the corners of Miss Black's mouth. 'Well, she wouldn't, would she? It's not the sort of thing a person likes to admit to.'

'So that's why the two women fell out,' Penny said. 'Miss Jackson stole from Mrs Melbourne.'

'Yes, and that wasn't the end of it,' Miss Black said darkly. 'She had a rather ill-advised liaison with a married gentleman.'

Emma felt her jaw drop. 'Miss Jackson?'

Miss Black gave her a knowing look. 'Mrs Melbourne heard all about it from one of the ladies at St James's.'

'I had no idea,' Penny said. 'No wonder she's so guarded – she has a few secrets she'd rather keep buried.'

Miss Black nodded in satisfaction. 'I never expected to see her in London again. But I suppose she thinks enough time has passed that people have forgotten. And perhaps most have. But I haven't. People like me have long memories.'

'Indeed,' Penny agreed. 'After all that, I'm surprised she was able to continue working as a governess.'

'I expect she left London and found work somewhere else, where no one knew her past,' Miss Black said. 'She must have conducted herself well after that – avoiding any further scandals. But that's why she's a spinster, you know. And she always will be.'

Emma hesitated before asking, 'Do you think Mr Ashford knows?'

Miss Black shrugged. 'I suppose he must do. I never spoke to him about it directly – it's not the sort of thing one discusses. The servants whispered about it, of course, but they wouldn't have dared mention it to him. However, I'd wager Mrs Melbourne told him. That's why it surprises me that he's spending time with her now. She must be charming him for some reason.'

'Perhaps they've rekindled their love affair after all these years,' said Penny.

Emma liked this thought. Twenty years had passed and yet they still held a fondness for one another.

Miss Black gave a sniff. 'She's only interested in him because he's inherited Mrs Melbourne's estate.' She gave them a pointed look. 'He'd do well to be careful, that's for certain.'

The afternoon light was beginning to fade as Emma and Penny left the lodging house.

'Miss Black has been helpful,' said Penny. 'I can understand now why Miss Jackson and Mr Ashford are being secretive about their relationship. Everyone must have disapproved at the time.'

'Yes!' Penny's eyes brightened as the realisation hit her. 'We know Mrs Melbourne was very fond of Christopher Ashford and no doubt hoped he would marry well. When she discovered he was in love with a lowly governess...'

'She wouldn't have been happy,' said Emma.

'No. And then a brooch went missing and Miss Jackson was blamed for the theft. It's the perfect reason to dismiss someone, isn't it?'

'Mrs Melbourne needed an excuse to dismiss Miss Jackson so she could separate her from her godson,' added Emma. 'Why would Miss Jackson steal a brooch from her employer? She doesn't seem the type of lady to do such a thing. It could have been a lie invented by Mrs Melbourne. And perhaps her supposed disgrace was an ugly lie too, just to ensure Mr Ashford would want nothing more to do with her.'

Penny nodded. 'Yes! I think that must be it. Mrs Melbourne ensured Miss Jackson's love affair with her godson came to an end. He went off to India... did she arrange that too?'

'She may have done. But I think we can be certain she separated them.'

Penny tapped her chin, her expression thoughtful. 'Then Mr Ashford returned from India... and the argument between Miss Jackson and Mrs Melbourne – do you think Miss Jackson confronted her?'

'I think she must have done,' said Emma. 'And years of anger and resentment could...'

Penny finished the sentence for her. 'Drive someone to murder.'

FORTY-SIX

Agnes Black sat in the wooden chair by her grimy window. She couldn't quite understand what Mrs Blakely and Mrs Langley were trying to achieve, but she felt pleased about what she'd told them. They needed to realise Lydia Jackson had a motive for murdering Mrs Melbourne.

Lydia didn't deserve to be with the handsome, wealthy Christopher Ashford. She hadn't deserved it twenty years ago and she didn't deserve it now. How had she managed to cast such a spell over him? Agnes felt a bitter taste in her mouth.

Nothing had pleased her more than when Lydia Jackson had been dismissed. For once, Mrs Melbourne had made a sensible decision.

But now Lydia was back. And she was with Christopher Ashford again. Agnes had never thought it possible.

There was a sharp knock at the door. Were the two ladies back again? No, the knock was different. It was louder and more officious.

She froze for a moment, her pulse quickening. Forcing herself to breathe, she smoothed the front of her dress, straightened her posture, and crossed the small room. When she opened the door, she found herself looking up into the familiar face of Inspector Paget.

A shiver of unease ran through her.

Standing beside him was a stockier man with a thick black moustache, his expression unreadable.

'Good afternoon, Miss Black,' Paget said. 'I trust you recall me?'

Agnes nodded, her mouth suddenly dry. 'Yes. What's this about?' Her gaze flicked to the other man, trying to gauge his purpose.

'This is Detective Inspector Peters from B Division,' Paget explained. 'He and I are working together on this particular matter. Would you mind if we have a word?'

A cold knot formed in her stomach. 'There's a parlour downstairs,' she said cautiously. 'We can talk there.'

'Very good,' said Paget, stepping aside to let her pass. 'We won't take up too much of your time.'

She wasn't sure she believed that.

A few minutes later, they were seated in the parlour. Agnes folded her hands tightly in her lap, willing them to stay still as Inspector Paget retrieved a notebook from his coat pocket and flicked through its pages.

'This is primarily a matter for Inspector Peters,' he said. 'Mrs Melbourne's former residence falls under his jurisdiction, and he has been investigating the fire that destroyed the house.'

Agnes stiffened. A slow, sickening sensation spread through her chest.

'The fire?' she repeated, keeping her voice neutral. 'Why are you investigating it?'

'Inspector Peters will explain.'

Detective Inspector Peters cleared his throat. When he spoke, his voice was low and thoughtful. 'We have reason to believe, Miss Black, that the fire at Mrs Melbourne's home was started deliberately.'

A chill ran down her spine. 'Not an accident?' she repeated, forcing a frown. 'That's awful. I... I assumed it was.'

'Our colleagues at the fire brigade are highly experienced in these matters,' continued Inspector Peters. 'And they found traces of paraffin in one of the fireplaces.'

Cold perspiration broke out across her forehead. 'Paraffin? How could they possibly tell? The house was burned to the ground!'

'Yes,' he said. 'And a considerable amount of it, which suggests someone intended the fire to spread quickly and thoroughly.'

'I... I don't understand,' she managed. 'I thought everyone assumed it was a stray ember or something of the sort. That's what people were saying.'

'One stray ember could start a fire, certainly,' Peters conceded. 'But not like this. Not so suddenly, and not with such intensity. The household was well maintained, every fireplace swept only the week before. Fireguards in every room.' He leaned in slightly. 'The butler confirmed as much.'

Her jaw clenched. The butler. He would always speak honestly.

'So, as you can imagine, Miss Black, the presence of paraffin significantly alters our perspective.'

She swallowed, her mouth dry.

'And,' he continued, 'after a thorough investigation, we've determined that the fire started in the study.'

A sharp, cold panic gripped her chest.

'The study?' she asked, her voice quieter now. 'How... how can you be certain?'

'Our colleagues at the fire brigade are certain, Miss Black,' Peters said, his gaze unrelenting.

She closed her eyes for a fraction of a second. She had thought everything had been destroyed.

Peters pressed on. 'We've spoken to nearly every member of the household now and pieced together their whereabouts at the time the fire began. So perhaps you can tell us where you were, Miss Black, when the fire started?'

'I was in the drawing room.' She fixed his gaze, keeping her voice as determined as possible. 'I was checking to see if the maid had done her dusting properly.'

Inspector Paget tilted his head slightly, watching her closely.

'The maid,' Peters repeated. 'Would that be Kitty Wilde?'

'Yes. That's right.'

Peters exchanged a glance with Paget before continuing. 'Kitty Wilde told us she was upstairs at the time. In one of the bedrooms. She barely made it out – smoke had already started filling the stairwell.'

Agnes pressed her lips together.

'Yes, that's right,' she said quickly. 'She was upstairs.'

Peters nodded, as if considering something. 'So she couldn't have been in the drawing room with you.'

Her pulse pounded in her ears. 'No,' she admitted. 'But she had been before. I went in there after she'd finished.'

'That's interesting,' said Peters, 'because three members of the household have told me you were in the study when the fire started.'

Her stomach gave lurch. 'Who?'

'I'm not at liberty to say. But two people saw you near the study shortly before the fire started and another claims they saw you running out of the study shortly before they smelled smoke. They said you ran to the drawing room.'

Her mouth felt dry as she tried to find the words to defend herself. 'I was in the drawing room already. I wasn't in the study. They were mistaken! You have no evidence, Inspector. Most of the household dislike me. They want to blame me for this. But you mustn't believe them! It wasn't me. I swear it!'

A silence stretched between them. The weight of their scrutiny settled heavily over her.

She clutched at the cross around her neck and swallowed hard. They didn't believe her.

FORTY-SEVEN

Clara Clifton smiled as she stepped into the little park nestled between the quiet backstreets of Clerkenwell. The wrought-iron gate creaked softly as she entered. Neat gravel paths traced tidy lines across the frosty grass, and although the trees stood bare against the cold sky, she could already imagine the transformation to come – blossom of pink and white and daffodils nodding their golden heads.

The park had once been the burial ground of St John's Priory. Just three years earlier, it had been a grim, shuttered corner of the city – overgrown and unloved. Now it was a place of renewal. Clara's heart lifted. This was exactly what she worked for. A space reclaimed, not erased: somewhere that paid quiet tribute to the dead while giving the living a chance to breathe.

She found a bench near a budding hawthorn tree and sat, clasping her gloved hands in her lap. It was too chilly to linger for long, but she wanted to be still for a moment – to let the hush of the garden settle her thoughts.

Her mind drifted to Penny and Emma. She had not told them everything. Not at first. And now she wondered whether she should have been more forthcoming. Since admitting she'd known

Mrs Melbourne, the memories had come back – fragmented, but stubborn.

Could there have been something in those brief interactions? A clue she had overlooked? A comment made in passing that now held weight?

She exhaled slowly, her breath misting in the air.

The last time she had seen Mrs Melbourne had been at a meeting of the Metropolitan Public Gardens Committee. It had been the second meeting Mrs Melbourne had attended, and she'd turned up unannounced wearing a fancy hat with a plume of brightly coloured feathers.

'I'm prepared to donate a considerable sum,' Mrs Melbourne had declared. 'I'm certain it will allow you to transform a neglected burial ground into a new public garden. But naturally, I must ask – how will my generosity be rewarded?'

A pause followed. The chairman, a mild-mannered man with half-moon spectacles perched low on his nose, had looked startled.

'Reward, Mrs Melbourne?' he'd said cautiously. 'We don't usually offer rewards for donations. We're simply grateful for the support.'

Clara recalled Mrs Melbourne's tight smile as she spoke. 'Perhaps I used the wrong word. Not a reward. Recognition. That's more accurate.'

The other committee members shifted uncomfortably in their chairs.

'Well,' the chairman replied, glancing at his notes, 'we always make sure donations are recorded in the minutes of our meetings, and also in our annual report, which is distributed to our members at the end of each year.'

Mrs Melbourne's smile thinned. 'How many people read your annual report?'

'All of our members do.'

'Yes, but I'm referring to public recognition. I'm offering to fund the restoration of an entire burial ground, and I would expect the finished garden to reflect that. Eleanor Melbourne Park – that has a pleasing ring to it, don't you think?'

The room had gone very quiet. Clara remembered the strained expressions, the way two members at the far end of the table had exchanged barely concealed smirks.

'I'm afraid that wouldn't be appropriate,' the chairman had said gently. 'We usually consult with the local community when it comes to naming these spaces. Often, they choose something historical, or a name linked to the church the ground belonged to. Naming parks after individuals is not our usual practice.'

'Even if that individual is responsible for the park's existence?'

'We receive many generous donations, Mrs Melbourne, and we are always grateful. But we cannot make exceptions to our process.'

Fury settled over Mrs Melbourne's features. Clara had been seated opposite her, and she remembered feeling the need to avert her gaze – the expression was too sharp to bear.

Clara and the other committee members had always believed in the goodness of their work – the quiet dignity of repurposed burial grounds. But Mrs Melbourne had brought something different to that meeting. Something acquisitive. It wasn't about the parks or the people who might enjoy them. It was about legacy. About being seen. About being remembered.

And now she was – although not in the way she would have chosen.

Clara shivered, although not from the cold. She looked around the garden, its tranquil silence at odds with the memory that still echoed through her mind.

FORTY-EIGHT

'I must say, I'm enjoying my piano lessons with you very much, Mrs Langley,' said Mrs Solomon brightly over breakfast the following morning. 'I even did a little practice yesterday – and for the first time, I truly feel like I'm making progress.'

'I'm pleased to hear it,' Emma replied with a smile.

In truth, she found Mrs Solomon a challenging pupil. The lessons often drifted off course, punctuated by monologues about her childhood, complaints about her forgetfulness, and the occasional tangent into local gossip. Emma frequently found herself repeating the same basic principles, but now, at least, it was clear that her efforts were being appreciated – which made the sessions more bearable.

'Before long,' said Mrs Solomon, reaching for the butter dish, 'I hope to play something lovely for Ronald. He'd like that, I think.'

'I'm sure he would,' Emma agreed. 'And if there's a particular piece you have in mind, let me know. I can find the music for it.'

Mrs Solomon smiled fondly. 'I'd like that very much.' As she spread butter on her toast, she glanced at the letters beside her plate. 'Oh, I nearly forgot – this one's for you. It ended up in my pile somehow. There's no postmark on it, it looks like it's been delivered by hand.'

She passed it to Emma. The handwriting on the envelope stirred something at the back of Emma's mind – familiar, somehow, although she couldn't place it immediately. A distant relation, perhaps? Someone from her husband's old circle?

She opened the envelope and read the first line. At once, her stomach dropped.

She had seen the handwriting before.

It was the same as the letters sent anonymously to Penny.

Except now, the threat had come directly to her. Delivered by hand to her home.

Emma felt the blood drain from her face as she read.

Dear Mrs Langley,

A widow should conduct herself with restraint and dignity. You have chosen to do neither. Your pursuit of this sordid little mystery does nothing to honour your husband's memory. Instead, it drags his name through the mud of scandal and speculation.

If you do not abandon this misguided course, I fear your reputation will not recover. Nor will your safety be guaranteed.

Emma folded the note slowly and placed it beside her plate, her hands trembling slightly.

She stared at a tea stain on the tablecloth, willing her expression to remain composed.

Someone knew where she lived.

Someone was watching her. Watching both her and Penny.

'Is everything all right, Mrs Langley?' Mrs Solomon asked worriedly. 'Who's the letter from?'

Emma forced a smile. 'Just something from the bank.'

'Oh dear. Nothing to worry about, I hope?'

'No,' Emma said quickly. 'No, it's routine. Nothing serious.'

'Well, if there's anything you need – any trouble paying the rent, heaven forbid – you come straight to me. We can sort something out.'

'Thank you,' said Emma, trying to keep her voice steady. 'That's very kind of you. But really, everything's fine.'

She stirred her tea with care, but her thoughts were already racing.

Emma didn't have a piano lesson to teach until the afternoon, so she decided to spend part of the morning practising – partly to keep her fingers nimble, and partly to distract herself from the letter.

Her hands moved over the keys, but her mind wandered. No matter how she tried to focus, her thoughts kept circling back.

As Penny had said, the anonymous writer was clearly fearful that they were close to uncovering the truth about Mrs Melbourne's death.

Emma paused mid-phrase, her fingers resting lightly on the ivory keys. She rose and crossed to the window, glancing at the quiet view of Northampton Square. A few people passed by: a man with a newspaper tucked under his arm, a woman leading a child by the hand, a tradesman wheeling a cart. No one loitered. No one stared up at the house.

Still, a shiver crept down her spine. Was someone watching her, even now? Or had the letter simply been intended to frighten her from a distance?

Surely that was all it was. A scare tactic. A coward's trick.

She returned to the piano, determined to shake off the unease. As the music filled the parlour once more, she felt her shoulders loosen slightly.

FORTY-NINE

Penny called in at the *Morning Express* offices the following day to hand her next article to Edgar Fish.

'This article is about preparing your young child for the arrival of their sibling,' she said.

'Is it indeed?' Edgar took the article from her. 'Do they understand?'

'Does who understand?'

'Do young children understand when you explain these things to them?'

'It's difficult to know exactly how much they understand, but I think it's a good idea to explain to them what's happening. You never know, some children understand more than you think.'

'I can't say Mrs Fish and I ever bothered. In fact, our third child has just been born.'

'Oh congratulations, Edgar! That's wonderful news!'

'It is indeed. A little girl this time and I'm immensely proud.' A broad grin spread across his face. 'She and her mother are doing extremely well.'

'And how are your other two children faring?'

'They seem indifferent to the baby to be honest. Although

when she's crawling about and causing a nuisance then they'll probably have stronger opinions.'

Penny smiled. 'I know exactly what you mean.'

Edgar read through the article and seemed pleased with it. As Penny got up to leave, she felt the need to ask him a final question. 'Have any more unpleasant letters arrived addressed to me?'

Edgar scratched his chin as he thought. 'No... I don't believe they have. That's good, isn't it?'

Penny nodded, relieved. 'It is indeed.'

Hopefully the anonymous letter writer wouldn't bother her again.

After leaving Edgar's office, Penny adjusted her hat and made her way down the corridor. Harry Wright emerged from the news-room. 'Mrs Blakely!'

'Hello, Mr Wright.'

'Any further developments on the curious case of Mrs Melbourne?'

'Not really,' said Penny. 'Emma examined the papers in her stationery box but didn't find much in them. Does the name Arthur Thornwood mean anything to you?'

Mr Wright shook his head. 'No. Did she find a mention of him?'

'Yes, she did. But the papers were so damaged, there was no context to them at all.'

'Well, if I come across the name, then I'll let you know.'

'Thank you, Mr Wright.'

'There's some news about the fire. Have you heard? The fire brigade believe it was started deliberately.'

Penny gave this some thought. 'I suppose that's not a great surprise.'

'My thoughts exactly. If someone in Mrs Melbourne's house-hold was responsible for her murder, there could have been incrim-inating evidence in that house. Perhaps they panicked, unsure how to dispose of it – and decided that fire was the best solution. It's an extreme thing to do, but certainly possible.'

Penny considered this, then offered another theory. 'Or someone wanted to destroy the home simply because they didn't want Christopher Ashford to inherit it.'

Harry's brows lifted. 'Ah, yes. Mrs Melbourne's godson.' He rubbed his chin. 'I don't see why anyone would object to him inheriting it – he seems an affable enough chap.'

'He does,' said Penny. 'But who can tell?'

'Who indeed?' The reporter let out a small sigh and shook his head. 'It's a puzzle, all right. I tried speaking to Mrs Harwell – the chairlady of the St James's Diocesan Home for Penitents that Mrs Melbourne was so devoted to. But she refused to talk to me.'

Penny allowed herself a small smile. 'She doesn't want to speak to news reporters?'

'Apparently not.'

'Mrs Langley and I managed to get an interview with her,' Penny admitted.

Harry's eyebrows shot up. 'Did you? And what did she say?'

'Very little. She's clearly shocked, but not personally saddened. There was something rather calculated about her demeanour – calm, controlled and giving almost nothing away.'

'You think she's hiding something?'

'It's possible.'

Harry's expression sharpened. 'Good, because that fits with what I've discovered. Since Mrs Harwell wouldn't talk to me, I spoke to a young lady who volunteers at the home. She helps the women with their babies. She told me she overheard arguments between Mrs Harwell and Mrs Melbourne before her death.'

Penny's interest piqued. 'Did she? So they weren't exactly friendly?'

'Not in the least. The young lady said Mrs Harwell only tolerated Mrs Melbourne's presence because of the generous donations she made. But apparently, Mrs Melbourne could be quite rude in the way she spoke to Mrs Harwell. The young lady said she was sometimes shocked by the way Mrs Melbourne treated her.' He glanced down at his notebook, flicking through a few pages. 'The young lady wasn't sure what the arguments were about. Sometimes, she thought they were over petty matters, but it was clear the two women had never been on good terms.' He tapped his pencil against the edge of his notebook. 'And let's not forget – Mrs Harwell was the last person to see Mrs Melbourne alive, apart from the hansom cab driver who took her to the churchyard.'

Penny nodded. 'That certainly makes her worthy of suspicion.'

Harry sighed. 'I'll keep asking around, and I'm sure you will too, Mrs Blakely. One thing's for sure though, I'll keep knocking on Inspector Paget's door and hopefully he'll give me some more information soon. He'll get so fed up with me that he'll tell me something just to get rid of me.'

'That's a good tactic, Mr Wright. Make a nuisance of yourself.'

'Oh, I intend to!' Then, as if something had just occurred to him, he added, 'So Mrs Langley isn't accompanying you today?'

'No, she's teaching at the moment.'

He gave a slight nod, but Penny caught the flicker of something else in his expression. Interest? Disappointment?

'Were you hoping she'd be with me today?'

'Hoping?' Harry repeated, suddenly looking flustered. 'Not hoping, exactly. Just... wondering.'

Penny suppressed a smile. 'Would you like me to pass on a message?'

His face turned a shade darker. 'A message? No. There's no message. In fact, I really ought to be getting on.' He checked his pocket watch hastily. 'Yes, I didn't realise the time – I must be going. Goodbye, Mrs Blakely.'

With that, he stepped back into the newsroom.

FIFTY

Penny stepped out onto Fleet Street, thinking about Mrs Harwell and Mrs Melbourne. She wasn't surprised to hear the pair had argued. But had the disagreement been strong enough to lead to murder?

'Well, I never,' said a large man in a dark overcoat. 'If it isn't Mrs Blakely.'

Penny halted mid-step. Dr Lloyd stood before her, tucking something into his inner pocket.

'Dr Lloyd,' she said, eyeing him warily. 'What are you doing here?'

'I was just paying a visit to a friend of mine – an editor for a medical publication,' he replied.

He glanced briefly towards the *Morning Express* offices and Penny wondered whether she should believe him or not.

'It was very interesting meeting you recently,' he continued, his small, close-set eyes looking her up and down. 'You and your delightful friend, Mrs Langley. How's your investigation coming along?'

'Very well, thank you,' Penny replied curtly.

She had no desire to converse with him. He made her skin

prickle. There was an unnatural smoothness to his manner, as though he enjoyed toying with people.

He stepped closer, lowering his voice. 'There are a few more things I could tell you about Mrs Melbourne, you know.' He gestured towards the street. 'Perhaps we could get a drink together somewhere? A quiet place to talk?'

Inwardly, Penny recoiled. The last thing she wanted was to be alone with him. But if he truly had useful information, should she pass up the opportunity?

As she hesitated, relief flooded through her when she spotted Harry Wright emerging from the *Morning Express* offices.

'Mr Wright!' she called.

The young journalist noticed her, smiled and strode over.

'This is Dr Lloyd,' she said, turning to him. 'Dr Lloyd, this is Mr Harry Wright, a reporter for the *Morning Express*.'

The doctor's expression soured slightly. Penny didn't miss the way his posture stiffened, as though displeased by the sudden addition of a younger – and more charming – man to their conversation.

'Pleased to meet you, Mr Wright,' he said coolly. Then he turned back to Penny, his tone clipped. 'So, what do you say? Shall we have our little chat?'

'Absolutely,' Penny said, seizing the opportunity. 'And Mr Wright must join us as well. You have half an hour to spare, don't you, Mr Wright?'

He hesitated, clearly reluctant. 'Well... I do have a rather tight deadline...'

Penny shot him a desperate, pleading look and he seemed to understand what she was suggesting. After a moment's deliberation, he nodded. 'However, I have some time now. Shall we go to Ye Olde Cheshire Cheese?'

Penny smiled gratefully. 'Yes. One of my favourite places.'

Dr Lloyd gave a small, stiff nod. For a moment, she thought he might change his mind. But then he sighed and gestured for them to lead the way.

. . .

Ten minutes later, the three of them sat at a wooden table in one of the dimly lit, panelled rooms of Ye Olde Cheshire Cheese. The scent of burning logs and ale lingered in the air, and a fire crackled in the grate.

'I reported on the court case, Dr Lloyd,' said Mr Wright.

'Did you?' The doctor wiped a hand over his fleshy jowls.

'Yes and I think the verdict was wrong. It was most unfair.'

He seemed keen to flatter the doctor and he was successful. Dr Lloyd's shoulders relaxed a little. 'You're not the first to tell me I was unlucky, Mr Wright. I should never have been sued in the first place, let alone lost the case. But what's done is done.'

Mr Wright leaned in. 'What do you think you can tell us about Mrs Melbourne that we don't already know?'

The doctor smirked and sat back in his chair, clearly enjoying the attention. 'Well now, let me see. People thought she was charitable, pious – some sort of saintly benefactor.'

'Yes,' Mr Wright said dryly. 'That's certainly how she liked to present herself.'

'Well, it's about time people saw the truth.'

'And what was the truth?'

'That she was an unpleasant, self-serving woman,' the doctor said bluntly. 'And I suspect you already know that.'

Mr Wright nodded. 'But someone detested her enough to kill her. Who do you think that could have been?'

Dr Lloyd gave a shrug. 'I'll be honest with you – I find the murder very interesting. As a medical man, I'm always fascinated by the details of how these things are done.'

Penny stiffened at the way he said it, his tone clinical and detached.

'I apologise if I'm being too graphic,' he continued, 'but Mrs Melbourne was killed with a rather unusual weapon.'

'It was a knife, wasn't it?' asked Mr Wright.

'An unusual knife.' The doctor swirled the ale in his tankard. 'The blade was very long and thin.'

'How do you know the details?' Penny asked.

'Inspector Paget consulted me,' he said with a nonchalant sniff.

Penny felt her brow creased as she considered this. Would Paget really have consulted Dr Lloyd?

'So was it a stiletto knife?' Mr Wright asked.

Dr Lloyd nodded. 'Similar to that, yes. A stiletto is an Italian weapon – thin and designed for stabbing rather than slashing. Now, the weapon hasn't been found. But if the police were to search the homes of everyone they suspect, they might just come across something interesting.'

'From what I've heard,' said Mr Wright, 'the police haven't searched anyone's home. They're dragging their heels. Every time I try to ask them about the case, they tell me to get lost.'

'That sounds about right,' said Penny. 'I've spoken to Inspector Paget myself – he's not particularly cooperative.'

Dr Lloyd chuckled. 'Well, can you blame him? He doesn't want journalists and amateur detectives getting in the way. He just wants to get on with the job.'

'But it's very interesting that you believe a stiletto knife was used,' Penny said. 'That's not a common item.'

'No,' the doctor agreed. 'Not something most people own. Which makes me wonder – was it purchased specifically for the crime? If so, that suggests premeditation.'

Harry nodded thoughtfully. 'If we could trace a purchase, we could trace the killer. But what was their motive?'

The doctor smirked. 'With a woman like Mrs Melbourne? There could be plenty of motives.' He sat back and steepled his fingers. 'She was a patient of mine for many years. So I knew her well and many members of her family and household.'

'And do you think any of them could have wanted to murder her?' Penny asked.

The doctor exhaled slowly, considering his answer. 'Murder? No, I can't say I can imagine any of them going that far. But did they like her? I doubt it. She wasn't the easiest woman to serve.'

'That certainly aligns with what we've heard,' Penny agreed.

Dr Lloyd lowered his voice and glanced around as if ensuring no one else was listening. 'Now, Miss Black – she's an odd character. I had dealings with her years ago when she first entered Mrs Melbourne's household.'

'What sort of dealings?' Penny asked.

The doctor hesitated. 'It's a rather private – one might even say shameful – matter.'

Penny stiffened. A person's medical history was their own affair. Dr Lloyd had no right to discuss such things. Yet, there was something about his manner – his eagerness to divulge – that suggested this was not simply idle gossip.

Mr Wright, sitting beside Penny, had gone completely still. She could sense his anticipation, his journalist's instinct kicking in. He was eager to hear whatever shameful secret the doctor was about to reveal.

Dr Lloyd tapped his fingers against the table. 'Miss Black was young then. Sixteen or seventeen, I'd say. And she found herself in trouble.' He paused, his meaning heavy with implication. 'She visited me and asked me if I could... remedy the situation.'

Penny felt her stomach turn. The topic was uncomfortable, and coming from Dr Lloyd, it felt even more distasteful.

'Did you?' Mr Wright asked bluntly.

Dr Lloyd straightened. 'Of course not. The procedure is illegal, as you well know. I refused to be involved. So it was my duty to inform Mrs Melbourne. She sent her away to a home in Fulham, I believe, although I can't be certain.'

Penny's stomach gave a flip. 'The St James's Diocesan Home for Penitents?'

'Possibly. Is that in Fulham?'

'Yes.'

'The home which is run by Mrs Harwell,' said Mr Wright, his eyes widening. 'What could this mean?'

'What could what mean?' asked Dr Lloyd. 'You've lost me.'

Penny and Mr Wright exchanged a glance. They had no words in that moment, but the same thought was surely running through both their minds.

Had that dark chapter in Miss Black's past somehow played a role in Mrs Melbourne's murder?

FIFTY-ONE

'Sorry I'm late,' said Penny the following morning. 'Florence didn't want me to leave her.'

'Oh no,' said Emma. 'That must have been difficult.'

They stood outside Walham Green railway station in Fulham and a cold wind pulled at their hats and coats.

'Mrs Tuttle assured me that Florence would be fine as soon as I left the house and I know that's usually the case,' continued Penny. She pushed up her spectacles and rubbed an eye with her finger. 'It's still a bit difficult. Oh, and I received another letter.' She retrieved it from her bag.

Emma's throat tightened. 'So did I. Delivered to my home. I've brought it with me today to show it to you.'

Penny's eyes widened behind her spectacles. 'So they know where you live too now?'

Emma nodded, aware of a bitter taste of fear in her mouth.

Penny sensed her concern and rested a hand on her arm. 'Don't worry,' she said reassuringly. 'They're just trying to frighten us.'

'And it's working!'

'Yes. They've got a way with words, haven't they? But that's all they are – just words.' She bit her lip and pushed the letter back into her bag. 'Let's not dwell on the letters for now, we need to examine them properly and see if we can find any more clues about the identity of the sender. In the meantime, we're here to speak to Mrs Harwell. Thank you for replying to my telegram late last night. I'm pleased you could make it.'

'I couldn't say no,' said Emma with a smile. 'What's made you decide to go to the St James's Diocesan Home for Penitents again?'

'I'll tell you all about it as we walk there.'

Emma listened as Penny explained about her unexpected encounter with Dr Lloyd the previous day.

'And it's lucky Harry Wright was there too,' Penny added. 'Dr Lloyd wanted to speak to me alone. I wouldn't have felt safe. There's something unnerving about him.'

Emma nodded. 'Yes, you were lucky.' She felt a pang of envy that she hadn't been there too. She would've liked to have seen Mr Wright again. 'So Mrs Melbourne sent Agnes Black to St James's Home to have her baby,' she said. 'To have found herself in such a desperate situation at such a young age – it must have been terrifying.' She hadn't particularly warmed to Miss Black, but now she saw her in a different light. There was a sadness behind the housekeeper's eyes, a weight she had presumably carried for thirty years. And now, all these years later, did those ghosts of the past still haunt her?

'And there's something else I haven't told you yet,' said Penny. 'James says the police suspect Agnes Black started the fire.'

Emma stopped and turned to Penny. 'Miss Black started it?'

'That's what they think.'

'So has she been arrested?'

'Not yet. They're trying to gather more evidence.'

They continued walking. 'It's funny,' said Emma. 'But Harry Wright suggested someone in the household started the fire to destroy evidence implicating them in Mrs Melbourne's murder.'

'Perhaps he's right,' said Penny. 'In which case, Miss Black seems a likely culprit, doesn't she? But before we decide it's definitely her, we need to bear in mind that Mrs Harwell and Mrs Melbourne were known to argue with each other.'

'How do you know that?' Emma asked.

'It's something Harry Wright found out after speaking to a woman who works at the home.'

'That's very interesting indeed,' said Emma. 'He's good at his job, isn't he?'

Penny smiled. 'Shall I tell him you said that?'

Emma blushed. 'You can if you want.'

'He was disappointed you weren't with me at the *Morning Express* offices.'

Emma gave a laugh which she hoped sounded dry and indifferent. 'He's just become used to seeing us together. He was probably being polite.'

'If you say so,' said Penny with a smile.

Emma felt her heart skip. She would never admit to anyone that she felt flattered Harry Wright had asked after her.

Inside the home, a young woman in a plain dress and apron led them along the austere corridor with its framed lists of rules and Biblical scripture on the wall.

'I'm afraid I'm rather busy,' said Mrs Harwell, barely glancing up from the papers in her hands. 'I don't have much time to talk.'

'We won't keep you long,' Penny assured her. 'In fact, we have a fairly straightforward question. How familiar are you with Mrs Melbourne's former housekeeper, Miss Black?'

For the briefest moment, Mrs Harwell hesitated. Then, with careful deliberation, she lowered the papers onto her desk.

'Why do you ask?'

Penny leaned forward slightly. 'She's an intriguing character. We've spoken with her a few times, and she strikes us as someone with a past she'd rather keep hidden.'

Mrs Harwell sat back in her chair and removed her spectacles. 'I don't like gossip,' she said. 'And I certainly won't indulge in it.'

'I can't say I enjoy gossip either,' Penny replied, 'but there's a difference between idle speculation and facts. We have reason to believe Miss Black came to this home thirty years ago.'

Mrs Harwell arched a brow. 'If you already believe that, then why are you asking me?'

'We'd like to confirm it.'

The older woman exhaled sharply. 'Remind me again why you two women are asking all these questions?'

Penny's expression remained composed. 'We're trying to discover the truth behind Mrs Melbourne's death.'

'Well, it's nothing to do with Agnes Black.' She placed her spectacles on again and picked up another pile of papers.

'We're simply trying to understand Miss Black a little better,' Penny said. 'And since you haven't denied she was here, I can only assume that she was.'

Mrs Harwell sighed impatiently. 'So you have your answer.'

'Were you running this home when she was here?'

'I have overseen its operation for nearly forty years.'

'Then you must remember her?'

'I don't get to know the girls here personally, Mrs Blakely. That would not be appropriate.'

Emma spoke up. 'Mrs Melbourne took Miss Black back into her service after her stay here, is that right?' Mrs Harwell confirmed it with a nod. 'And she worked for Mrs Melbourne for the next three decades.'

'Indeed. Mrs Melbourne believed in redemption. And, as expected, our home did its job well.' She straightened in her chair.

'How did you get on with Mrs Melbourne?' Penny asked her.

Mrs Harwell gave her a sharp look. 'Why do you ask?'

'There are rumours the two of you argued.'

The older woman gave a sniff. 'We had our differences from time to time. Quite normal for two ladies with strong opinions. Are you suggesting I followed her to the churchyard that night and murdered her because we argued?'

The challenge caused Penny to back down. 'No. I'm not suggesting that.'

'Good. Now, if that's all, I have more pressing matters to attend to. I don't have time for further questions.'

Realising they would get little more from her, Penny gave a polite nod. 'Thank you for your time, Mrs Harwell.'

As they stepped outside into the brisk air, Emma exhaled. 'So did Miss Black take revenge on Mrs Melbourne for sending her to this home?'

'I don't know,' Penny frowned. 'If she did, then why exact her revenge thirty years later? It doesn't make sense.'

FIFTY-TWO

Who had told those two meddling women about Miss Black?

Margaret Harwell drummed her fingers on her desk. The secret had been buried for three decades. And yet, somehow, it had resurfaced.

Was Miss Black aware of the whispers? Or worse – had she been the one to let something slip?

Mrs Harwell shook her head. No. Some things were meant to be forgotten, locked away in the past, never to be spoken of again.

But perhaps Miss Black only had herself to blame. It was she, after all, who had foolishly decided to seek the truth. After all these years, she had chosen to dredge up the past, to go looking for answers that should have remained buried. And somehow, in doing so, she had stirred up a secret that should never have seen the light of day.

Mrs Harwell had tried to warn her. She had told her that ignorance was often kinder than the truth. But Miss Black had been insistent. And now, she had to suffer the consequences.

Well, that was her own doing.

Mrs Harwell exhaled slowly, leaning back in her chair. It wasn't her fault. She'd done what she could as had St James's Home. Miss Black had lived a pious, sin-free life since those days.

And that was what Mrs Harwell had to remind herself.

A knock at the door interrupted her thoughts. Margaret Harwell inhaled sharply, composing herself as her secretary, Miss McKay, stepped into the room with her usual efficient stride.

'I have some letters for you to sign,' Miss McKay announced, placing a neat stack of papers on the desk. 'And a few pieces of correspondence which require replies.'

'Very well,' Mrs Harwell said, reaching for her pen.

The young woman hesitated before adding, 'And there's the invitation for the unveiling of Mr Harwell's plaque at the new office headquarters. I haven't sent your response yet, but I assume you'll be attending?'

Mrs Harwell blinked, momentarily caught off guard.

'Oh yes... I'd forgotten about that.' She set her pen down. 'I suppose I had better.'

She hadn't meant to sound so indifferent, but it was too late. She saw the flicker of curiosity in Miss McKay's expression – a slight tilt of the head.

'I'm looking forward to it,' she added, realising she should show some enthusiasm. 'It's a wonderful tribute to my late husband's career.'

Miss McKay nodded. 'Very well, I'll inform them you'll attend.'

'Thank you, Miss McKay.'

As soon as the door clicked shut behind her, Mrs Harwell reached for the stack of letters. She began signing them mechanically, but her mind was elsewhere.

She had let her guard slip. Only for a second – but that was all it took.

Most people never questioned her grief. They never looked closely enough. They saw only what they expected to see: the dignified widow carrying on with quiet fortitude. But there had been one person who had looked a little too closely.

Mrs Melbourne.

She'd made several remarks about Samuel Harwell's sudden

and unexpected passing. Little comments, seemingly offhand, but always delivered with that sharp, knowing glint in her eye.

Mrs Harwell had brushed them aside, feigned polite ignorance, but she had worried that something in her face or voice, had betrayed her.

Lying did not come naturally to her.

And Mrs Melbourne had always been adept at spotting weakness.

She had been clever. Far cleverer than Mrs Harwell had ever given her credit for.

She put down her pen and a cold perspiration broke out across her forehead as she recalled Mrs Melbourne's words to her. 'I'm rather tired of our arrangement, Margaret. Perhaps it's time the world knew the truth about dear Samuel. I wonder what the newspapers will say when they learn that his devoted wife was the cause of his tragic demise?'

FIFTY-THREE

Emma and Penny laid out the anonymous threatening letters on the table in the dining rooms at Victoria railway station. They'd received three in total: two addressed to Penny and one addressed to Emma.

They sipped their tea as they examined each letter and gathered their thoughts.

'The handwriting remains consistent, doesn't it?' said Penny. 'And I agree with your earlier theory that it seems genuine rather than disguised.'

Emma picked up one of the letters and rubbed a corner between her forefinger and thumb. 'It's quite thick letter paper too. Good quality. Let's make a note of when each letter was received.' She put down the letter and pulled her notebook out of her bag.

'Good idea,' said Penny. 'None of these letters are dated.' She pointed to the first letter. 'This one was delivered to the *Morning Express* offices on the tenth of March. You received one on the fifteenth and I received another today – the seventeenth.'

Emma sighed. 'Do they intend to send them daily from now on?'

'Possibly.' Penny took a sip of tea. 'We're clearly bothering them quite a lot now. Who had we called on when I received the first letter?'

'We had just visited Mrs Harwell for the first time,' said Emma. 'And in the days before that we spoke to Dr Lloyd, Lydia Jackson and Christopher Ashford.'

'All of whom are capable of writing eloquent letters in my opinion,' said Penny. 'And if I were to choose a suspect from the three of them, I'd say Dr Lloyd. But that's probably because I don't like him and my judgement is being clouded by my personal opinion.'

Emma smiled at Penny's honesty. 'And the skill of a detective is to investigate with a practised detachment, isn't it? Not always easy. I agree with you, Penny. I'm tempted to think Dr Lloyd has written these but only because I don't like him either.'

Penny put down her teacup. 'I've just remembered something! When I encountered him outside the *Morning Express* offices yesterday, he quickly put something away in his pocket. Perhaps it was a letter he was planning to deliver there? And when he saw me, he decided to quickly hide it.'

Emma caught her breath. 'Really? Well that could support our theory, couldn't it? Did he explain what he was doing there?'

'He told me he was visiting a friend of his. An editor for a medical publication. But he didn't name the friend or the publication. He kept his explanation suitably vague.'

'It's possible he was telling the truth,' said Emma. 'But I think he's suspicious. We need to find an example of his handwriting.'

'Yes, we do,' said Penny. 'Let's have a think about how we can do that. In the meantime, perhaps we can find out more about the paper. As you've said, it's good quality paper which someone of limited means might struggle to afford.'

Once they'd finished their tea, Emma and Penny searched for a stationer's shop and found one on Vauxhall Bridge Road. A sign in the window read: 'Fashionable Stationery at Lowest Prices'.

The brass bell above the door tinkled as Emma and Penny stepped inside. They were greeted by the smell of ink, paper and sealing wax. Shelves lined the walls from floor to ceiling, stacked with writing paper and envelopes tied in bundles. Cabinets with small labelled drawers stood behind the counter and a glass case displayed an array of pens, letter openers and paper weights.

'Can I help you, ladies?' A bespectacled man appeared from a door behind the counter. He had prominent teeth and wore a smart blue apron.

'I hope so,' said Penny pulling the letters out of her bag. 'We think this letter paper could be quite expensive. Can you tell us what you think?' She handed a sheet to the stationer.

He ran his fingertips over it, rubbed it, then held it up to the light of a gas lamp which hung above the counter. 'Rag paper,' he said. 'Quarto sized with a light cream tint. An unglazed surface which gives a nice biting texture for the pen nib. Quite thick, almost as thick as the papers we sell for commercial use.'

'Commercial?' asked Emma. 'Paper used in offices for example?'

'Yes, this type of paper could be used in an office. Some people buy it for personal use but many people would choose something a little lighter and thinner because it's cheaper.'

'So this paper is expensive?' asked Penny.

'Not enormously expensive, but certainly pricier than many people would usually pay. Let me see what we've got here which is similar...' His eyes narrowed as he glanced over at the shelves. Then he stepped out from behind the counter and beckoned them to follow him to one of the shelves. 'This is similar,' he said. 'Clarendon. It's rag paper which is a little more durable than pulp. It's priced at a shilling for five quires. I don't know what sort of letter paper you ladies prefer, but one of our most popular papers is the Regency Linen at ninepence for five quires. You can feel the difference.' He pulled out a sheet for Emma and Penny to touch.

'Yes it's thinner,' acknowledged Emma.

'And if you're looking for something even thinner then you'd probably choose the Larkspur,' he continued, pulling out another sheet. 'Sixpence for five quires. Good value but not the sort of letter paper you'd use if you wished to create a good impression.'

'Thank you, you've been extremely helpful,' said Penny, clearly keen to stop him going into any greater detail.

'My pleasure.' He paused for a moment, then frowned. 'I hope you don't mind me saying this but I noticed the content of the letter you showed me wasn't entirely... how should I say it... complimentary.'

'You're right,' said Penny. 'It isn't. The sender is anonymous and we're trying to learn more about who they could be. We've learned from you that they like to buy good quality letter paper.'

'They do indeed,' he said. 'Do you mind if I have another look at the letter?'

Penny handed it to him again and Emma watched as he peered closely at it. 'The ink's not quite jet black,' he said. 'More like violet black, I'd say. A popular brand for violet black is Thacker's but there are many more as I'm sure you're aware. It's a confident hand, isn't it? Someone quite accustomed to the written word. A regular letter writer perhaps, as well as someone with a broad vocabulary. What a shame they're writing such unpleasant things.' He handed the letter back to Penny. 'Having met the pair of you, I'd say they were entirely unfounded too.'

'Thank you,' said Penny. 'They are. And we'll find the person who's sending us these letters. They won't remain anonymous for much longer. Paper which is used in an office... that could lead us somewhere.'

Emma wished she shared Penny's confidence.

FIFTY-FOUR

A loud knock at the door startled Agnes Black from sleep. She stirred on the bed, blinking into the darkness. The air was stuffy and stale. Her hand brushed against the half-empty bottle of brandy on the mattress beside her. 'What time is it?' she muttered, her voice hoarse.

Her head ached, she pushed herself upright. The bottle fell onto the floor and she kicked it hastily beneath the bed with her foot.

The knock came again, sharper this time.

'I said just a moment!' she called, trying to keep the irritation from her voice.

She stumbled over to the small chest of drawers and fumbled to light the gas lamp. The flame hissed and flared to life, casting an amber glow over the faded wallpaper and cluttered room. The clock on the wall said half past five.

She ran a hand over her hair, then tugged at her bodice, straightening herself as best she could. Her heart beat faster as she approached the door. Was it the police again? Their repeated visits felt like slow torment. Better they arrest her and be done with it.

But it wasn't the police.

Standing at the door, jaw tight, was Margaret Harwell from St James's.

Agnes's mouth went dry. She opened it to speak but her words came out raspy. 'What do you want?'

'I need to speak to you, Miss Black,' Margaret replied, her tone clipped. 'What do you think I'm here for?'

Agnes glanced past her, down the narrow hallway. 'We can talk in the parlour downstairs.'

'Is it private?'

She hesitated. The landlady's hearing was sharp and her curiosity sharper.

Agnes gave a reluctant nod and stood back. 'Very well. Come in.'

Margaret stepped inside, her nose wrinkling at the musty smell. She remained standing, rigid and composed, while Agnes sat on the edge of the bed, her hands trembling faintly in her lap.

'I've been visited by a pair of ladies on two occasions,' Margaret began. 'Mrs Blakely and Mrs Langley. You know them, I assume?'

Agnes nodded, wary.

'They're trying to solve Mrs Melbourne's murder,' Margaret continued. 'They seem to think they're lady detectives.'

'Yes,' she murmured. 'They think they're quite good at it, don't they?'

'They do. They called on me today. Asking questions about you.'

Agnes looked up sharply.

'It seems,' Margaret said, her eyes narrowing, 'that your shameful little secret is no longer a secret at all, Miss Black.'

Agnes bowed her head. 'How did they find out?'

'I don't know exactly. But ever since your impudent visit to me it seems your past has crept back to haunt you.' Margaret's voice was cool, measured. 'It's reared its ugly head, just as I warned it would.'

Agnes stared at the folds of her dark dress. Her heart pounded, and a deep sense of dread twisted in her stomach. She'd spent years burying the truth. And now it was clawing its way back up.

She looked up at Mrs Harwell. 'But how did they find out? Have you told anyone?'

Mrs Harwell shook her head. 'Of course not. You know I don't go around disclosing the secrets entrusted to me. I may not approve of everything I've seen, Miss Black, but I'm not in the habit of spreading stories. However, you called on me to speak about it recently, so you must have spoken to someone else as well.'

'But I didn't,' said Agnes, panic rising in her voice. 'I only spoke to you. I called on you because I wanted to find out where—'

'Yes, I know exactly why you came,' Mrs Harwell cut in sharply. 'And we are not revisiting all that again. I've told you more than once – it's done with. It's over. Or at least, it should have been. But you couldn't leave it alone. And now, because you stirred the ashes, the smoke's spread. Your little secret is no longer so secret.'

Agnes rubbed her hands across her face, trying to make sense of it. Her thoughts reeled. Who else had ever known? The staff at St James's? The other girls who were incarcerated alongside her? But after all this time – surely they wouldn't have spoken of it?

There was Mrs Melbourne, of course.

And the doctor...

'None of this is my fault,' she muttered, although it sounded weak even to her.

'None of it's your fault?' Mrs Harwell's voice was shrill with disbelief. 'It's all your fault, Miss Black. It was your disgrace, remember? Your shame. You brought this on yourself.'

Fury seized her. She sprang to her feet, anger burning in her chest. She stood taller than the older woman now, and for the first time in years, she felt something powerful stir inside her.

Mrs Harwell instinctively stepped back.

'If people know,' Agnes said coldly, 'then perhaps it's time they knew about you too.'

The other woman's jaw tensed. 'I have no idea what you're talking about.'

'Yes, you do. And so did Mrs Melbourne, didn't she?'

'Mrs Melbourne meddled in other people's business,' Mrs Harwell snapped. 'She took pleasure in other people's suffering and lied to achieve her own end. You know that better than anyone.'

'Yes, she meddled,' said Agnes, her voice now steady. 'And she lied when it suited her. But what she truly relished was holding on to truth. She kept it close and ready to use. It was her weapon. She knew my secret but she also knew yours.'

Mrs Harwell's face had gone pale. She glanced towards the door, then back again, her eyes narrowing. 'I don't know what lies she told you.'

'It wasn't a lie. Your husband's death was sudden, wasn't it? Mrs Melbourne told me you poisoned him.'

The words landed like a slap. Mrs Harwell flinched, recoiling as though struck. 'I did no such thing!' she hissed. 'That was one of her spiteful fabrications, and you're a fool to believe it.'

'Well, if it was a lie,' Agnes said, stepping forward, 'then it doesn't matter if I repeat it, does it?'

Mrs Harwell's face twisted into a grimace of rage and fear. 'You wouldn't dare!'

'Oh, I might.' Agnes kept her voice low. 'You did nothing to save my daughter. You watched me suffer, and now you're here again, trying to shame me once more.'

'You shamed yourself,' Mrs Harwell said, although her voice had lost much of its sharpness.

'And you,' Agnes said coldly, 'are a murderer.'

Mrs Harwell gasped.

'Perhaps,' Agnes continued, 'you didn't stop at your husband. Perhaps you murdered Mrs Melbourne that night too?'

Mrs Harwell stared at her, trembling now, the bag in her hands clutched like a shield.

FIFTY-FIVE

Rain lashed the pavement as Dr Robert Lloyd stepped out of his club that evening.

'This wasn't forecast!' he muttered, blinking up at the downpour. He hadn't thought to bring his umbrella. With a grimace, he tugged his collar high and lowered the brim of his hat, then hurried along Pall Mall in search of a cab.

Carriage wheels sent up arcs of water as they passed, their lamps casting jittery reflections across the shining road. Robert raised a hand, hopeful, but no cab slowed. Up ahead, two figures were already stationed beneath a flickering gas lamp, trying their luck as well.

It was always the same in the rain – scarce cabs and too many people wanting them. Robert muttered under his breath and pressed on towards Trafalgar Square, water seeping into his shoes and his trousers clinging wetly to his legs.

The square was a blur of umbrellas and damp hats, the hiss of rain drowning out conversation. Every cab that passed was occupied, the drivers barely sparing him a glance. Frustration tightened in his chest. He made for Northumberland Avenue, jaw clenched, hand raised with fresh determination. Rain ran from the brim of his hat in steady rivulets.

Then – at last – a cab began to slow. Robert broke into a trot, his heart lifting as he saw the interior was empty.

'Bedford Square!' he called up to the driver, who responded by tugging the lever to release the door. The horse stamped and shook rain from its mane, steam rising from its flanks.

'Excuse me!' came a shout from behind. 'That's our cab!'

Robert ignored it and set a foot on the step.

A hand grabbed his arm.

'Get off!' he snapped, twisting round. Two young men stood glaring at him, both soaked through.

'We've been here twenty minutes!' one of them barked. 'The driver was stopping for us!'

'Nonsense. I've been waiting half an hour.' Robert wrenched free and climbed into the cab, water dripping from his coat.

'You'll regret this!' the second man growled as Robert pulled the door shut.

He thumped the roof. 'Drive on!'

As the cab lurched forward, Robert gave the pair a jaunty wave through the window. 'Regret it, will I?' he said, grinning to himself. 'We'll see about that.'

In Bedford Square, Robert paid the driver and climbed down from the cab. As it pulled away he fumbled in his pocket for his door key, impatient to get out of the rain which drummed on his hat.

Where was the key?

Frustrated, he pulled off his glove so he could feel better in his pocket. Somehow his pocket was damp. How had the rain found its way through his overcoat already? He'd paid a good price for it. He made a note to return to the gentlemen's outfitters and make a complaint. His fingers found the key and he approached the steps to his door, looking forward to having a nightcap before bed.

He forgot about the puddle which collected at the bottom of the steps when it rained. As the cold water soaked his foot, he gave a curse.

Then he heard something. A voice?

He spun round. The light from a nearby gas lamp didn't extend very far. He could just make out the silhouettes of the trees being lashed by rain in the centre of the square.

But was that? A movement?

He squinted at the darkness, trying to find it. Had it been near the railings which enclosed the square?

But there was nothing. As he turned back to his door, he heard something again.

'Excuse me!'

Now the sound was clear.

'Who's there?' he called out, staring into the darkness. He wasn't the sort of man who usually felt afraid, but he could feel the hairs prickling on the back of his neck.

No reply came. Rain drummed down on the square and he could hear the heavy trickle of an overflowing gutter.

Shaking his head, he turned and headed for his front door. Perhaps a drunkard was wandering around the square. Or a tramp wanting money or a bed for the night. He had no time for that. People were responsible for their own fortunes in life. He'd worked hard to get where he had. And then that woman had practically ruined him. But his fortunes would recover, they always did.

As he climbed the steps, the blow from behind sent him tumbling sideways. His arms wheeled, hands grasping at the empty air. He couldn't steady himself. Gravity pulled him back down the steps towards the wet cobbles. Even as his body thudded heavily to the ground, he felt sure he'd manage to get up again.

But the air had left his lungs. And now a dark figure stood over him. As he lay there gasping and helpless, a stream of blood mingled with the rainwater running into the gutter.

FIFTY-SIX

Emma received another letter the following morning. A chill ran through her as she saw the familiar handwriting on the envelope. But this letter had not been delivered by hand. The postmark showed it had been posted in the West End the previous evening.

Was the postmark a clue? Emma reasoned it didn't rule out any of the people she and Penny were considering; Dr Lloyd, Miss Jackson and Mr Ashcroft could all have posted a letter from that location.

Dear Mrs Langley,

I am dismayed to find that my earlier words have had no effect. You persist in meddling, as if you believe yourself above reproach – or above consequence.

Let me be plain: your continued interest in Mrs Melbourne's death is not only improper, it is unwise. You are poking around in matters you do not understand. Curiosity may seem harmless, but it has consequences. Dire ones.

It was written on the same paper as the previous letters. And appeared to be written in the same ink too. Thacker's violet black, the stationer had posited.

Emma crammed the letter back into its envelope. She didn't want to feel troubled by its contents, but she couldn't help herself. Even Mrs Solomon's banal chatter couldn't distract her from her anxious thoughts.

She had some time after breakfast to play the piano. It wasn't long before the music soothed her troubled mind. She'd just begun the second piece when a sudden knock at the front door made her fingers jolt on the keys. A dissonant chord rang out, sharp and ugly. Her breath caught.

Had the anonymous letter writer escalated from threats on paper to a presence on her doorstep?

She strained to hear voices from the hallway.

'Mrs Blakely,' said Mrs Solomon. 'Come on in!' A moment later, she ushered Penny into the parlour.

Relief flooded through Emma. At a time like this, her friend was a welcome sight. She rose from her seat, smoothing her skirts.

Penny's cheeks were flushed and her breath slightly quickened, as though she'd hurried to get here.

'You got another letter too?' Emma asked.

Penny frowned a little. 'No. Have you?'

Emma nodded, noticing her mouth felt dry. 'I thought that's why you were here.'

'No,' said Penny. 'I haven't received any post this morning.' Her expression darkened. 'I'm here to tell you about Dr Lloyd. He's been murdered.'

FIFTY-SEVEN

'So what happened to Dr Lloyd?' Emma asked.

She and Penny sat together in the parlour, each with a cup of tea prepared by Mrs Solomon. The fire crackled gently in the grate, but the comfort of the room couldn't warm the chill that had settled over them.

'He was discovered late last night,' said Penny. 'Just a few yards from his front door in Bedford Square. He'd been stabbed.'

Emma's eyes widened. 'Stabbed? Like Mrs Melbourne?'

'Yes,' Penny confirmed. 'Exactly the same. A long, narrow blade, according to James. It's peculiar, because when I met him the other day, he was describing that very weapon to me. He commented on how unusual it is.' She gave a shudder. 'And now he's a victim of it too! I can't pretend I liked Dr Lloyd – in truth, I found him quite loathsome. But to think I was speaking with him only two days ago, and now...' She trailed off, shaking her head.

'Do you know anything more about the circumstances of his death?' Emma asked.

'Only what James told me. Dr Lloyd had taken a cab home from his club. A passer-by discovered him on the pavement at around midnight.'

'So the killer was lying in wait for him?' Emma suggested.

'That's what James thinks. As you know, there's a garden in the centre of Bedford Square. It's dark at night with no lighting at all. Someone could have been lying in wait there, hidden by the trees. Once the hansom cab moved off, they struck. The driver didn't see a thing.'

Emma took a sip of tea. 'So we can be fairly certain now that Dr Lloyd didn't kill Mrs Melbourne.'

'Yes, quite certain,' said Penny. 'But the motive confuses me. Who could have wanted the pair of them dead?'

'Miss Black?' said Emma. 'She asked him to end her pregnancy but he refused and told Mrs Melbourne. She then sent her to that miserable home for penitents in Fulham.'

'Yes it's easy to understand her motive,' said Penny. 'But if she wanted to take revenge on the pair of them, why wait until now?' She paused to drink her tea. 'It's certainly a puzzle. Anyway, you mentioned you received another anonymous letter. May I see it?'

'Of course, I'll fetch it from my room.'

Emma finished her cup of tea as Penny read the letter then tossed it aside with a sigh. 'It's hardly original, is it?' she commented. 'You'd think they would have come up with something a little different by now.'

'It may not be original,' said Emma. 'But it's very worrying now that Dr Lloyd is dead too.' She felt a shiver run down her back.

Penny nodded. 'Yes it's a stark reminder of what this person is capable of. But we can't let it stop us.'

'I don't want to stop,' said Emma. 'But I'm also very worried about carrying on. This person could harm us! They know where we live.'

Penny gave a visible shudder. 'I don't like to think about it.'

'But don't you think we should? I know we've discussed the risks before but we have to think again about whether they're worth it. This person could break into our homes and—'

Penny raised a palm to stop her. 'I know.'

A pause followed and Penny stared down at the table, biting her lip.

Emma lowered her voice. 'When do we decide enough is enough?' she ventured.

Penny met her gaze. 'We don't.' Her eyes glinted with determination. 'This person has murdered two people now. They have to be stopped. And if we decide now to give up, then they've won, haven't they?'

'It's not about winning or losing,' said Emma. 'We don't have to do this.'

'I disagree. We need to win. Good needs to triumph over evil. I know Mrs Melbourne and Dr Lloyd were flawed people, they weren't even pleasant. But does anyone deserve to die how they did? No. So I do worry about our safety, but I also worry how unsafe this world will become if people are allowed to get away with this. We just have to look after ourselves and our loved ones and... well, hope that with luck and determination we'll get there. But if you want to stop, Emma, then—'

'No, I won't stop. I won't let you do this alone.'

Penny smiled. 'Thank you, Emma.' She picked up the letter again and ran her eyes over it. 'I suppose we can rule Dr Lloyd out as the author of this now. He wasn't the murderer. He seemed likely for a while, didn't he? The type to own some expensive letter paper. Or maybe it was paper he took from his office? But that's irrelevant now... It's unlikely he wrote the letters because I can't see how he would have wanted us to stop our investigations.'

'So that leaves Miss Jackson and Mr Ashford,' said Emma. 'And there's Miss Black and Mrs Harwell too.'

'We hadn't spoken to Miss Black about the murder before the first letter arrived,' said Penny.

'True... but perhaps she heard we were investigating?'

Penny pushed her spectacles up her nose as she gave this some thought. 'It's possible, isn't it? And as for Mrs Harwell, I can certainly imagine her sitting at her desk writing us horrible letters on nice writing paper. I wish now we'd got a closer look at her handwriting when we called on her! There must have been something lying about on her desk which we could have glanced at. How frustrating!'

FIFTY-EIGHT

'So, Dr Lloyd is dead,' said Christopher Ashford, frowning as he studied the article in the *Morning Express*.

'Yes,' said Lydia quietly. 'It's quite shocking, isn't it?'

They were sitting together in Christopher's study. Lydia had read the article that morning and hadn't been able to think of anything else. She had come to speak with Christopher, needing to hear his thoughts and, perhaps, steady her own.

He looked up from the paper, his brow creased. 'Did you ever meet him?'

'I can't remember,' she replied. 'I imagine he must have visited the house when I was working there. He was the Melbourne family's physician, wasn't he? For many years, I believe.'

Christopher nodded. 'Yes, he was. Although I never encountered him myself. And I didn't attend any of the court hearings when my godmother sued him. Still, it's rather unsettling that both of them are dead. And now, in such similar circumstances.'

'They might not have been murdered by the same person,' suggested Lydia.

'They might not have,' he agreed. 'But the similarities are hard to ignore. According to this, he was killed by a single stab wound. Just like my godmother.'

He folded the newspaper and laid it aside. 'It's not as if this sort of murder happens every day in London. And he and my godmother had a long and rather complicated history. They were once close, then fell out publicly. Whoever did this must have known them both.'

Their eyes met, a silent understanding passing between them. Lydia felt an ache stir in her chest. Every time she thought the worst was behind them, something new emerged – some fresh tragedy, another layer of sorrow. First Mrs Melbourne's murder, then the fire.

And now this.

She rose from her chair and moved to his side, sitting on the armrest and slipping her hand into his. He wrapped his arm around her, warm and steady.

'I want this to end,' she said. 'I want all of this behind us. I want us to be free of it. I want us to be happy together, somewhere far away from all of this.'

He looked up at her, his expression soft. 'So do I, Lydia. I can't begin to tell you how happy I am that we found each other again. I thought of you constantly while I was in India.'

Her cheeks coloured. 'Don't say that – you were married.'

'I was. And my wife was a kind and gentle person. But she wasn't you. She never made me feel the way you did.'

Lydia smiled faintly, the familiar flutter of emotion stirring in her chest. 'I thought you'd forgotten about me.'

'How could I?' he said. 'But I was told you'd gone.'

'You believed I was a thief,' she said, the old hurt rising again. She stood and turned away from him. 'You believed I'd behaved disgracefully with a married man.'

'I didn't want to believe it,' he said, rising and moving towards her. 'I was young and confused by the sudden turn in events. I respected my godmother back then. I had no idea what she was capable of.' He reached out, placing his hands gently on her shoulders. 'What matters is that we're here now. And yes, it's been difficult – everything about our reunion has been more complicated than we ever imagined. But we'll get through it. And then we can start thinking about a future. Together.'

She turned to face him. His expression was sincere, his eyes steady on hers. The pain softened just enough for her to smile.

'A future,' she said quietly. 'I'm forty years old, Christopher. We've lost so much time.'

'Then let's not waste another moment,' he said. 'We have time now. And I intend to make the most of every day with you.'

Before she could reply, the sharp chime of the front doorbell cut through the room.

They both stilled.

Lydia glanced at the clock on the mantelpiece. 'Are you expecting someone?'

Christopher shook his head. 'No. Not today. I'll go and see who it is,' he said, striding towards the door.

FIFTY-NINE

Lydia tried not to let her irritation show, but the interruption had come at the worst possible moment. She and Christopher had finally been speaking candidly about their feelings – about the past, about the future – and now here they were, seated stiffly in the sitting room, making polite conversation with Reverend Underhill over tea.

'I've been meaning to call on you for a while, Mr Ashford,' the reverend was saying. He smoothed a hand over his white thinning hair. 'We exchanged a few words at the service for your godmother, and again at her funeral. Naturally, I expected you would move into the house on Upper Belgrave Street, and I was looking forward to welcoming you as a new member of the parish. But, well' – he gave a sombre shake of his head – 'the fire has rather changed everything, hasn't it? I presume you intend to rebuild?'

Christopher gave a polite nod. 'Yes, that's the plan. Although I must confess, Reverend, it was never my intention to live there.' He glanced around the modest but warmly furnished room. 'This place in Fitzrovia may lack the grandeur of Belgravia, but I've grown rather fond of it. It's comfortable and quiet. It suits me.'

The reverend followed Christopher's gaze and offered a measured nod. 'It's a pleasant home, certainly. And, of course, one's comfort is not to be underestimated. Still, it is a pity you won't be joining us in the parish.'

'I appreciate you taking the time to visit nonetheless,' Christopher replied courteously.

The reverend's eyes drifted back to Lydia, curiosity flickering in his expression. Although Christopher had introduced her upon arrival, it was clear the clergyman hadn't quite worked out what to make of her presence. Sensing it, Christopher offered further explanation. 'Miss Jackson worked as a governess for my godmother – many years ago now. We knew one another during that time and, as it happens, we were reacquainted at the memorial service you conducted.'

The reverend's expression softened as comprehension dawned. 'Ah. I see. Well, that certainly explains it.'

Christopher smiled faintly. 'We hadn't seen each other for twenty years. There's been rather a lot to catch up on.'

'Yes, I imagine there has.' The reverend turned to Lydia with a more approving air. 'It's a pleasure to make your acquaintance, Miss Jackson.'

'And you too, Reverend. I have attended a few of your services. I worked briefly for the Brockhurst family in Upper Belgrave Street earlier this year.'

'Did you indeed? Then you're more familiar with me than I am with you,' he said with a genial smile. 'I hold the Brockhursts in high regard. A most respectable family. These recent events must have been deeply unsettling for them – as they have been for us all. First Mrs Melbourne's untimely death, and now the fire... It's quite beyond comprehension.'

He sighed heavily and reached for his handkerchief, dabbing his forehead. 'At times like this, I take comfort in the words of St Paul – the Second Epistle to the Corinthians, chapter four, verse seventeen, "For our light affliction, which is but for a moment, worketh for us a far more exceeding and eternal weight of glory".'

Lydia nodded politely, although the verse struck her as cold comfort. She wasn't sure what affliction the reverend believed they were enduring lightly. Certainly not murder and arson.

'And now there's Dr Lloyd to consider,' said Christopher.

The reverend blinked. 'Dr Lloyd... not the man Mrs Melbourne sued? The surgeon?'

'The same,' said Christopher. 'He was found stabbed outside his home in Bedford Square.'

The reverend sat back with a stunned expression. 'Good gracious. Murdered? When did this happen?'

'Late last night,' said Christopher. 'He'd returned home in a cab, and was found not long after – just a few steps from his front door.'

The reverend shook his head. 'The Lord preserve us. What is the world coming to?'

Lydia fidgeted with her teacup. It wasn't that she disliked the reverend – he seemed a perfectly well-meaning man – but she had little patience for small talk when matters so dark and pressing hovered just beneath the surface. The purpose of his visit seemed thin and she found herself wishing, with growing intensity, that he would take his leave and let her and Christopher return to their interrupted conversation.

'Well, it truly has been a series of tragic events, hasn't it?' said the reverend, folding his hands over the top of his walking stick. 'And I must say, Mr Ashford, I miss your godmother enormously.'

Lydia sipped her tea in silence as the reverend continued to speak warmly of Mrs Melbourne's generous contributions to the church and her involvement in charitable causes. She exchanged a glance with Christopher – his eyes had taken on a faraway look. Clearly, she wasn't the only one eager for the reverend's departure.

'I imagine the pair of you have fond memories of Mrs Melbourne,' the reverend added, looking between them.

Christopher gave a polite nod. 'Yes, of course. She did a great deal for me in my younger years. I was very grateful for her guidance and support.'

Lydia resisted the urge to raise an eyebrow. She knew he didn't mean a word of it. His tone was calm and respectful, but she could sense the practised diplomacy in it.

'Well,' said the reverend. 'I won't keep you any longer. It's been a pleasure to speak with you again, Mr Ashford. And although I know you won't be residing in Upper Belgrave Street after all, I do hope you'll still consider attending services at St Peter's from time to time. It would be a pleasure to see a familiar face in the pews.'

'I'll certainly consider it,' Christopher replied, casting Lydia a sidelong glance. She read it instantly: a shared understanding that he had no intention of doing any such thing.

Lydia stood, smoothing her skirts. The reverend did the same, leaning on his stick for support. 'Mrs Melbourne was a generous lady who touched the lives of so many.' He turned to Lydia. 'You must have fond memories of your time with her, Miss Jackson.'

Lydia hesitated. She wanted to respond graciously as Christopher had done. It was the polite thing to do. The sensible thing. But the words wouldn't come. Too many memories, too much anger, still sat unresolved in her chest.

'I'm afraid I must be honest, Reverend,' she said, her voice even but firm. 'My memories are not particularly fond. When I left Mrs Melbourne's employment, it was under difficult circumstances.'

The reverend's genial expression faltered. 'I see. That is... unfortunate. But I suppose we must accept that not all working arrangements are destined to be harmonious.'

'Indeed.'

'It was very gracious of you to attend her memorial service, despite the disagreements between you.'

Lydia had attended only in the hope of seeing Christopher again. But that wasn't something she could admit aloud. She swallowed. 'That's right. I believe in forgiveness.'

The reverend's face lit up with something close to reverence. 'Ah! Forgiveness. Quite so. "And be ye kind one to another, tender-hearted, forgiving one another, even as God for Christ's sake hath forgiven you." Ephesians, chapter four, verse thirty-two.' He beamed, clearly pleased with her answer and his response.

Lydia returned his smile, feeling guilty about her lie.

SIXTY

'What time are they all arriving?' asked James, watching as Penny adjusted the final piece of cutlery on the dining table.

'Eight o'clock,' she replied, glancing up. Then, noticing the slight downward tug of his mouth, she walked over and took his hands in hers. 'You don't seem particularly enthusiastic, James.'

He gave a sigh. 'It's been a busy day and it looks like the Yard is going to get involved with the murders of Mrs Melbourne and Dr Lloyd.'

'That's excellent news! And your help is much needed, James. Inspector Paget hasn't exactly made a lot of progress, has he?'

'It's a complicated case. And these letters you've been receiving bother me.'

Penny adjusted the position of a wine glass and said nothing. The letters bothered her too but she didn't want to think about them too much. The thought that the killer could turn up on her doorstep was terrifying. And as for the children...

She straightened herself and tried, once again, to bury her fears. If she listened to them too much, she'd never do anything.

'Why do the letters bother you?' she asked her husband.

'Isn't it obvious? They're threatening and the author knows where you live.'

'The author may not be the killer, James.'

He gave a laugh. 'I don't think anyone is writing those letters for their own amusement.' He stepped forward and took her hands in his. 'This person wants you to stay away. They want you to stop.'

She looked up into his eyes, instantly feeling reassured by the warmth and protectiveness in them. 'I've received nasty letters before.'

'I know.'

'And so have you.'

'Yes, I have.'

'I can't pretend they don't worry me, James. But I'm trying not to think about them too much. They're a sign we're on the right track...'

He smiled. 'That excuse again. I've used it myself.'

'So you understand, don't you?' She lifted a hand and rested it against his cheek.

'Of course I understand, Penny! But as your husband, I worry enormously.'

'I know. And as soon as we catch this person, it will all stop.' She smiled. 'We'll be safe again.'

He sighed. 'I suppose I feel a little better now the Yard is involved.'

'Good.' She leaned in and kissed him. 'And we can have a nice evening where we forget about it all for a few hours.'

His shoulders slumped a little. 'I don't mind seeing people. But hosting... it can be rather exhausting, can't it?'

'I've only invited four guests. Emma Langley, Francis Edwards, and Mr and Mrs Clifton. That's hardly a banquet.'

'The last time Francis Edwards was here, he and I ended up in a quarrel.'

Penny gave a patient sigh. Francis had mentioned the same thing. 'It wasn't exactly a quarrel, was it? Just a spirited disagreement about whether Sir Francis Drake was a hero or a pirate.'

'The trouble with Francis is that he considers himself an expert on every subject there is. Just because he works in a library.'

'He does have a mind like an encyclopaedia,' Penny agreed. 'But your brain is just as busy – and far more practical, might I add. Francis may be able to recite the dates of every Tudor battle, but you're the one who actually catches criminals.'

James's mouth twitched into a smile. 'Very tactfully said.'

She returned his smile and leaned in to kiss him. Tact was something she'd had to practise when the two men had been competing for her affections.

She drifted over to the table to lift and refold a serviette. James folded his arms and leaned against the sideboard. 'So if there's a risk of another spirited disagreement, I should diplomatically steer the conversation elsewhere?'

'Yes, I think that would be a wise strategy.' She straightened the serviette with care. 'I'd like everyone to feel welcome. And I would like my husband to enjoy himself.'

'I'll do my best,' said James.

She stepped back and admired the table, pleased with the arrangement of silver cutlery, polished glassware and their best crockery. Everything gleamed beneath the soft light of the gas lamp.

'The table looks good,' she said. She glanced down at her plain dress and winced. 'But I don't. And I've got about ten minutes to get ready before everyone arrives.'

'Really? I think you look lovely, Penny. There's no need to change.'

She gave him another quick kiss. 'Thank you, James. But I feel quite sure someone's going to notice Florence's dribble on my shoulder.'

The drinks before dinner went well. Clara Clifton seemed at ease and wore a stylish dark violet bustle dress. Her husband, Jonathan, had a thick dark moustache and a polite manner about him. He worked as a senior clerk in an insurance company but he was also a member of the Metropolitan Public Gardens Committee.

Discussion of Clara's work arose at the dinner table as everyone enjoyed their soup course.

'How did you find yourself in such an unusual occupation?' James asked her.

'I've always been interested in how London's neighbourhoods can be improved,' she replied. 'And when I heard about the work of the Metropolitan Public Gardens Committee, I realised I could do something to contribute.'

'I can't say it's something I would enjoy,' added her husband. 'Disused graveyards are dismal places. I may be on the committee but I leave the surveys to Clara.'

'It's lovely to see the graveyards turned into something beautiful,' said Clara. 'Such as the lovely little park which has recently been created from an old burial ground of St John's Priory in Clerkenwell.'

'That sounds like a nice place to visit,' said Emma.

'It is,' said Clara, her eyes bright with enthusiasm. 'And I'm not the first person to survey London's graveyards. It was done fifty years ago by a doctor, George Alfred Walker.'

Francis gave a knowing nod. '*Gatherings from Graveyards*,' he said. 'That was the book he published. "A detail of dangerous and fatal results produced by the unwise and revolting custom of inhuming the dead in the midst of the living."'

Clara gave a little laugh of delight. 'You can recall the subtitle of the book too, Mr Edwards?'

James glanced at Penny with a raised eyebrow. She chose not to respond.

'I don't think it's the full subtitle,' said Francis. 'But George Walker really didn't like the idea of everyone being buried in crypts and churchyards, did he?'

'No,' said Clara. 'And although it would be improper to go into details at dinner, his work helped influence the Burial Act of 1853 which gave the Home Secretary powers to close overused and hazardous burial grounds.'

Francis nodded enthusiastically. 'Such an important act. And we also now have the Disused Burial Grounds Act which prohibits building on any disused burial ground.'

'That's right,' said Clara with a grin, clearly impressed by his knowledge. 'It was passed just five years ago and work needs to be done on implementing it because some unscrupulous builders are doing their best to ignore it.'

'Excuse me a moment,' said her husband. He pointed his soup spoon in Francis's direction. 'How do you know all this, Mr Edwards?'

'He's a walking encyclopaedia,' said James. Penny shot him a sharp stare.

'I'm a librarian,' said Francis. 'And my days are spent surrounded by books in the reading room of the British Museum. I suppose information just... soaks in.'

Discussion about Clara's work continued with Francis contributing thoughtful facts and information. The more he spoke, the more impressed she became. Penny noticed her husband growing silent and sullen.

As they dined on chicken in white wine sauce, Penny leaned forward to involve him in the conversation. 'Which insurance company do you work for, Mr Clifton?'

'Harwell Insurance,' he replied. 'We're just about to move into new purpose-built offices.'

'Are you indeed?' said James. 'Fascinating.'

Although he probably hadn't intended it to, his comment had a tone of sarcasm. Penny gave him another look, willing him to come up with something more constructive.

'Harwell Insurance?' said Emma. 'Could that be anything to do with Mrs Harwell at the St James's Diocesan Home for Penitents in Fulham?'

Mr Clifton gave a shrug. 'I don't know I'm afraid.'

'The chairlady of the charity is Margaret Harwell,' continued Emma. 'She's a widow. I wonder if she was married to the founder of Harwell Insurance?'

'She may have been. Mr Samuel Harwell died about five years

ago. As I recall, his death was sudden and unexpected. And now that I think about it... I'm sure I've heard mention that his widow is a keen philanthropist.'

Penny and Emma shared an excited glance.

'Why do you ask?' added Mr Clifton.

'Margaret Harwell was with Mrs Melbourne on the night she died,' replied Penny.

'Goodness,' said Clara. 'So my husband works for a company which was owned by the husband of Mrs Melbourne's friend. I never realised that until now. What could it mean?'

'That's a good question,' said James, scratching his head.

SIXTY-ONE

The dinner conversation turned to the murder of Mrs Melbourne and Dr Lloyd. Penny realised it wasn't a relaxing evening for James after he'd spent the day discussing the case with his colleagues. However, it was a conversation which everyone seemed keen to take part in so she dared not change the subject again.

'The housekeeper, Agnes Black, seems particularly suspicious to me,' said James. 'It's believed she started the fire to destroy evidence she'd murdered her employer.'

'An entire house fire to destroy evidence?' said Francis. 'That seems quite extreme.'

'Someone could have destroyed the house to spite Christopher Ashford,' said Emma. 'They felt resentful he'd inherited it.'

'And it could still have been Miss Black for that reason too,' said James.

Penny nodded in agreement. The former housekeeper seemed to have a nervous disposition and her tragic past could have pushed her to emotional excess.

'I was recalling my encounters with Mrs Melbourne while I was sitting in the garden in Clerkenwell recently,' said Clara. Everyone listened as she recounted the two committee meetings when Mrs Melbourne had offered to make a large donation in return for public recognition.

'She had presence,' Clara said. 'And a sense of entitlement. When she didn't get what she wanted, she could be... unpleasant. Not outwardly cruel, just... cold. Cutting. She made it very clear that she expected to be rewarded for her generosity.'

'Did she threaten anyone?' James asked.

'No. Nothing as obvious as that. But the chairman of the meeting was flustered. And she was dismissive of the process, of the committee. Of the people around her. When it became clear at the second meeting that her suggestion wouldn't be accepted, she told us we'd regret humiliating her. That we'd be sorry for turning her down. And I remember she mentioned Dr Lloyd, and said we should all know what happened to him. The implication was clear – she believed she'd ruined him, and that she was capable of doing the same to any of us. She mentioned someone else who was going to get his comeuppance too, I don't know who he was. Another doctor maybe. I think his name was Thornwood.'

Emma jolted. 'Arthur Thornwood?'

'Yes. I think that's right. Arthur Thornwood.'

Emma turned to Penny. 'That's the name we found in the papers in the stationery box.'

Penny nodded slowly. 'Yes, it is.' She turned to Clara. 'And she didn't explain who he was?'

Clara shook her head. 'No. She said his name as though we were all supposed to know. But I didn't. I don't think any of us did. The way she said it, though – it stayed with me. Perhaps she mentioned other names too, but her outburst was so sudden, so theatrical, it all blurred together.'

'When was this?' Penny asked.

'Late November, I believe.'

'Arthur Thornwood,' Penny said, turning to James then Francis. 'We've come across the name twice now. We really need to find out who he is.'

A knock sounded at the door. Penny glanced at the clock; it was half past nine. 'Who on earth can that be?'

SIXTY-TWO

James went to the door and returned moments later with Margaret Harwell. She wore a black fur-trimmed coat with a matching hat.

'Oh, I see you're entertaining,' she said curtly. 'I'm sorry to interrupt but this won't take long. I'd like to speak to you, Mrs Blakely, and you, Mrs Langley. And Mr Blakely too, as you're an inspector at the Yard.'

Penny felt a surge of indigence at the manner in which Mrs Harwell was conducting herself. She got to her feet. 'You're interrupting our dinner!'

'And you'll find it worth your while when you hear what I've got to tell you, Mrs Blakely. I've decided it's time to finally speak up.'

Penny glanced at Emma whose eyebrows were raised in shock and surprise.

'If it's important, Penny, then we don't mind at all,' said Francis.

'Absolutely,' added Clara. 'We can talk between ourselves.'

'Very well.' Penny sighed. She felt happy her friends were understanding but the rudeness of Mrs Harwell astounded her. 'We'll go into the sitting room,' she said. 'And this can't take long.'

Mrs Harwell sat herself in James's armchair. Penny caught

James's gaze and rolled her eyes. He seemed keen in hearing what their visitor had to say, however.

'Ever since you called on me,' said Mrs Harwell, 'I've been thinking about this. And the more I think, the more I realise – I believe Agnes Black should be arrested for Mrs Melbourne's murder.'

James regarded her with quiet scrutiny. 'What makes you say that?' he asked. 'What evidence do you have that she could even be involved?'

'She found something out recently,' Mrs Harwell said, lifting her chin. 'Something which greatly upset her. I should have said something earlier... It's not easy, speaking of things like this. But I can see now that they may be... relevant.'

James leaned forward. 'What did she find out?'

Mrs Harwell paused, then turned her eyes to Penny. 'Mrs Blakely and Mrs Langley already know some of this. Miss Black was admitted to the St James's Diocesan Home when she was sixteen,' she said. 'At the time, she was pregnant. She gave birth to a baby girl – frail at first, but she survived.'

James's expression softened slightly, though his tone remained steady. 'And what happened to the child?'

'She was put up for adoption, as was customary,' said Mrs Harwell. 'The children are always adopted by good families, people with means. It's the best for everyone. However, I am occasionally visited by mothers and people who were born at the home for news. I refuse. It isn't appropriate. Our policy is to sever the ties completely. It's the only way to protect all parties involved.'

'Do you stay in contact with the adoptive families?' Penny asked.

'Not formally,' said Mrs Harwell. 'But sometimes – very occasionally – we might learn how a child is faring, especially if they live nearby. Even then, we never share that information. The children are told they were born into loving homes. And the mothers must accept that. They must be thankful.'

'And if they're not thankful?' ventured Penny.

'Then they're ungrateful,' Mrs Harwell said. 'Miss Black should have been grateful. But no – after all these years, she came to me asking questions. She wanted to know what became of her child. And that's when I realised she'd never truly forgotten. I warned her she was stirring up the past. A past that should've remained buried. I fear that discovery unmoored her. It changed her. She wasn't the same afterwards.'

'What do you mean?' asked Emma.

'In Miss Black's case,' Mrs Harwell continued, her voice hardening, 'the child was rather unlucky.'

A sinking feeling swept through Penny. 'Oh no,' she muttered. 'What happened?'

'She died,' said Mrs Harwell curtly. 'Six months after being adopted, the baby succumbed to measles. She was laid to rest in the burial ground behind the home.'

The weight of her words knocked the air from the room. Penny's throat tightened. 'Did you tell Miss Black that?' she asked, almost afraid to hear the answer.

'No! Of course not.' Mrs Harwell hesitated. 'Well... not at the time. But a few months ago, she came to see me. She turned up at the home quite unexpectedly – something I never relish, but it happens. She told me she wanted to find her daughter – thirty years old by now, she said. For all those years, she had believed the child was alive and thriving.'

'Because that's what you told her,' said James. His voice was low and cool with restrained anger.

'Yes. As we always do. Mrs Melbourne told her the same. It's what we must say. There's no alternative, is there?' Mrs Harwell gave a tight shrug. 'But Miss Black was persistent. She wouldn't take no for an answer. I warned her not to dwell in the past, but she wouldn't let it rest. And I'm afraid... well, in the end, I told her the truth.'

Penny exhaled slowly. 'You told her the baby had died.'

Mrs Harwell nodded. 'I wish now I'd lied. I wish I'd said the girl had moved abroad or changed her name. But I didn't. She was pressing me for answers, and I wanted her gone. So I told her.'

She looked down at the gloves in her hands for a moment. 'I've seen grief before, Mrs Blakely. Plenty of it. But I've never seen anything like that. She didn't cry or scream. She just collapsed. Fell to the floor and made these terrible sounds – like an animal. It was... unnerving.'

Penny had to press a handkerchief to her mouth, trying to steady herself. She thought of her own children. Of the fierce, protective love she carried for them. And then she thought of Miss Black, clutching to hope for thirty years, only to learn her baby had died alone, a stranger, half a lifetime ago. Her heart ached for her.

James, quiet beside her, rested a comforting hand on her arm. Neither spoke.

When Penny recovered herself, she noticed Mrs Harwell still staring down at her hands. Her expression was unreadable.

'Now you understand,' Mrs Harwell said at last. 'That sort of news could drive a woman to do something terrible. And I believe that's exactly what happened. She took her revenge.'

'On Mrs Melbourne?' James asked, puzzled. 'Why?'

'Because Mrs Melbourne was the one who brought her to the home. She was the one who insisted on it. It was the right thing to do, of course – any sensible woman would have done the same. But Miss Black never forgot. And even though Mrs Melbourne took her back afterwards, gave her a position, a wage, a roof over her head – it wasn't enough. Not in Miss Black's eyes.' She gave a shrug. 'Miss Black blamed her. All these years later, when that final hope was taken from her, she blamed the woman who had sent her away in the first place. That's why I believe she killed her.'

James remained silent, studying Mrs Harwell.

'And the fire?' Penny said. 'Do you think Miss Black could have started it?'

'Oh absolutely. The woman has been slowly falling to pieces in recent weeks. She's losing her mind. I called on her yesterday and she was drunk. At half past five in the evening!' She shook her head. 'Such a shame.' She turned to James. 'I think you will need to arrest her, Inspector. Murder... arson... and let's not forget Dr Lloyd.'

'What did Miss Black have to do with him?' asked James.

'She asked him for help and he refused. As he quite rightly should have done. So if you ask me my opinion on the matter, Inspector, I'd say she murdered him too.'

'What an unlikeable woman,' said James after Mrs Harwell had left. 'But we can't ignore what she's told us, can we?'

'No,' said Penny. She still felt saddened by Agnes Black's tragic story.

'I'll speak to Miss Black tomorrow,' said James. 'And I'll ask Paget to accompany me.'

SIXTY-THREE

'You're popular this morning, Mrs Langley,' said Mrs Solomon, handing her a pile of post at the breakfast table.

Emma's heart sank when she saw the handwriting on the envelopes. She flicked through them. There were eight in total.

Eight malicious letters. It would have taken someone a long time to write them all and address each individual envelope. They were clearly desperate to unsettle her.

'Aren't you going to open them?' asked her landlady, her expression curious.

'I will shortly,' said Emma, biting into a slice of toast. Her appetite had gone and her stomach gave an uncomfortable twist. She chewed the piece of toast, struggling to swallow it. When she finally did so, it stuck in her throat.

Mrs Solomon gave her a sidelong glance as Emma attempted to wash the ball of toast down with a mouthful of tea. She felt hot and uncomfortable.

Keen to present a calm appearance, she nibbled another piece of toast. But it was hard to swallow as her heart pounded so fiercely in her chest. Her palms felt damp and her fingers trembled.

She took another bite and tried to slow her quick, shallow

breaths. It was impossible to eat at a time like this. Consuming the half-eaten toast on her plate was becoming a feat of endurance.

'More tea?' asked Mrs Solomon, giving her another curious glance.

'No, thank you.' Emma had to admit defeat. 'I'm sorry, I can't finish my toast.'

'Oh don't worry about that. You appear to have come over all queer. Do you feel faint?'

'Yes, I do.' Emma excused herself from the table and picked up the letters.

'Have a lie down,' said her landlady. 'That will help.'

Emma left the dining room, clutching the letters in her hand. She didn't want to read the letters but... then again, she did. There had to be more clues which the author had inadvertently left in them. Some personal information, perhaps. A turn of phrase which she'd heard before.

Eight letters. Surely a sane person wouldn't write so many? It could be a sign the killer was getting more desperate – losing their grip on reality. Descending into madness, even.

The thought was chilling.

SIXTY-FOUR

Penny made her way to the reading room at the British Museum. James planned to interview Agnes Black and she felt hopeful he would get closer to the truth.

Emma was teaching but had told Penny she would join her in the reading room as soon as she could.

Even if Agnes Black was the murderer Penny was determined to find Arthur Thornwood. Her instincts told her he knew something. It would be no small task locating him, though Francis had offered to help.

As the omnibus rattled through the streets, Penny turned her mind to the fragments of words Emma had managed to salvage from Mrs Melbourne's ruined papers. "Remember me?" The phrase lingered in her mind. If it referred to Arthur Thornwood, then he must have been someone from Mrs Melbourne's past – perhaps someone she had known long ago and, for some reason, never forgotten.

Then there was the mention of Africa. That, Penny found concerning. If Arthur Thornwood was living somewhere on that vast continent, finding him would be next to impossible. But had Mrs Melbourne ever been to Africa? There had been no indication she had travelled that far.

She mentally sifted through the other words Emma had noted – stole, truth, secret. What had been stolen? And by whom? Had someone kept a secret from Mrs Melbourne, or had she been the one concealing something?

And yet, there was also the very real possibility that Arthur Thornwood had nothing at all to do with her murder. The letter – if it even was a letter – remained a mystery. Had Mrs Melbourne written it, intending to send it? Or was it something she had received from someone else? Could it have been a draft, a message she had struggled to put into words but never sent?

The questions spun in Penny's mind, each thought tangling with the next until she feared she might lose her train of thought entirely.

'Hello, Penny.' Francis whispered the greeting warmly. 'Thank you for dinner last night.'

'It was a pleasure. I apologise for the interruption.'

'Don't worry. It was still an enjoyable evening. Let's get to work, shall we?'

Penny pulled the Post Office Directory from the shelf and turned to the listings under Thornwood. Her heart sank as she scanned the seemingly endless list of names. Even when she limited her search to those with the initial A, there were still far too many to sift through easily.

She frowned in thought. From what she knew, Mrs Melbourne had lived in both Putney and Belgravia. That was something, at least. For now, she methodically noted down every A. Thornwood she could find in those areas, though it was impossible to tell which – if any – was the Arthur she sought.

It was frustratingly inconclusive. She needed another approach.

'If Arthur Thornwood is a man of any importance,' said Francis, 'he might be listed in *Debrett's Peerage* or another directory of note. Failing that, we could try the electoral register.'

'Now that's a good point,' Penny said, her spirits lifting. 'If he owns property, he could be listed there.'

'Do you know anything else about him? His age, profession, any connection beyond his name?'

Penny exhaled. 'Nothing. Just Arthur Thornwood. No address, no occupation, not even a rough idea of how old he is.'

Francis chuckled, shaking his head. 'Penny, I think this might be one of our most obscure searches yet.'

She grinned. 'Quite possibly. But you know how much I enjoy a challenge.'

Francis disappeared for a short while and returned carrying two thick volumes, setting them down on the desk with a satisfying thud.

'This one,' he said, patting the first book, 'is the Register of Persons Entitled to Vote in the City of Westminster. It covers Belgravia. And this other one here,' he added, lifting the second volume, 'includes the Wandsworth district, which covers Putney.'

'Thank you, Francis.' Penny wasted no time opening the Westminster register, pleased to see that it listed both first names and surnames. But as she flipped through the pages, she quickly realised the register was organised by street rather than by name.

She sighed. 'Goodness, this is going to take a while.'

Francis sat beside her and helped with the search.

'I think this could be him,' Penny said after a while, tapping her finger on the page. 'There's an Arthur Thornwood listed on Albert Street in Belgravia. Do you know where that is?'

Francis leaned over to glance at the entry. 'Albert Street?' He frowned. 'Not off the top of my head. But give me a moment – I'll fetch a map.'

He returned moments later, unfolding a large sheet of paper across the desk. 'This is an Ordnance Survey map,' he explained. 'Scale of six inches to a mile. We should be able to find it on here.'

Together, they scanned the intricate web of streets. 'Mrs Melbourne lived here,' Penny said, tracing her finger over Upper Belgrave Street. 'If Albert Street is in Belgravia, it can't be far.'

'Exactly,' Francis agreed. 'Belgravia isn't that big – surely it should be easy to find.'

But as they continued searching, Albert Street remained elusive. Penny paused, slipping off her spectacles to wipe them with her handkerchief. Was this even worth the effort? Was Arthur Thornwood truly the key to uncovering the truth?

'Here it is,' Francis said in a triumphant whisper.

Penny leaned in as he pointed to a narrow little street tucked between Lower Grosvenor Place and Victoria Square.

'Oh, well done, Francis!' she said, smiling. 'That was extremely well spotted. Now all that's left is to pay him a visit and find out whether he knew Mrs Melbourne.'

SIXTY-FIVE

Emma reached the reading room just as Penny was leaving.

'What good timing!' said Penny. She looked bright and cheery, not at all weary from their late night.

'Have you found out who Arthur Thornwood is?' Emma asked.

'Yes.' Penny grinned and patted her bag. 'I've written his address in my notebook.'

'Excellent! That was quick.' Emma felt relieved to hear some good news.

She and Penny opened the letters as they travelled by omnibus to Victoria.

'Oh dear,' said Penny, reading the first one. 'More of the same I'm afraid.'

Emma opened the next one and skimmed her eyes quickly over the words to protect herself from their full impact. 'What a sad, desperate person they must be,' she said.

'I'm so sorry you've received these, Emma.' Penny rested a hand on her arm. 'The person who wrote them doesn't know you. They're just trying to frighten you.'

Emma nodded, tears pricking the backs of her eyes. 'I realise that,' she said. 'But as much as I try to not let the words bother me...' She trailed off, worried she might cry if she said anything else.

'I know,' said Penny. 'I'll read the last one and then we'll put them away and forget about them.'

She picked up the final envelope. And although she approached the task with nonchalance, the brief look of horror on her face betrayed the letter's contents.

'What does it say?' asked Emma.

'It's just nonsense.'

'I know but I still want to read it.'

'You don't...'

Emma held out her hand for the letter and Penny reluctantly handed it to her. It contained just a few words:

I am watching you.

Emma's blood chilled. Was it true? She glanced around the lower deck of the omnibus as if the author of the letter could be there right now.

'It's just a lie,' said Penny.

'But you don't know that for sure, do you?'

'We can't let this person upset us.'

They disembarked at Victoria station and made the short walk to Albert Street.

'Thank you for hosting dinner last night,' Emma said. 'I really enjoyed it.'

'Good.' Penny smiled. 'We didn't really stay off the topic of the investigation, did we? But it was interesting to discuss it. Until Margaret Harwell interrupted! It will be interesting to see if her accusation of Agnes Black has any substance to it.'

'Yes, I'm looking forward to finding out. And I've been thinking about Clara...'

'In what sense?'

'It was nice to see her last night and I think she spoke frankly and honestly. I realise she wasn't immediately truthful with us but I don't think she's suspicious either. I think she held back some information because she was being cautious.'

'Because she didn't want to be arrested by Inspector Paget,' added Penny. 'I agree with you, Emma. I like to think I can trust Clara. I don't think she's suspicious.'

They reached Albert Street. The narrow lane was wedged between the grand terraces of Belgravia and the modest streets of Victoria. Nearby stood the wall of the Royal Mews with the gardens of Buckingham Palace just beyond it.

'Hopefully, Mr Thornwood will have some answers for us,' said Penny as they approached the address.

The house they sought was a modest, three-storey building squeezed between two slightly more well-kept properties. Penny knocked, and they waited. Moments later, the door creaked open to reveal a man of about sixty. His greying hair curled slightly at the edges, and thick muttonchop whiskers framed his face. He wore a woollen jacket, its elbows patched with care, and a pair of spectacles perched on the end of his nose. He peered at them in puzzlement.

'Mr Thornwood?' asked Penny. 'Arthur Thornwood?'

'Yes? What is it?' he asked gruffly.

'We're sorry for disturbing you.' She offered a polite smile. 'We'd like to ask you about Mrs Melbourne.'

His bushy eyebrows lifted slightly. 'Mrs Melbourne? Who's she?'

'She was a lady who lived near here, on Upper Belgrave Street,' Penny explained. 'She was murdered recently, and her body was found in St Anne's churchyard in Soho.'

Recognition flickered across his face. 'Ah, yes. I remember reading about that now.' He adjusted his spectacles. 'But why would you want to speak to me about her? Who are you?'

Penny briefly explained their connection to the case, how a

friend was under suspicion, and their efforts to prove her innocence. As she spoke, the man's brow furrowed deeply.

'I see,' he said slowly. 'But I don't see what that's got to do with me.'

'We discovered some of Mrs Melbourne's papers,' Penny said. 'Among them, the name Arthur Thornwood was mentioned.'

His frown deepened. 'She mentioned me? That's odd – I never even knew the woman.'

Emma studied his face, watching closely for any flicker of dishonesty. Yet his puzzled expression and unwavering tone made her feel almost certain he was telling the truth.

'Are you sure you didn't know her many years ago?' Penny pressed.

'Quite sure.'

'She married a textile manufacturer – Patrick Melbourne.'

He shook his head. 'Never heard of him.'

'They were married about forty years ago,' Penny continued, undeterred. 'Before that, she lived in Putney.'

Another shake of the head. His lower lip jutted out slightly, as though in emphasis. 'No, sorry. Are you sure you've got the right Arthur Thornwood?'

'Well, I can't be completely certain,' Penny admitted. 'We found the name, you see—'

'Yes, you've explained that,' he interrupted. 'But I'd wager there's more than one Arthur Thornwood in London. I read about that poor lady's death in the papers, but I swear I never set eyes on her in my life. Even years ago. My memory's still sharp, and I'd know if I had ever had any dealings with her.' He paused before adding firmly, 'You must be looking for another Arthur Thornwood. I don't know anyone else by my name, so I'm afraid I can't help you.'

Emma felt a weight of disappointment settle over her.

'Well, thank you for your time, Mr Thornwood,' Penny said. 'Apologies for troubling you.'

'Not at all,' he said, although he looked mildly bemused. 'I hope you find the fellow you're looking for.'

'So do we.'

They took their leave, walking briskly back towards the main street.

'I really thought the name Arthur Thornwood would lead us somewhere,' said Emma.

'It might do,' Penny said. 'Once we find the right gentleman.'

Clara Clifton pressed a gloved hand against the heavy oak door of St Anne's Church and slipped inside. The outside world – clamorous, chaotic – was swallowed the moment the door closed behind her. Silence met her, solemn and complete, broken only by the distant creak of old wood and the faint rustle of fabric in the pews.

Coloured light spilled from the arched stained-glass window above the altar, casting fragments of crimson and gold across the flagstones. Clara paused in the nave, letting her eyes adjust to the dim interior. The air smelled faintly of incense and old stone.

Her footsteps echoed down the central aisle; she eased her pace, conscious of disturbing the stillness. A few figures knelt in silent prayer, their heads bowed.

Near the altar, Clara hesitated, scanning the shadows for someone to speak to. From the gloom beyond the choir stalls, a robed figure emerged, his movement soundless, almost spectral.

'Mrs Clifton, isn't it?' he said, his voice gentle and low. 'It's good to see you again. How may I assist you?'

Clara offered a polite nod. 'Hello, Reverend. I'm looking for a gentleman by the name of Arthur Thornwood. I wondered if you might know of him.'

SIXTY-SIX

James looked weary when he returned home that evening.

With Florence in her arms, Penny watched as her husband sank into his armchair and pinched the bridge of his nose with thumb and forefinger.

'How did you get on with Agnes Black?'

James exhaled slowly, his eyes still closed. 'I'm discovering it's one woman's word against another's.'

He sat forward and rubbed his hands together as though trying to summon energy. 'Most of what Mrs Harwell told us last night was true; Miss Black confirmed it. Although it was obviously difficult for her. She became quite emotional, and I don't blame her. It's clear she's carried this shame for years.'

'Do you think she murdered Mrs Melbourne and Dr Lloyd?'

'I don't know yet. She certainly had a strong motive. But... she had some rather surprising things to say about Mrs Harwell.'

Penny raised an eyebrow. 'Surprising in what way?'

James met her gaze. 'Apparently, Mrs Melbourne believed Mrs Harwell had poisoned her husband.'

Penny gave a laugh. 'What? That sounds utterly absurd.'

'I thought so too,' James admitted. 'At first, I assumed it was just a desperate counter-accusation – something Agnes Black had clung to in order to discredit Mrs Harwell. But the more I looked into it, the stranger it became.'

He leaned back. 'Samuel Harwell died five years ago. I managed to find the doctor who treated him in the weeks before he died. The man said Harwell had consulted him several times. He was complaining of lethargy, persistent nausea, stomach discomfort... nothing very specific. The cause remained unclear.'

'And then he died?'

'Yes. Just a few weeks later.'

'What was listed as the cause of death?'

'Heart failure. He was sixty-four. It wasn't questioned – at least, not formally.'

'Did the same doctor certify the death?' Penny asked, intrigued now.

'No, and that's the peculiar part. Mrs Harwell summoned a different doctor when she found her husband unresponsive at home one evening. Someone who hadn't seen him before. He examined the body, presumed heart failure and signed the certificate.'

Penny frowned. 'How convenient.'

'That's what I thought. So I asked the original doctor whether he now believed poisoning could explain the symptoms. He said yes – it was plausible. Arsenic or another slow-acting toxin. He admitted it had never crossed his mind at the time.'

Penny let out a low breath. 'So no one suspected anything, and nothing was ever investigated.'

'Exactly. There was no post-mortem. No reason to doubt the widow. Everything appeared above board.'

'But if Mrs Melbourne did suspect her...'

'Then she may have been right,' said James. 'And if she confronted Mrs Harwell about it – or even hinted that she knew – it would certainly give Mrs Harwell a motive.'

'And now Agnes Black says Mrs Melbourne told her about the poisoning. Which means... Mrs Harwell had a secret to protect.'

James nodded grimly.

'What will you do?' Penny asked him.

'I plan to speak with Mrs Harwell tomorrow. I'll ask her directly about her husband's death and see what she's willing to reveal.'

'And if you do believe she poisoned him?' Penny asked softly.

'We can search for evidence.'

Penny pulled a grimace, knowing what this meant. 'An exhumation?'

'I'm afraid so. And let's consider the facts of that evening again, Mrs Harwell was one of the last people to see Eleanor Melbourne alive. And she certainly had reason to silence her.'

SIXTY-SEVEN

'Mrs Harwell poisoned her husband?' said Emma at lunch the following day.

'Apparently so,' said Penny, tucking into her consommé au riz in the ladies' dining room at Café Monico. 'Hopefully James is finding out more as we speak.'

Emma paused from eating and gave a slow exhale. 'So Miss Black and Mrs Harwell are both keen to blame each other. Surely this is little more than a long-held grudge between them?'

'It could be,' said Penny. 'And we need to remember there are other people to consider. Lydia Jackson and Christopher Ashford.'

'It seems Mrs Melbourne deliberately separated them. She told people Miss Jackson had stolen from her and claimed she'd disgraced herself with a married gentleman. Why don't we ask Miss Jackson about it?'

Penny bit her lip. 'She won't like it.'

'No, she won't. But she and Mr Ashford have got away with being secretive, haven't they? You'd think Mr Ashford would want to do more to find his godmother's murderer but instead he merely comes up with polite platitudes.'

Penny rested down her knife and fork. 'That's a very good

point,' she said. 'Perhaps he's doing so to protect Lydia Jackson? Perhaps he doesn't want to find his godmother's murderer because the murderer is the woman he loves?

SIXTY-EIGHT

Margaret Harwell sat in the dingy interview room at Vine Street police station. The air was stale and heavy, the gaslight casting thin, wavering shadows on the peeling walls. Opposite her sat Inspector Paget, his face lined and unreadable, and beside him, the calm but sharp-eyed Detective Inspector Blakely from Scotland Yard.

She kept her handbag clutched tightly on her lap. Had it been a mistake to call on the Blakelys two nights ago? At the time, it had seemed like the best course of action – to steer suspicion in the direction of Agnes Black. But now, seated in this room under the full attention of two seasoned investigators, her confidence was beginning to unravel.

She cleared her throat. 'Why am I here?' Her voice sounded too thin. 'I've told you everything I know about Mrs Melbourne.'

Inspector Blakely nodded slowly, flipping through the file before him. 'You have indeed been very forthcoming. And we appreciate your cooperation.'

Paget leaned forward, his fingertips steepled. 'But we're not here to discuss Mrs Melbourne today.'

A cold prickling sensation ran down the back of her neck. 'Oh?' she said. 'Then... what are we going to discuss?'

Blakely sat back, his gaze steady. 'Your husband, Mrs Harwell. Samuel Harwell.'

She held her breath. For a moment, her mouth refused to move. 'What of him?' she asked carefully, but her voice was tight, her throat constricting.

'He was a successful man, wasn't he?' Paget said. 'The founder of a reputable insurance firm. Built it up from nothing, I believe.'

She gave a small nod. 'Yes.'

'And I understand the firm is soon to move into new offices,' Paget continued. 'There's to be a plaque unveiled in his honour. A fitting tribute, surely. You must be very proud.'

Margaret didn't answer. She was aware of the way their eyes lingered on her – not unkindly, but with intense scrutiny. She could feel their silent calculation, the way they studied every movement of her face. She tried to hold herself still, lips pressed into a tight line. But her chin trembled, just once.

She turned her eyes to a corner of the ceiling, pretending to focus there, but she could feel the heat rising under her collar. Her wall – so carefully built over the years – was beginning to crumble.

Blakely's voice was soft but insistent. 'Mrs Harwell?'

She didn't reply. She dared not. Words felt too dangerous. Her silence had served her well until now. But the air in the room seemed thicker than before, weighted with things unspoken.

'Is there something you'd like to tell us?' Blakely prompted. 'This would be the right time to do so.' His tone was gentle and kind.

The tightness in her chest collapsed in a shuddering sob. She covered her face with her hands. The tears were sudden, hot, unwelcome. She pulled off her glasses with trembling fingers and pressed her palms to her cheeks, as if trying to contain the flood.

'I'm sorry,' she choked.

Blakely and Paget said nothing, allowing the silence to coax the words from her. And it worked.

She sat straighter, hands falling into her lap, the resolve coming back. Her voice, when it returned, was steadier.

'I suppose you know,' she said, glancing between them. 'You've pieced it together, haven't you?'

Paget nodded. 'We have suspicions. But we need to hear it from you.'

Margaret took a breath. 'He was a violent man. A bully. Behind closed doors, he was cruel – especially when he drank. No one would've believed me. Everyone saw the successful industrialist, the philanthropist. They didn't see the bruises. The threats. The way he'd—'

Her voice faltered. She straightened again, clinging to her resolve.

'I couldn't take it anymore. I tried to leave, once. He made sure I knew what would happen if I tried it again. So I stayed. And eventually, I did what I had to do. I put an end to it.'

'Put an end to what, Mrs Harwell?' asked Inspector Blakely, his voice low and steady.

Margaret Harwell drew in a shuddering breath. 'His cruel words. His domination. His bullying. His temper.' She paused, then pressed her lips together before whispering, 'The violence.'

The room seemed to shrink around her as the words left her mouth. The memories surged forward – sudden and unwelcome. Her body still remembered the pain: the way his anger would erupt without warning, the blows that left bruises she had to explain away.

She leaned forward, her eyes wet once more. 'You have to understand – I was trapped. I couldn't get out. I wasn't thinking clearly. I was desperate. I even tried asking for help.'

'Who did you ask for help?' Blakely asked.

'I went to the police. My local station. I told them what was happening and begged them to speak to him.' She gave a bitter smile. 'And they did. Just a polite word. A warning.' She shook her head. 'And when he found out I'd gone to the police...' Her voice faltered. 'That just made everything worse.'

Blakely scribbled a note, then glanced up. 'We'll be able to check that. There should be a record of your visit.'

'Oh, there'll be a record,' she said fiercely. 'Because I'm telling you the truth.'

She leaned back in her chair. The relief of speaking openly was unexpectedly profound. For years she'd borne it all in silence. But now, her voice, once hidden behind fear and respectability, had found its strength.

'The police wrote everything down,' she said. 'But nothing more was done.'

'I'm sorry to hear that,' said Blakely. 'From what you're describing, your husband should have been charged. And the officers you spoke to should have done more.'

'Yes, they should have!' Her voice cracked. 'But Samuel was clever. He had charm when he needed it. And money. I wouldn't be surprised if he tried to bribe them. He would've done anything to protect his reputation. And so, I endured it. For years. Until I couldn't anymore.'

Blakely allowed a few moments to pass before continuing. 'How did Mrs Melbourne find out?'

'It was a mistake I made. I once joked about putting something in his tea which would finish him off. I shouldn't have said it because it formed an idea in her mind that I'd be capable of such a thing. Before I made the joke, I'd confided in her, just a little, about how bad things were with Samuel. I thought perhaps she'd understand. Offer support. But she didn't. She took that knowledge and stored it away.'

'So she used it to control you?'

'She exploited it,' Margaret said, feeling a bitter taste in her mouth. 'When Samuel was dead, she asked me if I'd poisoned him. As blatant as blood on snow! I denied it of course but I know I wasn't convincing enough. I can't lie easily when put on the spot like that. Something in my manner or expression must have given me away. She was sharper than most people realised – and she had a talent for sniffing out weakness. I was weaker than her. Most people were. She made it clear that she knew exactly what I'd done. And if I didn't do her bidding, she would tell someone.'

'And what did her bidding involve?' asked Blakely.

'She dictated how everything ran at the home,' said Margaret. 'She wanted reports about the girls, about their families, about anything she could gossip about. She liked to play the benevolent benefactor – but only if it gave her power. I was to protect her reputation at all costs. If anyone criticised her, I was to defend her. That was the arrangement.'

Inspector Blakely sat back in his chair. 'How could Mrs Melbourne have proved you'd poisoned your husband?'

'She couldn't prove it. But she could have persuaded someone. If she'd reported me to the police then it's possible they would have believed her. It would have been her word against mine. And I worried that it would be resolved with an... exhumation.' She shivered at the word. 'I read the newspapers. I know poison can be detected in a corpse long after death. I couldn't risk that happening! I had to make sure she kept quiet. And I so had to appease her.' She shook her head at the memory. 'Just what she wanted.'

'And then the pattern repeated itself,' Blakely said. 'You murdered your husband because you couldn't bear the situation any longer. You found yourself in a similar position with Mrs Melbourne. And you killed her too.'

'No!' Margaret slammed her hand on the table with a sharp crack. The sound echoed off the walls. 'I didn't kill her!'

Both officers stared at her. She sat back, taking a breath and nursing the pain in her hand. 'Yes, I thought about it,' she added quietly. 'I can't pretend I didn't. She made my life miserable. And yes, I may have even planned it in my mind – wondered how I might do it. But if I had, I wouldn't have used a knife.' Her voice dropped to a near-whisper. 'Poison. That's how I did it before. It would've been poison again.'

The inspectors exchanged a glance.

'I didn't kill her. I wanted to be free of her, yes. But I didn't murder her!'

SIXTY-NINE

Christopher Ashford didn't greet Penny and Emma with his usual warmth. His posture was guarded, and there was a flicker of apprehension in his eyes as they stood on his doorstep.

'What is it?' he asked, voice clipped.

'Is Miss Jackson with you?' Penny asked.

He didn't respond immediately. His hand rested on the door frame. 'Why are you asking?'

'Mr Ashford,' Penny said, stepping forward slightly, her tone calm but firm, 'I know you probably think we're a nuisance. But we're here because we want to tell you that we understand.'

He looked sceptical. 'Understand what, exactly?'

Penny took a breath. 'We know about you and Miss Jackson – about your love for one another. We know how it began twenty years ago, and how Mrs Melbourne tore it apart. We suspect she told lies about Lydia in an attempt to ruin her reputation. We also think you were sent to India under the guise of duty and encouraged to forget her. And yet – despite all of that – you didn't forget. Because you never stopped loving her. And now, after everything, you're finally back together.'

She glanced at Emma, who gave a quiet, heartfelt nod. She felt a lump in her throat.

Mr Ashford's expression faltered. The stiffness in his shoulders softened. He studied Penny for a moment. 'How do you know all this?' he asked, his voice quieter now.

'We discovered parts of it,' said Penny. 'And the rest we pieced together.'

He gave a bitter smile. 'Tell me, Mrs Blakely – have you ever been torn from someone you love for twenty years?'

Penny hesitated, then shook her head. 'No. I haven't. But I do know what it is to love someone fiercely – and I can imagine what it would feel like to be forced away from them. Maybe I can't fully grasp what you and Miss Jackson have endured, but I believe I can understand why you would guard what you have now with such determination.'

He looked away, his jaw tense.

Penny continued, gently, 'And I understand the secrecy. It makes sense. Keeping your love hidden now protects it – from judgement, from interference. No one can separate you again.'

A figure appeared behind him in the hallway. Lydia Jackson. Her expression was composed but weary.

'Let them in, Christopher,' she said. 'It's better to talk inside than have this conversation on the doorstep.'

He hesitated before stepping aside. Emma and Penny entered, the tension between them all slowly easing.

A short while later, they were seated in the comfortable sitting room.

'So,' said Miss Jackson, folding her hands in her lap. 'You're here for the truth?'

'To be fair,' said Mr Ashford, 'you've uncovered most of it already.'

Penny leaned forward. 'Then perhaps there's only one question left to ask.' She looked from one to the other. 'After everything Mrs Melbourne did to the two of you – after she destroyed your happiness and kept you apart for two decades – did you seek revenge?'

Miss Jackson gave a sigh. 'Twenty years ago, I was a governess. Just as I am now. My father was a shopkeeper – not a wealthy man, but determined that his daughters would have every opportunity he could afford. He gave us an excellent education, which was more than many girls of our class could hope for. I was – by all accounts – a respectable young woman.' She paused, her expression thoughtful. 'But that wasn't enough for Mrs Melbourne. In her eyes, I was only fit to instruct her niece in needlework and French. Nothing more.'

She paused and cast a glance at Mr Ashford. 'I never expected Christopher to fall in love with me,' she said with a wistful smile. 'I adored him from the moment I first met him. He was handsome, yes, but it was more than that. He was clever, intelligent and funny. And above all, he treated me as an equal. I wasn't used to that.'

Her eyes drifted down to her hands, clasped in her lap. Her left hand rested slightly beneath the other, the underdeveloped fingers curling inward. 'Especially not with this,' she said, gently raising her left hand. 'People have always noticed it. Children stared, and even adults couldn't hide their discomfort. I learned to expect rejection. I certainly never imagined I'd be admired – let alone loved. But Christopher saw past all of that. I still don't know why.'

Emma did. Miss Jackson carried herself with a quiet, self-possessed dignity. Her features were still striking – fine cheekbones, large violet-blue eyes, the sort of face that hinted at beauty and sadness in equal measure.

'We kept our courtship secret,' Lydia continued, her voice lowering. 'The difference in our backgrounds was too great. But we spoke of marriage.'

Emma felt a tug of sympathy. There was something earnest in Lydia's voice, a lingering ache that hadn't dulled over two decades.

'I don't know who told Mrs Melbourne,' Lydia went on. 'But someone in the household must have noticed. Miss Black, perhaps.

She saw us together once or twice – nothing improper, but enough to raise questions. I always had the feeling she resented me.'

'Resented you?' Emma asked gently.

'Yes. I never quite understood it, but there was something in the way she looked at me. As if I'd stolen something from her. I suppose she wasn't a happy woman, even then. And unhappy people rarely like to see others joyful. Especially when it's something they believe they'll never have for themselves.'

She fell silent then. Mr Ashford reached out to her and took her hand.

'Did Mrs Melbourne confront you about your relationship?' Emma asked.

They both shook their heads. 'No,' said Miss Jackson. 'Instead she accused me of being a thief. And she told people that I'd had a romantic entanglement with my previous employer. I had to leave. I went to stay with my sister in the country, too ashamed to face anyone. I was certain everyone believed Mrs Melbourne.'

She pressed her lips together before continuing.

'I wrote to Christopher asking to see him. But my letter never reached him. I received a reply from his family telling me he'd gone to Bombay.'

She turned to him and he held her gaze, squeezing her hand as he did so.

'You must have felt a great deal of anger towards Mrs Melbourne,' said Penny. 'When did you realise she had manipulated everything?'

'I knew she wanted to be rid of me,' Miss Jackson said. 'But I didn't realise just how involved she'd been in separating us until I saw her again. That was when she humiliated me.'

'What did she say?' asked Emma quietly. 'You wouldn't tell us before, but I imagine it must have been dreadful.'

Lydia nodded. 'It was dreadful. And I've struggled to repeat it because...' Her voice faltered. 'Because I fear it may be true.'

Emma leaned forward slightly. 'What do you mean?'

'She was visiting the Brockhursts one day. I heard her loud

voice coming from the drawing room and ensured I stayed away. And then, a little later, I encountered her on the stairs. I don't know what she was doing there and there was no one else around. She stopped on the staircase and looked me over. Then she said something to me, quite calmly.' Lydia's voice shifted, quiet and sharp as she recalled the words. '"I did you a favour, Lydia. Christopher would never have been happy with a girl like you. Especially a girl with a deformity – imagine the scandal! Now, let's not pretend you hold a grudge, dear. After all, you did rather bring it upon yourself."'

A silence followed. Emma felt a heaviness in her chest.

'She said that?' whispered Penny.

Miss Jackson nodded. Her expression was composed, but her hands trembled slightly in her lap.

'And you could never forgive her for that remark,' said Penny. 'Understandably so. Not only was it cruel, but it reminded you of the love and happiness she'd denied you.'

She nodded again, her eyes watery.

'So you took revenge,' said Penny. 'You killed her.'

A tear spilled down Miss Jackson's face. 'I considered it,' she said. 'But it's something I really couldn't do.' She turned to Mr Ashford. 'And neither could Christopher.'

He nodded solemnly. His eyes also damp.

Emma felt puzzled. Were the pair of them really innocent?

Miss Jackson addressed them both. 'I've told you the truth now. I didn't harm Mrs Melbourne but I'm glad she's dead.'

SEVENTY

'I believe everything Miss Jackson told us,' Emma said to Penny as they left the Fitzrovia townhouse. 'Do you?'

Penny nodded. 'Yes. When someone speaks to honesty, the truth is unmistakeable. I like to think my years of working as a news reporter have helped me develop an instinct for whether I'm being lied to or not.' She stopped and turned to Emma. 'But if Miss Jackson and Mr Ashford aren't suspects, we don't have many ideas left now, do we?'

'Perhaps James has got a confession from Mrs Harwell.'

Penny smiled. 'That would solve it, wouldn't it? It will be interesting to find out how he gets on with her.' They headed towards Tottenham Court Road, sidestepping a lady who tried to sell them overpriced bunches of heather. 'We need to think about what we do next,' added Penny.

'Arthur Thornwood,' said Emma. 'We still don't know who he is, do we?'

'Of course! Arthur Thornwood, we need to find him. He could hold the answer, couldn't he?'

'I hope so. We tried to find him once and failed. Where do we look this time?'

Penny scratched her chin as she thought. 'It could take a lot of research. But perhaps we could ask Clara and Francis for help.'

'I like that idea.'

Penny continued to think. 'We need to work quickly now,' she said. 'The killer could strike again and they need to be stopped. If Arthur Thornwood doesn't hold the answer, then we can rule him out and move onto the next theory.' She turned to Emma. 'How do you feel about working tonight?'

'Tonight?'

'Possibly all night.'

The question surprised Emma but the idea sounded intriguing. 'Why all night?'

'Because it will hopefully give us the time we need to find Arthur Thornwood. I'll ask Francis if we can use the library and we'll have it to ourselves. And if we find out who Arthur Thornwood is, we can call on him tomorrow and hopefully get some answers. I'll speak to James and make sure he's all right minding the children tonight. What do you think?'

Emma found it difficult to ignore the spark of enthusiasm in her friend's eyes. 'Very well,' she said with a smile. 'Let's work tonight. Let's see if we can solve this case once and for all.'

SEVENTY-ONE

After a flurry of telegrams sent back and forth, Emma met Penny outside the looming silhouette of the British Museum at nine o'clock that evening. The streets were quiet, the gas lamps casting long, flickering shadows along the pavement.

They stood close together in the dark, their breath misting in the cold air, and spoke in hushed voices.

'I hope they haven't forgotten,' Penny said.

'I wouldn't blame them if they had,' said Emma. 'It's a chilly night and this feels rather risky.'

Before Penny could reply, a voice emerged from behind them.

'Good evening, ladies.'

Emma let out a sharp breath and Penny gave a tiny yelp, clutching Emma's arm.

'Don't worry,' said Francis, stepping out of the shadows. 'It's only me.' He was barely discernible in the dark.

'Francis!' Penny scolded, her hand to her chest. 'You gave us a fright. You really ought to have announced yourself.'

He chuckled softly. 'Forgive me. But we're trying to be discreet, aren't we?'

'Did you manage to speak to the head librarian?'

There was a pause and Francis cleared his throat. 'I decided against it in the end.'

'You didn't ask him?' Penny said in disbelief. 'Then how exactly are we getting inside?'

'I have a set of keys.' They heard a jangle.

'I thought you were going to speak to the librarian, ask for his discretion and keep it quiet from the museum director,' whispered Penny.

'That was the plan,' Francis admitted. 'But I worried he might say no. And we can't afford that. It's safer if no one knows we're here at all.'

Penny sighed. 'And what happens if we're caught?'

'Well...' Francis hesitated. 'I might lose my job but it's a small price to pay.'

'A small price to pay? Francis, that's your livelihood!'

'If we uncover something important tonight, maybe it will all be worth it.'

'Hello!' came a soft voice from nearby.

'Clara,' said Penny. 'Thank you for coming.'

'I like an adventure. If there's anything I can do to help, I want to be involved.'

'Well,' said Francis, 'since we're all here, follow me. I'll lead you to the side entrance.'

'But how are we supposed to follow you?' asked Penny. 'We can barely see a thing.'

'We'll walk very slowly,' said Francis. 'And perhaps...' He paused for a moment. 'We'll have to hold each other's hands.'

Emma smiled as Penny groaned softly beside her.

Francis lit a cluster of candles once they were safely inside the large, domed reading room. The golden flames cast flickered shadows across the polished desks and shelves. Francis set the candles at a desk furthest away from the door. 'If anyone does happen to peer in,' he whispered, 'we'll have just enough time to snuff these out and hide.'

Emma shuddered at the thought. She didn't like the idea of someone catching them here.

Francis set off at a brisk pace between the towering shelves, pulling out volumes with practised ease. Each time he returned with a heavy book or bundle of documents, placing them on the desk muttering titles and references with scholarly enthusiasm.

He darted off again before they could ask questions.

The women exchanged glances, half amused, half bewildered.

'I think this is the sort of thing Francis enjoys more than anything else,' Penny said, watching him disappear into the shadows again. 'And with luck, he'll tell us exactly what we're looking for.'

Emma smiled faintly. 'I certainly hope so. Because I haven't the faintest idea where to begin.'

Eventually, Francis returned with one final stack of volumes. He made himself comfortable in a chair rubbing his hands together briskly.

'Right,' he said, pushing his spectacles up his nose. 'Let's get started. If you need anything else, just say the word.'

Emma looked at the pile in front of them. The books were heavy and some were old with cracked spines. It looked like more work than one night could possibly contain.

She stifled a yawn, trying not to let the others see. The candle-light shimmered softly across the pages, and the scent of old paper hung in the air.

It was going to be a long night.

SEVENTY-TWO

'Before we begin,' said Clara, 'I found out something which may or may not be useful.'

'What's that?' asked Penny.

'I called at St Anne's in Soho and spoke to the reverend there. I've spoken to him a few times about my survey of the churchyard. I asked him if he knew an Arthur Thornwood and he told me he didn't. I asked to look through the parish records and I found a few things of interest. Firstly there was the record of Mrs Melbourne's marriage there.'

'Was Arthur Thornwood a witness?' asked Francis.

'Unfortunately no. There was no sign of a Thornwood on the register for her marriage. But I continued looking and I found a burial record for Maria Thornwood. She died in 1831 at the age of thirty-three. I realise it doesn't sound like anything promising in our search, but it provides a possible connection between Mrs Melbourne and Arthur Thornwood.'

'She was murdered in the churchyard where someone who could be related to him was buried?' said Penny.

Clara nodded. 'I realise it's not much but...'

'Every little piece of information is a possible piece in the jigsaw,' said Francis. 'Let's bear Maria Thornwood in mind as we get to work.'

They worked diligently through the night, their heads bowed over registers, directories, and yellowing volumes. Candlelight flickered across the desk, casting shadows on tired faces and stacks of books.

Emma flipped through yet another electoral roll register, her hand cramped from hours of note-taking. She wasn't sure how much of it was useful – half the entries blurred together in her aching eyes – but still she wrote, as if sheer determination might lead her to the truth.

Every now and again, one of them would speak – a soft exclamation, a discovery, a name read aloud – but nothing stuck. They had found several Arthur Thornwoods, but none they could confidently tie to Mrs Melbourne.

It was approaching one o'clock when Emma leaned back in her chair with a long sigh, rolling her shoulders and stifling a yawn.

'No,' said Penny, 'you're making me yawn now.'

'There's no time for yawning,' Francis muttered from behind a mound of books, scribbling furiously into his own notebook.

'I'll try to pretend I'm wide awake,' said Emma, giving a half-hearted smile. She rubbed her eyes and reached for the next volume on her pile – *Crockford's Clerical Directory*. She'd leafed through so many like it that the process had become mechanical.

As usual, she turned instinctively to the letter T. To her pleasant surprise, she found the name Arthur Thornwood.

And then she saw it. 'Putney,' she said aloud.

Penny straightened. 'What did you say?'

'There's an Arthur Thornwood listed here,' said Emma. 'He was a vicar in Putney.'

'Mrs Melbourne grew up in Putney,' Penny said.

Francis leaned in. 'When was he there?'

Emma squinted at the entry. 'From 1845 to 1847. He studied at Chichester Theological College and then he was at St Mary's Church in Putney.'

Clara sat forward, her voice suddenly alert. 'Was Mrs Melbourne living in Putney then?'

'Mrs Melbourne was sixty-five when she died,' said Penny. 'That means she was born in 1822 or '23.'

Francis's eyes narrowed in thought. 'So she would've been twenty-two or twenty-three when he was vicar in her parish.'

'She married in 1851,' said Penny. 'And that's when she moved to Belgravia.'

Emma looked again at the listing, her heart quickening. 'He joined the Church Missionary Society in 1847. Posted to Abeokuta, Yoruba Country, West Africa.'

Penny's eyes widened. 'Africa! That was mentioned in the stash of papers, wasn't it?'

Emma nodded. 'It was.'

'So Arthur Thornwood left for Africa,' said Clara. 'And never came back?'

'Or did he?' said Penny, her eyes glinting.

They looked at each other, the flickering candlelight dancing in their tired, excited eyes.

SEVENTY-THREE

'Explain this to me again,' said Inspector Paget early the following morning. He sat with Emma, Penny and James in the coffee room at the Continental Hotel near the British Museum.

Emma was exhausted. She wrapped her hands around her coffee cup and breathed in its sharp aroma, willing it to wake her.

She listened as James patiently explained what she and Penny had told him after their night of research in the reading room. Paget made notes, his brow furrowed.

Once James had finished, Paget looked at his notes and scratched his head. 'You really think this solves it?' he said.

'I'm convinced by it,' said James. 'But better still, let's go there now and speak to him.'

SEVENTY-FOUR

Twenty minutes later, they disembarked from a four-wheeler cab outside St Peter's in Eaton Square.

Fog hung low over the church as they stepped through its grand portico and went inside. The two inspectors led the way and Emma and Penny followed.

Reverend Underhill sat on a pew opposite the altar, his head bowed in prayer. As he heard them approach, he slowly got to his feet, leaning on his stick for support. A kindly smile spread across his round face. With his thin, white hair he looked frail.

Emma felt a stab of regret.

What if they had got it wrong?

'Welcome to St Peter's,' said the reverend. 'To what do I owe the pleasure of your visit?'

'I'd like to speak to you about Mrs Melbourne,' said Inspector Paget.

'Of course.'

'And Dr Lloyd.'

'Who?'

'Dr Lloyd. He was murdered outside his home three days ago.'

'Oh yes, I recall reading about that now.'

'Am I addressing Reverend Godfrey Underhill?' asked Paget. 'Or Arthur Thornwood?'

'I'm sorry?' He stared at them, narrowing his eyes.

'Arthur Thornwood,' said Paget. 'Is that your name?'

'No,' replied the reverend curtly. 'I'm Godfrey Underhill.'

Paget turned to James, his expression exasperated. 'Are you sure about this, Blakely? I've already told you I'm unsure about this one.'

James turned to the clergyman. 'Reverend Underhill,' he said. 'Your real name is Arthur Thornwood and you were once a vicar at St Mary's in Putney. Am I right?'

The reverend shook his head.

'I can see you're not ready to agree with me just yet,' said James. 'So I'll let the two ladies talk and we'll see what you have to say after that.'

Emma and Penny stepped forward. 'Reverend,' said Penny. 'We're going to tell you what we've learned about Arthur Thornwood. He was a young curate at St Mary's in Putney from 1845 until 1847. During that time, a young woman called Miss Eleanor Patterson also lived in the area and regularly attended the services at St Mary's with her family. They – like many other parishioners – were dismayed when Mr Thornwood was discovered to have stolen funds from the church. His disgrace had been swift and unforgiving, leading to his dismissal from the parish and the collapse of his standing in the community.

'Arthur Thornwood left Putney and the country. He joined the Church Missionary Society and went to work at a mission in Abeokuta, Yoruba Country, West Africa.'

'Do you mind if I take a seat?' said the reverend. 'It sounds as though this is going to take a while.' He sat back down in his pew, rested his stick next to him and fixed his gaze on the altar.

'Arthur Thornwood appears to have vanished in Africa,' said Emma. 'No record of him can be found after that time. But we're quite sure that West Africa is the place where he became Godfrey Underhill.'

The reverend gave her a sharp glance then followed it with a smile. 'Nonsense,' he said. 'You seem a pleasant young lady but you're talking nonsense.'

'For the few decades, you built a new life under this false identity,' said Penny. 'By the time you returned to England ten years ago, your past had been erased. No one suspected that Reverend Underhill of St Peter's was, in fact, Arthur Thornwood, the disgraced curate from Putney. On your return you secured a post in Dulwich on the strength of your excellent references from a mission in Cairo.'

'Cairo?' said Paget. 'It seems you moved around quite a bit, Reverend.'

'Eventually, you were offered a position here at St Peter's,' said Penny. 'There was always a risk that someone from your past might recognise you – after all, Belgravia is only a few miles from Putney. But a lot of time had passed, and you must have reasoned that your secret was safe. That was until you met Mrs Melbourne. Unlike others, she had not forgotten your face. Despite the years, despite the change in name, she knew exactly who you were.

'You probably spent years convincing yourself that your past was buried. But Mrs Melbourne refused to let it remain so. She took great satisfaction in knowing something about you that others did not. And then, true to her nature, she decided to use it to her advantage.'

The reverend raised his hand. 'Just a moment,' he said. 'You have no proof of any of this. This is all just...' He flapped his hand in the air. 'Fantasy.'

'If so,' said Emma. 'Then why is the entry for Godfrey Underhill in *Crockford's Clerical Directory* inaccurate?'

'I'm sorry?'

'Your entry lists you as having attended Chichester Theological College. Remarkably you supposedly attended the college at the same time as Arthur Thornwood. But when we sent a telegram to the college asking them to confirm it, the college confirmed that no one by the name of Underhill had been a student there at that time. The college did confirm, however, that an Arthur Thornwood had studied there during the same period.'

Reverend Underhill finally lost his temper. 'This is all nonsense!' he snapped, his face darkening with indignation. 'I have never heard of Arthur Thornwood, and I certainly would never have stolen money. This is a fabrication – an outright slander against a man of the cloth! You should be ashamed of yourselves, accusing me of such heinous crimes.'

Emma took a measured step closer, her eyes never leaving him. 'Who's Maria Thornwood?' she asked him.

His lower lip trembled slightly. Then he looked away without answering.

'She's buried in St Anne's churchyard,' said Penny. 'Do you visit her grave there?'

He gave no response.

'Maria Thornwood died in 1831,' continued Emma. 'Perhaps she was Arthur Thornwood's mother? Perhaps her son visited her grave there. Maybe he knew St Anne's churchyard well?'

'Enough!' he snapped.

'Do you mind if we look in the vestry, Reverend?'

'Yes, I do mind!'

'May I ask why?' asked Penny. 'If you're innocent of any wrongdoing, then surely you wouldn't mind us looking in the vestry.'

'The vestry is out of bounds,' he retorted. 'Only members of the clergy and trusted parishioners may go in there.'

Inspector Paget cleared his throat. 'It would satisfy my mind if the ladies were granted access to the vestry, Reverend,' he said. 'We're here because you're suspected of two very serious crimes. Your compliance would help your cause greatly.'

The reverend sniffed then gave Emma and Penny a distasteful glance. 'I'm unhappy about these women looking in the vestry,' he said. 'But I don't wish my reluctance to be misconstrued as guilt. If you must look in there then go.' He gave them a dismissive wave. 'But kindly treat the room with respect.' He sat back in the pew and folded his arms.

SEVENTY-FIVE

Emma and Penny made their way to the small vestry doorway to the left of the altar.

Inside the room, grey daylight streamed in through an arched mullion window. A simple cross stood on the stone windowsill and candles rested on the mantelpiece of a small fireplace. A large walnut wardrobe took up one corner of the room and in the centre stood a small table covered with a red linen cloth.

Books and papers were stacked in neat piles on the table. Emma and Penny began to look through them, both knowing what they were searching for.

'Here's a diary,' said Penny, turning the pages. Meanwhile, Emma opened a leather-bound Bible which had sheets of paper tucked between its pages.

'These look like notes for sermons,' she said, examining the papers.

'Written in the same handwriting as these diary entries?' asked Penny.

Emma compared the two and nodded.

Penny stepped over to a small dresser and searched its shelves. 'Here are some blank sheets of writing paper,' she said. 'Thick and good quality.' She picked them up. 'How did the stationer describe it? Rag paper, isn't it?'

'Light cream and quarto sized with an unglazed surface,' replied Emma.

'I think that describes this paper perfectly,' said Penny. 'Let's take this, the diary and the sermon notes and show them to Inspector Paget. And there's something else I've noticed too.'

'What's that?'

'The reverend's walking stick. My father took a very similar one with him on his travels to South America.'

Emma listened intently as Penny described it to her.

Reverend Underhill glared at them as they rejoined him, Paget and James a short while later. Having been made aware of the reverend's stick, Emma noticed it still rested against the pew beside him.

She and Penny showed Paget what they'd found in the vestry.

'What's the meaning of this?' he asked.

Reverend Underhill gave a laugh and added, 'They're wasting your time, Inspector.' He turned to them. 'I want everything you've taken from the vestry to be returned to its rightful place please.'

'We'll do that,' said Penny. 'After we've shown Inspector Paget the anonymous letters we've received over the past few weeks.'

Penny pulled the bundle of letters out of her bag. 'You'll need some time to examine these carefully, Inspector,' she said. 'But Mrs Langley and I are quite certain that the handwriting in these threatening letters matches the handwriting in the diary and the sermon notes from the vestry. The handwriting belongs to Reverend Underhill.'

The reverend shook his head in mocking disbelief.

'The writing paper the anonymous letters were written on is the same as the supply we found in the vestry,' added Emma. 'It's good quality paper which befits the position of a clergyman.'

'You'll need some time to read through the letters, Inspector,' said Penny. 'And you'll discover their tone is malicious. Designed to frighten us into stopping our investigation. That's why we're certain Mrs Melbourne's murderer wrote them. He noticed we were investigating and he wanted us to stop.'

'He was scared we'd discover the truth,' said Emma.

Paget turned to the reverend. 'Would you like to explain any of this, Reverend?'

He gave a dismissive wave. 'There's nothing to explain, Paget. These women have forged those letters in my handwriting. It's a setup.'

Paget frowned.

'Nonsense!' snapped James, stepping forward. 'I can clearly recall each time my wife received one of your malicious letters, Underhill. She tried her hardest not to let them bother her, but they did. And the same can be said for Mrs Langley. Both ladies were needlessly upset by your poisonous cowardly words!'

'Thank you, Blakely,' said Paget, clearly keen to keep the mood calm.

'Don't believe him, Paget,' said James. 'These letters are genuine and this man wrote them.'

'I'll need some time to look at them,' said Paget. 'But even if the reverend did write them, they don't prove he's a murderer.'

Reverend Underhill gave a smug nod. 'Thank you, Inspector. The voice of reason. And let me remind you all, that only the Lord holds the power to judge.' He lifted his chin and raised his voice to the altar. '"There is one lawgiver, who is able to save and to destroy: who art thou that judgest another?"'

Penny responded with a sigh. 'It's disrespectful to use scripture to create a false impression of piety. You seem to think that all this' – she gestured at the altar then the rest of the church – 'all this means you're blameless. That no one will suspect you. You disgraced yourself at the beginning of your career and ran away to Africa, cloaking yourself in your religion. While there you forged a new identity for yourself. And who would question it? No one. No one wants to question a man of God.'

A pause followed and Reverend Underhill wiped his brow. 'It's time for you to leave,' he said. 'You're not welcome in the Lord's house any longer.' His face twisted into an ugly sneer. '"Depart from me, ye cursed! Into everlasting fire, prepared for the devil and his angels"!'

Emma and Penny exchanged a glance and Penny nodded. Without a word, Emma reached for the walking stick leaning against the pew.

The reverend stiffened. 'What do you think you're doing?' His voice sharpened with sudden alarm. 'That's my stick! I rely on it to get about – put it back this instant!'

Emma ignored his outburst. Holding the cane horizontally in both hands, she adjusted her grip – her right hand tightening on the handle, her left gripping the shaft.

Then, with a single, decisive movement, she pulled.

Inspector Paget stepped back as the stick separated into two distinct parts.

In Emma's right hand gleamed a long, narrow blade – its surface polished to a deadly sheen. In her left remained the hollowed casing, the unassuming wooden sheath that had concealed the murder weapon all along.

'A sword stick,' Penny said, her eyes wide.

'Indeed.' Emma turned the blade slightly, mesmerised as she watched the light glint on the metal. 'Everyone was wondering where the murder weapon had gone. But all this time, Reverend Underhill was carrying it with him – hidden in plain sight.' Emma turned to Penny, her mind racing. 'It's as we discussed last night, Penny.'

'My father had one just like it,' added Penny. 'He carried it on his plant-hunting travels through the jungles of South America – it was a discreet weapon, meant for protection.' She turned to the reverend. 'But Reverend Underhill used it to murder his victims.'

Emma caught a movement from the side of her eye, but the reverend had flung an arm around her neck before she had time to react. Her grip on the sword loosened as the pressure increased on her airway. The clergyman seized it from her and pointed it at Penny.

He was much stronger and quicker than she'd realised. But this prowess served to remind her how he'd confidently killed two people.

'No one move!' he threatened.

SEVENTY-SIX

Penny remained where she was. Her eyes wide. Emma stared at her as she gasped for breath and tried pulling at the arm around her neck. Her breathing felt laboured. The reverend's grip was like a vice.

'Let her go!' demanded Penny.

But the clergyman didn't flinch.

'This is all a silly nonsense,' said Inspector Paget, stepping forward. 'You're outnumbered, Underhill. Leave these two women alone.'

But to Emma's dismay, the inspector seemed reluctant to tackle the clergyman. Her eyes moved to James who appeared to be quietly weighing up the situation. She felt sure he had a plan, but there was no telling what it was.

Penny stepped away.

'I warned you!' shouted the reverend. Now he brought the sharp end of the weapon up to Emma's chest. She felt her knees weaken. She'd heard all about the deep fatal wounds which Mrs Melbourne and Dr Lloyd had received to the torso.

The reverend let out a cry and the sword stick fell to the floor. James had used his own walking stick to whack the reverend's hand. Paget leapt forward and pulled the reverend's arm from Emma's neck. She staggered back, relieved to get her breath back.

James picked up the sword stick from the floor and Paget bundled the reverend back into his pew. The reverend paled. 'This is – this is preposterous!' he blustered; his voice had lost its earlier strength. Then he let out a small cry, clutched at his chest and tumbled onto the stone floor.

A pause followed then James spoke. 'You're not fooling anybody, Reverend. The evidence is overwhelming now. Continuing to deny it will only make you look foolish.'

Reverend Underhill lay on the floor, groaning dramatically.

James crouched down next to him. 'Despite everything we've just heard,' he said, 'I still believe you're a man of God.' He gestured to the altar in front of them. 'Why not make your confession now, in the Lord's house? It's a much better place to do it than in a miserable police station. And who knows? Perhaps a little more mercy might be shown to you here?'

The reverend glanced at the altar then back at James. Although he'd undoubtedly pretended to be taken unwell, Emma could hear a raspiness in his breath. A vulnerability.

She couldn't resist stepping forward. 'Let me help you up, Reverend,' she said, holding out a hand. 'And we shall all listen while you tell us your story.'

To her surprise, he allowed her to pull him up on his pew with the help of Penny and James.

A long silence followed. Everyone seemed to hold their breath.

Then, at last, the reverend exhaled slowly. His shoulders slackened, and his expression shifted – less defensive, more resigned. 'That doctor was cleverer than he looked,' he muttered.

James narrowed his eyes. 'Dr Lloyd?'

The reverend nodded.

'He suspected you of Mrs Melbourne's murder?'

'He did more than suspect. He accused me outright. And the trouble was... he had a rather good case against me. For some reason, he took note of the fact that I left the Athenaeum Club at half past eleven that evening.'

'You were both members of the Athenaeum?' asked James.

The reverend nodded. 'We weren't friends. He was an odd chap.'

'And he saw you leave the club on the evening Mrs Melbourne was murdered?' asked Penny.

He nodded. 'Why he remembered it, I couldn't tell you. But he did. And you weren't the first to suspect my walking cane was a sword stick. Dr Lloyd suspected it as well, and the mistake was entirely mine. We were both dining at the club one evening, seated at neighbouring tables. My cane was resting against my chair when a waiter, careless fool, knocked it over.

'I reacted rather... enthusiastically,' he admitted. 'I grabbed it as quick as I could. But it was knocked out of its sheath a little. Just an inch or so. I had to replace it. The doctor noticed and gave me an odd smile. He probably wondered why a reverend carried a weapon with him.'

Emma was suddenly struck by a memory of young Thomas picking up the stick when they'd visited the reverend. She recalled now how the old man had quickly taken it back from him. Now that she knew it was a weapon, she understood why.

'Dr Lloyd saw the way I guarded it, how protective I was over something that should have been an ordinary walking stick,' continued Reverend Underhill. 'And that was when I saw it – the flicker of suspicion in his expression.'

'Did he confront you directly?' Penny asked.

The reverend let out a slow breath. 'I suppose he did. A few days later he told me I ought to speak to the police. He said he'd seen me leave the club that night and that he knew I was carrying a weapon. I laughed it off, of course. I ridiculed him and acted as though the very suggestion was preposterous. I assured him I had no reason to murder Mrs Melbourne. But from that moment on, I felt... uneasy. Unsettled. I couldn't stop thinking about it. I had been so certain – so convinced – that I had got away with it. No one suspected me. No one had even entertained the thought. But then... one man did. And I knew I wouldn't be able to rest until I was sure he wouldn't tell anyone.'

James's expression hardened. 'On the night of his death, Dr Lloyd had been to the club. Did you follow him home?'

He responded with a slow, deliberate nod. 'Yes. I did. I couldn't risk him mentioning his suspicions to someone who would go to the police. I had to eliminate the threat.'

Emma felt a chill creep down her spine. 'How did you do it?' she asked, although she wasn't sure she wanted to hear the answer.

'I saw Lloyd in the club that night and left before him, knowing he would be heading for his home soon. And I waited for him there. There are a lot of good hiding places in Bedford Square at night. I made sure I wasn't seen. And then, when the moment was right... I struck.'

His voice was eerily calm, as though he were discussing a mere inconvenience rather than the brutal murder of another man.

'And Mrs Melbourne?' said James. 'How did you persuade her to meet you in the disused churchyard that night?'

'That wasn't very difficult,' he said. 'I sent her an anonymous note telling her I was willing to pay her a lot of money in return for keeping my secret.' He gave a little chuckle. 'She couldn't resist. I met her outside the churchyard and suggested we speak inside, away from the street. She was so desperate to hear how much money I was willing to pay that she agreed.'

'And you chose St Anne's churchyard because you know it so well,' said Emma. 'Your mother is buried there?'

He took his time to answer. 'She is,' he said quietly. 'I was eleven years old when she died.' He fixed Emma's gaze. 'She understands I had to do this! I prayed at her graveside and I had her blessing!'

'But before you met Mrs Melbourne that night,' said Penny, 'she confronted you about being Arthur Thornwood?'

'Oh yes, she didn't waste any time with that.'

'How did she recognise you?'

His gaze drifted to the flagstones. 'She and I... when we were young. We got on well. Believe it or not, she was a beautiful young woman then.'

'You had a love affair?' asked James.

The reverend gave a sharp exhale. 'Not as such. It could have happened but... there was the incident with the money and I had to leave. Everyone was disappointed but no one was as disappointed as she was. We had strong feelings for each other but I never thought I'd see her again. I was gone away for so long... and I was forty years older. I spent decades in Africa working in different missions. I travelled a great deal and lived in many different places. But I always wanted to return home one day. My last mission was in Cairo and home I went. After some time in Dulwich, I came here to St Peter's.' He glanced up at them. 'And who did I encounter on my arrival? Her!'

'And she recognised you after forty years?' said James.

'Yes. She seemed familiar to me too but I couldn't recall where I'd seen her before. We were in the middle of a conversation when she mentioned it and then... I couldn't believe she remembered me. My appearance had changed quite a bit but I suppose there was my voice, my mannerisms... she worked out who I was.'

'And she confronted you,' said Penny.

'Oh yes. And she taunted me about my disgrace for a few months. She never forgave me for it. She told me I'd betrayed her as well as the church. She told me I didn't deserve to be a clergyman and she was right. But what else could I do? I love my work. What else could I do with my life? And I didn't want to be pushed out from a parish once again. So when she saw me by the churchyard gates that night, she understood immediately that I wanted to come to an arrangement. She was expecting money from me to keep my secret quiet. She met me there ready to discuss it. But I...' His eyes rested on the sword stick in James's hand. 'I didn't give her the chance.'

SEVENTY-SEVEN

A solitary figure dressed in black moved quietly through the mist towards the small burial ground on the marshy banks of the River Thames. The fog drifted in from the water, soft and ghostlike, curling around the leaning gravestones and clinging to the grass like a shroud. The air was still, heavy with the silence of remembrance.

The mist coiled particularly thick around a single stone – unremarkable in shape, but solemn in purpose. It marked not one name but many: the countless infants born at St James's Diocesan Home for Penitents who had not lived beyond their first year. The forgotten. The nameless. The lost.

The figure knelt and laid a simple posy of white flowers at the base of the stone. Her hands, worn and trembling, reached for the small cross at her neck. She pressed it to her lips and murmured a prayer – not only for her own daughter, but for all the tiny lives buried beneath the earth, their cries long silenced.

She bowed her head, staying there for a time, until the chill began to creep through her coat and into her bones. Then she rose, turning away from the grave with quiet resolve.

Agnes Black followed the narrow path back to the road, her

steps slow but certain. She would return. This graveyard would always draw her back.

As she walked, a faint smile spread across her face. That morning's newspaper had brought unexpected satisfaction: Margaret Harwell had been formally charged with her husband's murder. At last, justice had found its way to her.

But the smile faded when her thoughts turned to Reverend Underhill. A man of the cloth, twice a killer. How could someone so devout fall to such sin? And yet... hadn't they all sinned in their own ways? He had acted, as so many had, out of fear. Fear of Eleanor Melbourne.

Agnes closed her fingers again around the cross, drawing strength from its cool metal. She could forgive him. In time. She prayed that the Lord might do the same.

And the fire... Yes, the police suspected her. But they had no evidence. The ruins were already being cleared, and Christopher Ashford was planning a grand new house to rise from the ashes.

Let him. The fire had at least scorched away something of Mrs Melbourne's legacy. And if it had caused Ashford some inconvenience along the way, well, so be it. That pleased her more than she cared to admit.

But some memories still lingered. Too many. When they pressed in too tightly, the brandy helped keep them at bay.

She reached the road and passed St James's Home without so much as a glance. Word had it the place was to be closed and pulled down. The thought brought a rare sense of peace.

That day couldn't come soon enough.

SEVENTY-EIGHT

'I take it you've read the papers today?' Christopher asked as he and Lydia set off through Hyde Park. A cold, blustery wind tugged at their coats, but spring was beginning to show: daffodils swayed at the base of trees, and the oaks were dusted with the first green haze of budding leaves.

'No, I haven't had the chance,' Lydia replied. 'I was visiting a lady who's considering me for a governess position.'

'And? Have you accepted?'

'I have.'

'That's good news.' He smiled, but the smile didn't reach his eyes. His hand brushed her arm, a touch more thoughtful than celebratory.

She tilted her head. 'You don't sound particularly pleased.'

'I am, Lydia.' But he looked away, jaw set.

She slipped her arm through his, sensing the shift in him. 'Tell me – what was in the papers?'

He slowed, glanced at her, and said quietly, 'They've charged someone with the murder of Mrs Melbourne and Dr Lloyd.'

She stopped in her tracks. 'Who?'

He turned to face her. 'Reverend Underhill.'

Her lips parted in shock, and for a moment, she forgot to breathe. Then she closed her mouth, quickly, self-conscious. 'A reverend?'

'Yes. The dreary fellow who led her memorial service at St Peter's. He called on us, remember?'

He began walking again, and Lydia stared across the windswept park, her thoughts whirling. 'Yes, I remember,' she murmured. 'A clergyman?'

She hurried to catch up. 'Why would he do such a thing?'

'I don't know. The papers haven't said yet. But I'll tell you who's bound to know – those two nosy ladies, Mrs Blakely and Mrs Langley.'

'Oh, those two,' Lydia said with a laugh. 'It wouldn't surprise me if they solved it before the police did.'

'You should ask them,' Christopher said. 'Then we'll finally understand what drove the reverend to it.'

'I will.'

He stopped again, turned to her, and removed his hat, the wind ruffling his hair. There was an urgency in his eyes now, something raw and purposeful.

'Lydia,' he said, voice low, 'I think you should tell that lady you saw this morning that you're no longer seeking employment.'

'What? I can't – I need the position. You've seen where I'm living. I haven't a penny to spare.'

He reached out, his hand warm against her cheek. 'Forget about money. You don't have to worry about that anymore.'

She gave a disbelieving laugh. 'Easy for you to say. But I—'

'Marry me, Lydia.'

The world stilled. Her breath caught.

'What?'

'Will you marry me?' His eyes searched hers, earnest and bright. 'I was going to ask you twenty years ago. Then life pulled us apart. But now – now that we've found each other again, it all seems so clear. Do you feel it too?'

Emotion rose in her like a tide. Her heart swelled, and before she could stop herself, a smile bloomed across her face.

'Yes, Christopher. I do. I will. I never imagined you'd still feel this way – I... I can't think of anything more wonderful.'

SEVENTY-NINE

Emma and Penny met Clara for lunch at Café Monico, just off the bustle of Piccadilly Circus. Inside the elegant dining room, calm prevailed. Crisp linen, gleaming silverware, and the gentle hum of conversation made a welcome change from the chaos of the past few weeks.

Once they'd placed their orders, the conversation turned to recent events.

'I wonder what Christopher Ashford will do with his godmother's fortune,' said Penny. 'It must be strange inheriting so much from someone you never really liked.'

'Hopefully he'll marry Lydia Jackson so she can benefit from it too,' said Emma. 'After hearing how Mrs Melbourne separated them, I think they deserve some happiness together.'

'I agree,' said Clara. 'From what you've told me, they were apart for twenty years – both believing the lies Mrs Melbourne had told them. I hope they can be happy together now.'

'James isn't sure what to do about Margaret Harwell,' said Penny. 'Although she's admitted to poisoning her husband, she did so because he was so brutal to her. I know I always say no one deserves to be murdered, but when someone has suffered as much as Mrs Harwell clearly did – should she escape punishment?'

Emma agreed it was a difficult dilemma. 'In the eyes of the law she's done wrong,' she said. 'But to be mistreated for many years like that... I can't imagine how awful that must be. If some leniency could be shown towards her I think that would be the best outcome.'

'A short prison sentence, perhaps,' said Penny. 'Although I don't know if the law allows it. She was determined to get Agnes Black arrested, wasn't she? All because Miss Black knew what she'd done to her husband.'

'And what will Miss Black do now?' said Clara.

'I'm sure she can find another job in service,' said Penny. 'If that's what she wants. Mind you, she's a rather sombre individual, isn't she? Not exactly the sort of person you'd want around your home all the time. It could become quite depressing after a while, I'm sure.'

'Mrs Melbourne didn't seem to mind, did she?' said Clara. 'But then, I think everyone can agree she was a very strange woman.'

Emma nodded. 'What she inflicted on others was terrible. She didn't deserve to die... but I can understand how Reverend Underhill felt cornered enough to act out of desperation.'

'She was insufferable,' Clara said bluntly. 'But no one has the right to decide who lives and who dies.'

'The reverend was terrified she'd expose his past,' said Penny. 'He couldn't bear the thought of enduring that disgrace again. Not that it excuses what he did.'

'If he were truly a man of faith,' said Emma, 'he would have accepted the consequences. He would have found a way to carry the burden with dignity. However impossible life may feel, there's always a way through. You just have to trust that you'll find it.'

'You speak like someone who knows,' Penny said, giving her a small, admiring smile. 'Underhill was a coward. Like most murderers. So frightened of their own downfall, they'd rather destroy someone else.'

'Fear,' Clara murmured, nodding. 'Yes. That's it exactly. I

hadn't thought of it that way. I must say, I always enjoy lunch with you two – the conversation is always intelligent.'

Emma laughed. 'I don't think you've spent enough time with us yet!'

'I hope I get the chance to spend more time with you both. If you'll allow it.'

'Of course!' said Penny. 'I love getting to know ladies with interesting jobs. Especially now that my own job is little more than writing an occasional column for a newspaper.'

'In that case,' said Clara said, 'perhaps you'd like to join me on a survey of a disused graveyard in Shoreditch?'

'I'd love to!' Penny's eyes lit up. 'Emma, will you come too?'

Emma smiled, but her enthusiasm didn't match theirs. 'I'll probably be busy teaching.'

'You don't even know when we're going yet.'

'I know,' she replied. 'But I'll be busy. You'll just have to tell me all about it afterwards.'

Penny narrowed her eyes playfully. 'Very well. But we'll keep trying to tempt you.' She turned to Clara. 'And how are things with the Metropolitan Public Gardens Committee? Are they treating you fairly again?'

Clara nodded. 'Thankfully, yes. I've even received a few apologies. I'm still astonished that anyone thought I could have harmed Mrs Melbourne. But I suppose once suspicion takes hold, it's hard to shake. No one ever imagined the real killer would be a reverend.'

'Least of all us,' said Emma. 'We did well, though. It wasn't an easy case. Thank you, Clara, for your help.'

'Oh, I hardly did anything.'

'You helped us in the library. And you found the reverend's mother. Mentioning her unsettled him – he began to lose his composure after that.'

Penny raised her glass of water. 'I propose a toast. To friendship.'

Emma raised an eyebrow. 'With water?'

'I can't find the waiter. We'll ask for something stronger shortly. For now – raise your glasses!'

Emma and Clara joined her.

'To friendship,' they echoed, and sipped.

'London water,' Emma said, setting her glass down. 'The finest in the land.'

Penny chuckled. 'It's improved in recent years, at least.'

Clara grimaced. 'Actually, I have a good story about water leaching from an old graveyard into a public supply. Would you like to hear it?'

'Yes!' said Penny eagerly.

'No!' said Emma, recoiling. 'That sounds revolting. If we must, can't it wait until after lunch? I don't want to lose my appetite!'

After lunch, Emma and Penny travelled by omnibus to Emma's lodgings in Clerkenwell.

'I was thinking earlier how frightened I was by the reverend's letters,' said Emma once they'd disembarked from the bus. 'Do you think he would ever have attempted to attack you and me?'

'Judging by his behaviour in the church when we confronted him, I think he would have tried it if he'd had the opportunity,' said Penny. 'He was carrying his weapon around with him all the time! Not a nice thought. But we worked out who he was before he planned any sort of attack. And I feel grateful we managed to do that. It's the reason we have to work quickly on cases like this; the culprit is always planning their next move.'

'It's the reason we had to work all night in a library?' said Emma with a smile.

'Yes. That was fun, wasn't it? Although tiring. Cases like these always are. It will be nice to have some peace and quiet for a bit.' She stopped for a moment and laughed. 'Peace and quiet! When I have two young children, one of whom is crawling everywhere at the moment...'

· · ·

'Now then,' said Mrs Solomon, flexing her fingers as she sat at the piano in the parlour. 'Is everyone ready?'

Emma and Penny exchanged an amused glance.

'Is everyone what?' asked Mr Solomon. He was hard of hearing.

'Ready!' shouted his wife so he could hear. 'Are you ready, Ronald?'

'Ready? You're the one playing it.'

'Yes, I am. But are you ready to hear it?'

'I think so,' said Mr Solomon. Then he turned to Penny and muttered, 'This won't be easy on your ears I'm afraid, Mrs Blakely.'

'I heard that!'

Mr Solomon chuckled and sat back in his armchair.

A silence fell as Mrs Solomon lifted her hands and began to play a haltingly slow version of 'Für Elise', correcting all the incorrect notes as she went.

Emma, Penny and Mr Solomon listened politely until the end.

At the end, Mrs Solomon turned to them, a wide beam on her face. 'So what did you think?' she asked.

'It sounded like someone strangling a cat,' said Mr Solomon.

'Oh Ronald!' scolded his wife.

'But other than that, it sounded lovely,' he added. Then he turned to Emma. 'Make sure you give her a few more lessons please, Mrs Langley.'

'Very well,' said Emma. She turned to her landlady. 'I think you did a very good job, Mrs Solomon. But there's always room for improvement.'

A LETTER FROM THE AUTHOR

Thank you for reading this Emma Langley mystery. I hope you enjoyed it!

Would you like to know when I release new books? Here are some ways to stay updated:

Click here to be the first to know about my latest releases with Storm:

www.stormpublishing.co/emily-organ

Join my mailing list and receive a free short mystery, *The Belgrave Square Murder*:

emilyorgan.com/the-belgrave-square-murder

And if you have a moment, I would be very grateful if you would leave a quick review of my books online. Honest reviews of my books help other readers discover them too!

emilyorgan.com

f facebook.com/emilyorganwriter

g goodreads.com/emily_organ

BB bookbub.com/authors/emily-organ

HISTORICAL NOTE

Clara Clifton is inspired by Isabella Holmes, a pioneering social reformer who undertook the monumental task of surveying every burial ground in London in the late nineteenth century. Her research helped shape the work of the Metropolitan Public Gardens Association, an organisation dedicated to creating public green spaces across the city. In 1896, Holmes published *London Burial Grounds: Notes on their History from Earliest Times to the Present Day*. Despite its formidable title, the book is both accessible and thought-provoking. It sparked debate on how graveyards were maintained and used.

The Association's efforts led to the transformation of many disused burial grounds into public parks. One notable example is Victoria Park Cemetery in East London, which was redesigned by the charity's landscape gardener, Fanny Wilkinson, and reopened as Meath Gardens in 1894. The organisation still operates today, continuing its campaign to preserve and create green spaces in London.

For centuries, London's dead were buried in small parish churchyards. But as the population more than doubled in the first half of the nineteenth century, these spaces became dangerously overcrowded. Coffins were crammed into deep pits, often just inches below ground, and older remains were disturbed to make room.

By the 1840s, the health risks were clear. Disused burial grounds turned to rubbish dumps, and the fear of 'miasma' led to public outcry. Surgeon George Alfred Walker, known as 'Graveyard Walker', surveyed the city's graveyards and published his damning findings in 1839, calling for reform.

One solution came in the form of the 'Magnificent Seven' cemeteries, established in the 1830s and 1840s – including Highgate, Kensal Green, West Norwood and Abney Park, all of which feature in Penny Green books! Brookwood Cemetery opened in Surrey, with coffins transported there from Waterloo Station by the Necropolis Railway – as featured in Penny Green's second adventure, *The Rookery*.

But the new cemeteries didn't solve the problem of London's disused burial grounds. Many were in poor condition and reformers believed they could be repurposed.

St Anne's Church, Soho, was first built in the seventeenth century on land which was then countryside. As London quickly expanded around it, the church became a central location in the West End and there was much demand for burials in its churchyard. George Alfred Walker reported: 'There is only one burying ground belonging to this parish; it is walled in on the side next to Princes Street; close to this wall is the bone house; rotten coffin wood and fragments of bones are scattered about... The ground is very full, and is considerably raised above its original level; it is overlooked by houses thickly inhabited.'

Sixty years later, Isabella Holmes reported an astonishing number of burials in St Anne's churchyard which was only half an acre in size: 'It is estimated that in this small ground and the vaults under the church 110,240 bodies were interred during 160 years.' The Metropolitan Public Gardens Association successfully converted the burial ground to a public garden in 1892 and these days it's a popular little city park – enjoyed by many people just as Isabella Holmes had hoped!

St Anne's Church has been repaired and restored over the years, most recently in the twentieth century after the building was severely damaged by fire during the bombing of London in World War Two.

St James's Diocesan Home for Penitents opened on Fulham Palace Road in 1871 as a refuge for so-called 'fallen women'. It was one of many institutions established in the nineteenth and early twentieth centuries to house unmarried mothers. A late nineteenth-century map shows the building situated in a semi-rural area near the River Thames. The women and girls sent there must have felt deeply isolated. Today, the area is a densely built-up residential suburb. The home closed in 1936 and was later demolished. A block of flats now occupies the site.

Belgravia was developed in the early nineteenth century, and its grand terraced houses have long attracted the wealthy. Eaton Square – the largest square in London – is among the city's most prestigious and expensive addresses. Today, many of the area's grand homes have been converted into apartments and offices. St Peter's Church, where Mrs Melbourne worshipped, is an elegant neoclassical building which has twice been rebuilt after devastating fires in 1837 and 1987.

The Plumbers Arms pub on Lower Belgrave Street – where Emma and Penny share a drink with Agnes Black – gained notoriety in November 1974 when Lady Lucan ran inside seeking help. Her husband had just murdered the family's nanny, Sandra Rivett, and attempted to kill her. Lord Lucan famously disappeared after the attack and was never seen again.

Printed in Dunstable, United Kingdom